MW00331228

GAMBLER'S CHOICE

To Jason —

Thank you for all of your
help, from beginning to end.

ABOUT

One horrific encounter haunts a world of characters nearly two decades later, just as a Silicon Valley startup promising a cure for aging sparks a startling chain of events. In this unconventional novel built along the zodiac's wheel, you'll explore an elaborate tapestry of pivotal moments staged in a variety of settings, from the Chicago theatre scene and life in South Louisiana to the world of paid plasma donations and hemophilia during the tainted blood era. Following twelve connected stories, you'll also examine the absurdity of plague, the complexity of truth, and the struggles we all share in our quest to understand ourselves. Here is your opportunity, dear reader, to experience a Gambler's Choice, where your decisions define your character in the face of obstacles along your path. And it begins right now, with your decision to choose this book.

Copyright © 2020 by Luna Sophia Publishing, LLC

All rights reserved.

The characters and events portrayed in this book are fictitious. Any similarity to real persons, living or dead, is coincidental and not intended by the author.

No part of this book may be reproduced or transmitted in any form or by any means, electronic or mechanical, including photocopying, recording, or by any information storage and retrieval system, without permission in writing from the publisher.

ISBN: 978-1-7350260-0-8

Digital edition published in 2020
eISBN: 978-1-7350260-1-5

Library of Congress Control Number: 2020908487

Cover Art and Graphics by Marina Kozak
Book Design by Mary A. Karnath Duhé

Luna Sophia Publishing, LLC
www.lunasophiapublishing.com
3861 Ambassador Caffery Parkway, Suite 100
Lafayette, LA 70503

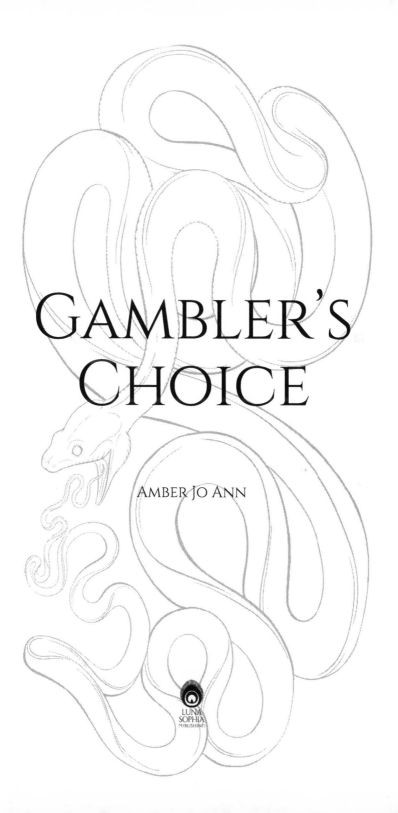

GAMBLER'S CHOICE

AMBER JO ANN

LUNA
SOPHIA
PUBLISHING

Behold, my love, for I am Death,
That Angel between Night and Day.
You feel my kiss with every breath
And see my face in shades of gray.

Fear not, my love, for I am Life,
Forever shifting as the Moon.
I prune your ego with my Knife
So that the Sun may rise at noon.

Be still, my love, for I am Time,
That slow process of Becoming.
Though I destroy with rot and grime
A new age is always coming.

And hold me, love, for I am Birth,
An infinite dance with the Light.
I am the seed born of this Earth
The Dawn that conquers every Night.

For We are One, and One is All,
In this cycle of creation.
Where those who rise must also fall
To our rhythm of Salvation.

MATILDA KARL PRAYED FOR BLOOD as the hot water of the shower fell down onto her head. Her eyes affixed to the white porcelain basin of the tub, she searched desperately for a spot, a drop, a slither of darkest red, feathering out across the stream of running water before reaching the rusty drain. Intently, she gazed upon the inside of her thighs with savage determination. *Blood, blood, blood,* her mind chanted, as if she could manifest a certain result to appease her frantic state of denial. The trash bin was out of sight, separated from her by the thin, translucent shower curtain. She retained a reluctant knowledge of its contents: four acid-stained sticks, each reading "Pregnant." It would have been more fitting had the screen read "Death."

She could still feel that poison rushing through her veins, spreading through her mind, body, and soul. The wound itself was invisible, cloaked by bone and tissue. No one knew about that deathly sting, not even Sarah, and she told Sarah everything. Instead, Matilda had pushed the only person she'd ever loved as far away from her as possible, then pushed a little more. Something had died in her that night, and even now, two months later, she felt the rot of her own mortality as a new life fed on it, like a fungus on the forest floor. Matilda wanted to reach out for Sarah, nestle her face against her soft, welcoming breasts and sob into the gentle folds of her skin. For the first time in her life, Matilda wanted to be held, for she had unwittingly discovered an unfamiliar connection between her mind and body, in the worst possible way. The pain was too much to manage alone.

Her mind felt salty now, floating inside a dark cavern of regret and remorse. She'd never noticed before how sensitive her brain truly was, how that soft jelly might turn against her with memories and phantom sensations. That silver fruit suddenly felt cold, foreign, and sealed. It was little more than a computer now, one she felt determined to reprogram. She longed to forget, to shed those dancing particles of a past painted black with shame, yet they clung to her. Those particles held tightly onto her frame and haunted her, day and night, while Sarah, beautiful, tender Sarah, was nowhere to be found.

Matilda had once read that being raped was like getting beat up: punched in the face, kicked in the gut, mercifully abandoned by a brutal stranger in the gutter of a disgusting alley somewhere with blood on your tongue and an eye swollen shut. Yet as she exited the shower and caught a glimpse of herself in the mirror, she could not ignore the apparent disconnect. Two months had passed, and still Matilda expected to see bruising, cuts, purple, black, blue, *anything*. In a way, she expected to see the Elephant Man in her reflection, with huge, bloated chunks of flesh mutating her face as her complexion throbbed and ached. She felt that everyone could see it as she walked down the street. On occasion, she thought she saw children stare at her hideousness, mouths agape; but the mirror always showed the same round eyes, small nose, and uneven lips. Her golden eyes were no different from how they had always appeared, and her gummy smile still showcased her strong, tiny teeth. Everything was in perfect order: not a dark brown hair, not a pore, not a cell appeared out of place, let alone damaged.

This constant reminder of outward continuity only served to make Matilda more aware of her inner turmoil, as that concealed poison brought with it the deepest melancholia. It was as if Greyson Carter had taken a serrated spoon and scooped out mighty chunks of her spirit, as one might remove small orbs from a melon. Now, with so many gaping holes, she could feel her soul slowly seep out, like the clear goo that oozes from a wound, no matter the size. No one could know of this. Matilda swore to herself that no one ever would.

On the Wednesday night of that fated week, she'd had consensual, albeit disappointing, sex with a man from Louisiana. Charles Price was his name. She didn't love him. It would be a stretch to say that she even liked him. No, she found Charles to be extremely dull, if not pretentious and fake. He seemed to be shopping around for a more passive female, but somehow found himself with Matilda instead. Their conversation over dinner had been agonizing, with his perfectly formed, grammatically correct sentences slowly dripping onto her forehead in an unnatural, forced rhythm. Nothing but talk about classical music, the industrial film for his family's company, and how his only real girlfriend had left him "for work."

When pressed about his life back home, if only to end the awkward lulls of silence between them, Charles briefly, if not vaguely, spoke of his mother's death and his father's controlling nature. For a man in his late thirties, he seemed like a disgruntled child, not the heir to a multi-million-dollar company. In bed, he seemed to be working out these frustrations through penetration, jackhammer style, with no consideration whatsoever for the pleasure of his partner, or knowledge of what a woman might actually need in order to reach orgasm. Her vagina was practically forced to recoil in response while her mind wandered to more interesting, if not purely entertaining, thoughts. Then again, his sexual ignorance was completely irrelevant to the situation, and not at all shocking. Matilda wasn't looking to marry the man, or even see him again for that matter. She just wanted to have sex with someone, anyone, to get back at Sarah for sleeping with Theodore Walsh. It wasn't personal. It was business.

Little did Matilda know that the following Sunday afternoon, after her final performance in a challenging new play, her co-star and director would get drunk on whiskey, trap her in the tiny closet of a dressing room backstage, and simply overpower her, as if she were nothing more than a poppet made of cloth. Sex with Sarah had always had its fair share of biting, scratching, hair-pulling and humping; but beneath that primal, animalistic activity, there had always–*always*–been love. With Greyson, the volition was very different. She scratched at him, bit his arms, pushed him away. Still, he was so much bigger than her, stronger, wider, drunker. If he'd only asked nicely, she probably would have slept with him, willingly and without fuss. Truth be told, she'd always found Greyson to be very attractive, with his china-blue eyes and dark red hair. In her mind, there had been no reason to rape her. She wouldn't have told him no. But this cruel operation wasn't really about sex—it was about power—and Matilda, despite being mentally strong, wasn't physically powerful enough to stop him. And no battlefield strategy her mind could concoct could have saved her from this event once it began.

She tried to disconnect, to escape into her mind, as any actress might; but the force she felt against her body shattered all illusions of control. With each thrust, the light within her was strangled, constricted, and dried out until her entire body felt as if it might break into pieces. And between each torn seam of her spiritual being awoke earthquakes of violence and war, until Matilda's eyes were glowing in red and ochre hues rich with hunger for wild revenge. And as his wicked seed sowed into her frightened earth, a fine dust of reddish-pink seemed to swallow her with a newfound knowledge she dared not share. So was born her depression and lethargy, her cruelty and vicious bite, all things that pushed Sarah out of their quiet nest so that she might breathe and slowly lick those infected wounds.

Almost immediately after the event, she cut her hair. Her long, dark chocolate brown locks had betrayed her as soon as Greyson had entered that dressing room. As if she were nothing more than a hunting dog, she cropped that superfluous tissue so that no boar might pierce her again. Once her hair had kissed her shoulders in fine, straight lines. Now she had a pixie cut shaved close along the sides, numbing her antennas purely as an act of survival. Matilda couldn't bear to feel any more than she already did, so she sheared those delicate tendrils of individuality as a way to cut herself off from the past. While serving as an initiation of sorts, this humble act was meant to prepare her for the greatest of personal wars.

However, she couldn't slice the flesh from her face where Greyson's fingers had gripped her jaw. She couldn't drown out the memories of his voice ringing in her ears, forever driving the hammer towards the anvil to find home within the stirrup. The very molecules in the air seemed to torment her, spiraling within that complex labyrinth designed to gather waves of sound rolling along fragile coils of consciousness. In this newfound wilderness of Matilda's exile, she could not find balance, let alone direction. Even her nose deceived her, forever catching the scent of Greyson on her clothes, bedding, and skin, no matter how frequently she washed them. Walking down State Street, she caught a whiff of his cologne. The scent curdled in her stomach as emotions rushed up and down her throat, burning her with unwanted thoughts.

There were times when Matilda wanted to tell someone, anyone, about what had happened; but who to tell? Non-union theatre had no protocol for violations such as these. Greyson owned the theatre and was artistic director of the company. He'd won three Jeff Awards over the years, which now seemed to be nothing more than cheap pieces of plastic fashioned into the shapes of shooting stars. These were barriers to truth that Matilda had never anticipated. Those credentials seemed to form a gag of sorts, preventing her supple cheeks, elastic lips, and fierce tongue from uttering a single word. Even her teeth couldn't cut through the red tape between the truth of the moment and the truth desired by the theatre community. Why risk damaging her reputation and hard-won career if nothing would be done, if even believed? Her golden eyes became the sole proprietors of this secret, and even if people noticed the twinge of sadness woven into those plentiful threads of amber and gold, no one would be able to solve the puzzle of her misery, not even Sarah.

"You could have left at any time," Greyson said, zipping his jeans while she cried, as if the sex doll has any choice as to what happens to her, or when. He had reduced her to such a role, an inanimate object unworthy of respect. And now, forcing herself to accept her own vulnerability as a human being, that she of all people could fall prey to such a crime, Matilda had to determine how best to move forward. Charles had used a condom. Greyson had not. Charles had a future, security, stability. Greyson was a monster on a power trip as far as she was concerned; but in all likelihood, this was his child. The thought of abortion crossed her mind, but that seed didn't take root. She didn't believe that violence could be solved with death, even if this pregnancy marked the death of the life she knew and the person she had always been. Instead of life and creation she felt nothing but darkness and chaos, especially as it pertained to her career as an actress in Chicago. An abortion would only feed the flames of her guilt.

As she looked around the small, one-bedroom apartment, all she saw were signs of a life dedicated to theatre. There were half-finished props on the floor, half-read plays on the table, playbills pinned to the walls, and abandoned scripts scattered across the couch. Matilda had met Sarah in their very first Meisner class at a local acting school. The two women had been inseparable ever since. Over the years, they helped each other memorize lines, dive deeper into character motivations, and prepare for auditions. They ushered at Steppenwolf together to see plays for free and had each worked at the Goodman's call center, a job almost every unemployed actor in Chicago was eventually fated to have. They studied Shakespeare and Chekov, commedia dell'arte and clown, circus arts and singing, dance and improvisation—always returning to the solace of this very apartment. Although solace was probably the wrong word.

Rage, passion, unbridled emotions—these were never left behind in the classroom or on the stage. Instead both actresses were equally guilty of bringing such heated feelings home to stew within. What's worse, the competition between them was fierce. If Sarah got cast in a show, Matilda became all the more determined to get cast in another. If one took a class, the other took the next one. If one got a new coach, so did the other. If Matilda received a compliment from casting, Sarah went out searching for her own. And since Matilda got cast in Greyson Carter's latest production, Sarah was hellbent on finding an equivalent accomplishment elsewhere. That's how she met Theodore Walsh, and, at least in Matilda's mind, why she had slept with him almost immediately. If Greyson was the hottest new director in Chicago, then Theo had the potential to become the best new playwright. Sarah had suggested bringing him home for a threesome. When Matilda refused, Sarah had simply gone home with him by herself. "Are you angry?" she asked, her opal eyes sparkling with sinister glee. "Not at all," Matilda lied. "In fact, I'm seeing someone too."

She hadn't been seeing anyone. Greyson had been awfully determined to single her out among the other cast members, but that didn't count as dating. It was more intense and confusing than that. Greyson demanded absolute vulnerability, for actors to be stripped naked, both literally and emotionally, on stage. He was passionate, charismatic, and possessive. "I love you *so* much," he'd say, but Matilda knew he didn't mean it. If Greyson loved anyone, it was Greyson. And you can bet your ass if he made a mistake, *any* mistake, an actress would be blamed for it. "You missed your mark. You're too sensitive. It's your fault for not being honest on my stage." If you didn't like it, if you weren't "tough enough" to hang with the *true* artists of the Chicago storefront theatre scene, well then, you could leave. "Bring your real life to the stage," he'd say, "or don't bother coming in at all."

As a co-star, he was overwhelming. Matilda often left re-hearsals and then shows with bruises on her skin and a head-ache pounding behind her eyes, his screaming voice bouncing between her ears; but the material itself was violent, gruesome, demanding. "If you're a real actress, you can handle it," he'd say. And Matilda, above all, considered herself to be a *real* actress. It was in her blood. Her grandfather had been an actor, and her father after him. She'd never known her mother, but she'd grown up in the wings of black box theaters and vaudevillian performance halls with her half-brother, J.J., often sweeping the stage, running the box office or concessions, and filling in casting gaps as needed. This was the only world she had ever known; yet she doubted her own intuition when it came to those who had garnered more success. Her instincts had told her something was wrong when she'd first started rehearsals for this final play, but Greyson was famous in Chicago for produc-ing the darkest and edgiest work, which also turned out to be the most applauded. The city had practically thrown awards at his feet. Who was she to question his methods? And why would she complain at home when Sarah was so terribly jeal-ous that she'd even gotten the opportunity?

In comparison, Theo was practically no one. He'd written two historical plays that had gotten some mild acclaim, but other than that, he had nothing, just potential. There were no plastic shooting stars in his apartment. The *Reader* hadn't profiled him. The *Tribune* probably didn't even know who he was. Still, Sarah rubbed Theo's promising future in Matilda's face at every opportu-nity. "He's the next David Mamet, just you wait and see." The only problem was that Sarah never gave her the time to wait. Instead she vanished into thin air mere days after the show with Greyson had closed. The story was that she and Theo were working on a new play together, with Sarah serving as his muse. Matilda couldn't blame her girlfriend for wanting to enhance her career through a strategic partnership, but over the past two months she'd needed Sarah more than ever, and the fact of the matter was that Sarah simply wasn't there.

Matilda had gone to work at a sports bar in Wrigleyville night after night, as she had for years, getting her ass grabbed and her tits ogled by drunken Cubs, Bears, and Blackhawks fans as she served Chicago dogs and cheap beer by the pitcher, only to come home time and time again to an empty apartment. She waited desperately by her phone for a call, a message, an update, but none came. She stopped by Chicago Dramatists to check in on rehearsals for Theo's public read-thru, only to discover that rehearsals had been moved to another, undisclosed location. She turned to mutual friends to fish for information, but no one had really heard from Sarah. A few people had seen her at plays around town, but she'd basically fallen off the face of the earth in a state of complete and utter bliss with Theo Walsh. And for the first time in their five year relationship, Matilda felt deeply, woefully bitter.

Here she was, sleeping alone at night, reaching out for someone who was no longer there. She'd wake up in the morning from her nightmares to discover the same heartbreaking circumstances. Then, slowly but surely, things began to vanish from the apartment while Matilda was away at work. Sarah's piles of clothing began to dwindle, her shoe collection halved in size, her books disappeared from the shelves, her artwork was removed from the walls, and even her Vitamix went missing. It wouldn't be the first time Sarah had liquidated her "assets" for cash, or had provided props for low budget theatre. Such disappearances were concerning, but not necessarily unusual. Meanwhile, Matilda continued to rationalize this affair with Theo as a mere fling, an obsession, something that Sarah would soon grow weary of before returning home. She even considered that perhaps the truth had somehow leaked, that she and Sarah were lesbians and secretly cohabitating in Ravenswood. If certain people believed that, neither Matilda nor Sarah would be able to get cast in certain plays by certain theaters alongside certain players, no matter how evolved the theatre community advertised itself to be. Maybe that was why Sarah was so hellbent on making public appearances with Theo, she thought. Recently, Matilda had heard they'd been seen at the Chopin Theatre, Timeline, iO, and even The Second City. Rumors swirled throughout the community that the couple was working on a play that might even premier at Victory Gardens, which would be a huge opportunity for them both, especially since that theatre also happened to pay the most. Armed with all of this information, Matilda still held on to hope, despite the fact that Sarah couldn't even be bothered to call her back.

Then again, the very last thing she had told Sarah was to leave her alone, so Matilda felt that she couldn't be mad at her for doing so. She was even willing to take on all of the blame, so long as Sarah came back. It didn't have to be today or tomorrow, but if she came back soon, all would be forgiven. No questions asked. Every day she lovingly studied pictures of Sarah and dreamed about her perpetually frowning mouth, her sparkling eyes, her fantastic breasts, and her perfectly round ass. She wanted to kiss her skin, from her hairline to her curling toes. She yearned to hear her vibrant laugh, as well as her earth-shattering moans. The neighbors had already left two notes on their door, one typed and one handwritten, each warning them to keep their lovemaking to a lower volume, *but oh*, how Matilda wanted to earn another warning. She wanted to watch Sarah wriggle helplessly beneath her and twitch frantically against her touch. Her ears ached to hear her panting, gasping for breath, as another scream danced in muffled tones within her throat. Instead, Matilda distinctly heard a key enter and turn the lock before the heavy white door to their unit slowly creaked open.

Sarah had her thick, blonde hair slightly curled and loose, the Chicago wind having provided its look of just-fucked freshness. Her long runner's legs were covered by her jeans and trench coat, but Matilda's eyes could imagine their monumental presence despite the layers of fabric. Her lover's pale complexion had been teased and tormented by the sun, causing her creamy skin to blend into bright shades of red along the tip of her delicate nose and across her freckled cheeks. Her jacket was tight across her large breasts while her lips were chapped and worn. In that moment, Matilda realized that she was willing to die for this woman, so powerful was her never-ending love.

"Oh, I didn't realize you were home," Sarah said, freezing in the doorway.

"I had an audition for a local commercial this afternoon, so I got someone to cover my shift."

Sarah smiled, revealing her perfectly aligned, perfectly shaped, perfectly white teeth. "How'd it go?"

"Awful."

"Don't say that. I'm sure you did great."

"The director said he didn't believe I was passionate about carpeting." Sarah snorted. "I guess that depends, now doesn't it?"

Matilda walked towards her, hopelessly craving affection. She reached out, pulled Sarah close to her and kissed her soft, warm cheek. "I'm so glad to see you," she whispered. "There's so much I need to tell you." She wanted Sarah to know everything, from beginning to end. The words were ready to pour out of her as those walls of pride and ego began to lower. She wanted to come clean about Charles Price, Greyson Carter, the unexpected pregnancy, everything. Matilda didn't have a maternal bone in her body. Sarah was the nurturer. Surely she'd understand and know what to do. She might even be delighted. Matilda needed her. She couldn't raise this child alone. She didn't want to. But to Matilda's surprise, just as she was ready to release all of her suffering and let the truth air out, Sarah pulled away.

"I have to talk to you too," she said, walking across the room and taking a seat on the couch. "I don't have much time. Theo's waiting for me downstairs."

"He can come up."

"NO...no. This is something I should do alone."

Matilda lowered herself into the opposing armchair as panic flooded her mind. "You're breaking up with me, aren't you?" The words were more breath than sound.

Sarah—all-American, girl-next-door Sarah—pursed her lips then sighed. "Yes."

"For Theo?"

"He asked me to move in with him."

Matilda sank even deeper into her chair, her voice cracking as she squirmed. "So I need to move out, don't I?"

"My father said he'll pay next month's rent, while I make the transition..."

"Gee. Thanks." The words came out as sludge.

"It's the least I could do," Sarah said.

"Sure is."

"We're just not...this isn't working anymore. I've realized, well, I think I always knew, but *I know* for sure now...I'm not gay, Tilly. You are, *and that's great*, but...I'm not. I'm in love with Theo."

That poison was racing again, from head to toes then toes to head, making a figure-eight throughout Matilda's body. She could feel the nausea in her stomach, the sourness in her gut, but it was her mind that felt sickly cold. She could see that Sarah was still talking, making excuses, using her hands for emphasis, but all thoughts and emotions Sarah expressed felt horribly empty. Matilda couldn't make eye contact as Sarah rambled. It was far too tempting to cry. She wanted to defend herself, to plead her case, but instead her mouth and teeth and tongue used words that only served to sever the connection between them. Her mouth felt armored, bloodthirsty, cruel. Matilda chose to cut, tear, grind and chew whatever justifications Sarah threw her way. She ground them up and spit them back out into the ether, as if her words could become arrows dipped in her own poisonous blood.

"*Why are you being so mean?*" Sarah cried.

Matilda couldn't answer that question. She couldn't even control her face. As if suddenly cast in one of life's cruelest plays, she now had a cold mask secured to her flesh. She didn't know what it looked like to Sarah. She hardly even cared. She just wanted to burn their connection to the ground, then plow that ground with salt. Words, words, words came spiraling out from between her teeth, as her ears searched for ways to dig even deeper into those unseen cuts and make Sarah hurt all the more.

"Is this because of Greyson Carter?" Sarah asked. "Because he told Theo yesterday that you were drinking too much during the run and that you've lost your mind; that you've been lying about him all over town and he'll never work with you again. I don't know what you did Tilly, but don't take it out on me."

The sound of Greyson's name formed crystals along Matilda's spine and turned her aura, that ethereal egg of energy, into a treacherous fortress covered by lethal spikes. Maybe Sarah couldn't see the change in her, but with that poison pumping through her veins, tissue and soul, her words didn't leave much to the imagination. She was going for blood with her sharpest teeth. The smell of fear reached her nose. *Yes, Sarah should be scared*, she thought. *Let her run back to Theo and tell him how manic I've become.*

"If we can't talk about this like rational people, then I don't need to be here," Sarah cried behind a flood of tears. "I thought you'd understand."

"Understand that you're leaving me for Theo Walsh so he can help your career?"

"Understand that I love him!"

"Well if you love him, *GO! LEAVE! I won't stop you.*"

"Fine, Tilly. Fine. I tried to do a nice thing for you, to make sure you had a place to live for at least a month—"

"You'll abandon him the same way you're abandoning me. Don't give yourself credit for the pathetic crumbs you leave behind."

Sarah fled the apartment with tears running down her face as Matilda was engulfed by her own madness. She was no longer the Matilda of the past. She saw quite clearly now that the past was gone, dead, dissolved. Another act had begun in this living theatre of mysteries, this dark and treacherous masquerade. Her anger was building up knots within her body and spirit. She could feel them, as if some ghostly sailor was tying up every loose end of her being. She could sense the tension held between every negative emotion, every painful thought, every vengeful fantasy. Anger, hatred, animosity—these were the names of her knots. They grew and spread throughout her physical structure, across all mental planes, building eternal tension that twisted and tightened every second. The pain and the misery dug deeper and deeper with each and every knot, from the surface level of her person to the darkness of her unconscious. Each knot became subtler and subtler, from thick rope to the spider's finest thread.

These knots formed a solidified wall between Matilda and her own feelings. Slowly it turned to iron, all to protect the smallest vein of buried gold that was the sole remnant of her Self. This armor, this protective layer of knots, numbed her senses. It closed her off from the pain she felt both inside and out, from her shins to her chest. A helmet formed across her skull, protecting her silver mind. That same poison was still rushing throughout her body, but now she had armor to protect her exterior. She would never be hurt again because she would never let anyone in again. These knots would serve as diamonds, harder than anyone's good or bad intentions. And this impenetrable barrier would be her only protection as she moved forward into the unknown, for there were no other options available. A new life had to begin, whether she was ready for it or not. The cards had been chosen and she alone could decide how best to play.

It was a shadow of her former self that went shuffling through the random papers on the desk. Soon, that shadow found the scrap she most needed in this entire apartment. It was a single page of the script from the industrial film she had done for Price Plasma, a small Louisiana company that had chosen a Chicago media firm in order to seem more important. Even if she still had the money from that acting gig, the sum wouldn't even cover her

rent. The script read: "At Price Plasma, we work tirelessly to ensure the safety of our samples, only collecting plasma from qualified donors who have been verified as healthy and able to meet
the strict criteria outlined by the FDA. As a family business we
believe in protecting families, and that is what we do every day by
providing the raw materials needed to create life-saving drugs for
the rarest diseases known to mankind. This is our mission. This is
our business. And this is what's in our blood."

Matilda grabbed her phone and dialed the number scribbled
at the bottom of the script. "Hi? Charles? It's Matilda. From Chicago. From the industrial? *From The Drake*? Well…is this a bad
time? We really need to talk."

As the conversation continued, Matilda could almost feel iron
being poured over her tomb. She felt buried alive by her circumstances, as if the person she had always believed herself to be had
been snuffed out by the reality of the moment. She had no choice
but to commit murder against her old self and to wage a war
against the future. And with that coffin lid closed, a curtain of
lead fell; but the end is only the beginning.

NATALIE ROSE PRICE WAS SMILING from ear to ear as the waiters delivered her personal birthday cake made of delicate layers of light sponge, fresh berries, and delicious Crème Chantilly. A single candle in the shape of the number eighteen flickered in the center, and when the waiters finished their song she blew the candle out, wishing that her deepest desires would quickly manifest. Then she opened her eyes once more to the world she had always known, if only a little brighter, just for today. It was good to see her father smiling, she thought. It had been such a long time since she'd seen him happy, she'd forgotten what his brownish teeth looked like, completely stained from smoking countless cigars. Unfortunately, his happiness also gave her pause, because she still didn't know how she was going to tell him about her acceptance to SCAD.

The Savannah College of Art and Design in Georgia was far away from their home in Lafayette, Louisiana, and she didn't trust that he'd take care of himself in her absence. Despite his long, lean build, her father tended to go for ice cream and salty treats when he was stressed, especially fresh cracklins from local boudin vendors. Recently a node had been discovered on his gallbladder, and his blood pressure was through the roof. The thought of him turning to junk food for comfort formed a lump in her throat. Who was going to cook healthy meals for him, make sure he wore his rain jacket in the winter, or took a break from work every now and

again if she left? Her mother certainly wouldn't. In fact, she didn't
want to leave him home alone with her at all. They already couldn't
communicate properly. How would they fare without her frequent
translations? Then there was their maid, Ms. Helen, who seemed to
indulge her father's worst habits, always making the exact foods his
doctors warned against, as if she somehow knew better than they
did. The entire situation was terrible, if not absolutely toxic.

Then there was another issue to consider. She hated to even think
on it. It would break her father's heart if he knew what she'd done. It
was selfish, she knew that. Terribly, terribly selfish; but she couldn't
help herself. It had been her father's idea in the first place. He was
the one who had wanted her to observe and learn from the managers
at various Price Plasma donation centers across the state. She took
photographs of everything and everyone. How could he expect her
not to take photos of the donors? She had them all sign a copy of a
release form she found on the internet, just in case; but his permission
was really the one she needed, and she knew she'd never, ever have
that. The business had been started by her grandfather in the late
1940s and had survived major global scandals through the decades.
Preserving the business was her father's top priority, but Natalie didn't
care about any of that. She cared about those people standing in line.

Her father often joked that the donors would sell him their shadows if they could. She didn't think that was very funny. Her own parents were little more than shadows themselves. They moved, looked,
and even spoke like parents; but there was no substance to them, just
darkness blocking the light. And instead of clear features to tell them
apart, Natalie knew those shadows by their habits: her mother with
her Negronis, her father with his cigars, the sound of ice being stirred
and the smell of fermented tobacco burning. Her mother was noc-
turnal, her father an early riser. Each had their own bedroom, and
neither liked to be in the same room at the same time. Like two
magnets of similar polarities, they were constantly pushing the other
away. Natalie was simply the resting point at the center, a gentle cushion between their opposing sides. She feared leaving them alone with

each other. The entire world might crumble if she did, for neither head nor body could survive without a uniting neck.

Her father was scratching his skin again. That was never a good sign. It meant that he was stressed, and had been for some time. He seemed to live in three-piece suits, but when the rash started to peek past his sleeves, sneak onto his hands, or even crawl up his neck like devil's ivy, that's when she knew things were especially bad. And if he started drinking scotch, well, it was time to prepare for the worst. Right now, as she ate her delicious Chantilly cake, he was doing both: scratching and drinking, then chewing on the ice. *Oh no*, she thought. *Maybe he already knows.*

"How was San Francisco?" she asked, filling her fork with cake.

"Good, good," he replied. "Once you graduate, I'll take you there. Let you see what this business is really about."

"Jesus, Charles, don't get her wrapped up in your nonsense," her mother replied, reaching for her cocktail. "That woman is a charlatan. I swear it on my father's grave."

"Matilda, I don't get involved with your business. Stay out of ours."

"What business?" her mother screeched. "All I do is babysit aging debutantes all day and give them gold stars for philanthropy that doesn't mean jack shit. It's like teaching drunk, shriveled up mermaids how to walk on land, with their diamonds, pearls and all."

"I've told you before that I don't care for your cursing at the table," he warned.

"There's a lot you don't care for, and I couldn't care less."

Natalie tried to change the subject. She hated when her mother interrupted, especially when she was negative, which she often was. The poor man was already stressed. Why couldn't she see that? Why was she hell-bent on making their evening worse? "Tell me Daddy, what's Delilah Russell really like? She's been all over the internet. Is she really that beautiful in person?"

"I still can't believe you went to California, when there's disease spreading there about as fast as their damn wildfires. I swear, if you get me sick…" her mother warned.

"You don't seem too concerned," her father replied. "What is that, your third Negroni in an hour?"

"I'm trying to kill your germs."

"I haven't even touched you!"

"Yeah but you breathe."

"Daddy?" Natalie chirped.

"Oh, yes, Delilah's beautiful, but nowhere near as beautiful as you, Peanut."

Natalie blushed as her mother rolled her eyes. "When can I try the elixir?" the teenager asked, practically bouncing in her seat.

"You *are not* putting that shit in your body," her mother barked. "I don't care how *beautiful* the founder is."

"My god, Matilda," her father howled. "The woman graduated from Stanford. Where did you go again? Oh, that's right: clown school."

"For the millionth time, it's called *physical theatre*, and I don't give a flying fuck where the bitch graduated from. Do you even know what's in that 'golden' shit? Because I'd like to know before our daughter starts tapping her veins."

Her father gave her mother a dirty look, then turned towards Natalie. "Gotta be thirty-five to qualify, Peanut, but don't you worry. I'll make sure you never grow old. You're gonna stay young and beautiful forever. I promise." He grabbed her hand and kissed it.

Those words seemed to wrap around Natalie's neck and squeeze, like a bejeweled collar fastened just a bit too tight. She feigned a smile; but remaining forever young, well, the thought filled her with dread. She already felt trapped in a tower, with her mother serving as the fire-breathing dragon and her father a blindfolded king who could be both generous and cruel; but that tower wasn't their Antebellum home out in the country, it was childhood itself. She couldn't blame her father for wanting to keep her there, in a permanent state of innocence, nestled in a ruffled bed of chiffon and silk, all shimmering in muted pastels; but ever since she'd gotten her first period, her mother had been especially domineering, as if that dark flow threatened the very balance of their lives. Natalie realized there was power in that blood, if only because it represented the demise of the tower itself. And in her imagination, every cramp, every headache, every tender pang was a necessary evil inching her closer to the freedom she most craved. Truth be told, despite her baby blush tulle dress and an assortment of sterling silver charms and bracelets from Tiffany's, Natalie didn't want to be a little girl anymore. And now that she was finally eighteen, she had plans on how to remedy the situation. She felt that she finally understood the story of the Garden of Eden— that temptation was inevitable and golden fruit was meant to be eaten. She was willing to eat *anything* that might break her free from those shackles of childhood, to be able to admit the hunger she felt vibrating deep within her, or to act on her darkest secrets, those impulses and fantasies that sweet little Peanuts were never meant to have. Natalie wanted to have it all, and then a little more. It was as if she had awakened from a dream, or emerged from an impenetrable veil of clouds. She was burning from within, and her ravenous lips already had ideas as to how she might mark a man with her shiny gloss.

"It's eight thousand dollars, Charles," her mother continued to fuss. "How are you, *of all people,* okay with that? If we buy brand-name groceries you fly off the handle."

"By the time she's thirty-five, the treatment will probably only be eight hundred."

"Don't put poison in your body, Natalie," her mother said. "You only get one."

"Says the woman who's having a relationship with gin."

"It's good for my circulation!"

"I promise, the Blue Lotus elixir is perfectly healthy. The military might even use it!"

"Right," her mother mocked. "At least I know what's in my drink. Natalie, be careful. I don't trust women with secrets, and Delilah acts like she's got a really big one."

"You have no idea what you're talking about," her father barked. "And Natalie's an adult now. She can make her own decisions."

"Well then Natalie, I hope you choose to treat your body like a temple, not a fucking guinea pig."

At least she could agree with her mother on that point. Natalie knew better than anyone that her body was a precious temple. She was actually very careful about what she put into it, and she only ate sweets once a year. Today just happened to be that day. She pulled out her little red notebook from her handbag and marked her estimation of calories: 620 for the slice of cake alone. She'd hardly eaten all day, knowing that this dinner would take place. It had been worth the wait. She imagined that other, more savory feasts would be worth the wait as well.

"Have you booked your flight to Chicago yet?" her father asked her mother. "You know the longer you wait, the more expensive it will be."

"If you're trying to get rid of me, you could've hired Matt to fly me there last week."

"Absolutely not. Business class is perfectly fine. I just need to know your schedule."

"Well if you'd look up from your damn phone once in a while, maybe you would've heard what I said, or was solitaire more important?"

"Just text me the dates."

"Got plans?"

"Call me old-fashioned, but I'd like to know when my *darling* wife is leaving so I can be sure to kiss you goodbye."

"Oh yes, *darling*," she snapped back with a laugh. "I'm sure you have nothing but the best intentions for my well-being, Charles."

"Then let's just pretend. You're an actress, aren't you?"

"You narcissistic son of a bitch. *How dare you!*"

The two of them continued to bicker and bitch as Natalie finished her birthday cake. Yes, her body was a temple. That's why she took such great care to moisturize, tone and tweeze. Her bathroom was overflowing with all kinds of lotions, perfumes and enhancers. One drawer held over a hundred tubes of lipstick, another housed her bronzers and highlighters. Her cabinets were filled with defrizzing serums and gels for her strawberry blonde curls, and the antique vanity in her room was covered with powders, all boasting exotic scents. She was a flower, reaching out towards the sun, her delicate petals luring in the bees with ultraviolet messages and electric vibrations. "All desire is sexual desire," David had once told her. Had truer words ever been spoken?

Natalie ignored her parents as she dissolved into the fantasy of her favorite equestrian. In her mind's eye, she could see his strong legs highlighted by his tight breeches, his heels driven down into the stirrups as his powerful forearms held firmly onto the reins. She wanted him to grab her long, tousled hair with those hands, which she thought Rodin would have begged to replicate with a sculpture. She wanted her head pulled back so that her spine could arch into him. As she sat at the table, she imagined his muscular fingers gripping the sides of her long neck, then running down her graceful shoulders, as one might run their hands down the length of a finely groomed show horse. She yearned for his stern lips to meet hers while his hands pulled her up against him, so that he might find rest within the puffy pillows of her blossoming flesh. Natalie wanted to be bound up in those leather reins, and slowly, deeply explored by David's agile tongue and eager fingertips. She was a flower meant to be plucked; soft, fertile earth begging for the plow. And like a fertility goddess of centuries past, her mouth ached to swallow those seeds of sacred knowledge, which could multiply like the grain. She licked the last of the white whipped cream off of her silver fork and dreamed of what David might taste like.

In reality, she was a virgin, and the only penis she'd ever actually seen up close had been the one belonging to her show horse. Before the Irish gelding had been sold, Natalie had held that penis plenty of times, with her childlike hands wrapped around his girth, cleaning his sheath and removing any waxy beans buried within the folds of the head, but that was different. She'd never seen a man naked, and thanks to her enrollment at the local all-girls Catholic school from kindergarten through her current status as soon-to-be graduating senior, she didn't know any boys. The only man she really knew was David Hall, her riding instructor, and she could only imagine what he might look like once his often suggestive clothing had been removed. David's hands were the first and only to grasp her hips and rotate them. His eyes were the first to openly study her body intently for any deviations in form. And his words were the first to stir the energies within her. His voice alone could bring her to a state of secret convulsions, and Natalie wanted more. She wanted his face between her legs, humming against her nerves. She wanted to be filled with him, in every possible way, to feel his weight within her. She wanted to become a slave to his desires, if only to be saved from her own.

He had already taught her so many life lessons, from how to give her horse intravenous injections and wrap its delicate legs with soft bandages, to navigating complex courses in the show jumping ring. When she'd fallen off of her horse in Blowing Rock, North Carolina, suffering a concussion, David was the one who had carried her in the rain to the First Aid tent. When her horse was struck by colic in Germantown, Tennessee, David was the one who had driven them to the nearby vet. He had taught her about literature, politics and life, more so than anyone else ever had. And he touched her in ways that no one had ever dared. There were hugs that lingered, frequent kisses on her cheeks, his large hand occasionally grazing her eager thigh as they watched other exhibitors ride. She spent more time with David than she did with anyone else, including her parents, and she believed that if anyone could guide her to the other side of childhood, he was the one to do it. She envisioned David riding towards her on his sorrel red horse, there to rescue her from the dragon and finally free her from the tower once and for all, so that she might find safe passage to perfectly divine bliss.

On the other hand, there were complications, just a few minor obstacles in their way. Her parents were one. David's girlfriend Renée was the other. But Natalie was convinced that she knew David better than Renée ever could, that she suited him better, and that their lovemaking would be infinitely better; because she believed, more than anything, that David truly loved her, in a way that he had never loved anyone before. And while her parents were constantly fighting, David offered solace, peace, harmony, the only things she'd ever truly wanted. Then again, her parents never took David seriously. Her mother didn't like him, but her mother didn't like anyone. Her father preferred Renée, always pointing out how much harder she worked than David ever did. It was true, Renée worked very hard: grooming horses, braiding manes, training students, schooling mounts, and handling every administrative task at Pine Grove Farms; but Pine Grove was her family's farm, her sole inheritance, and David was a trainer for hire who just happened to be living with her. It was a system that seemed doomed to fail, as David was the talent and Renée the frustrated owner. It was only a matter of time before the entire system fell apart. And just as David had made Natalie earn her white breeches to wear during classics and big money classes, she would earn his eternal love and devotion too.

"You don't even know how the technology works," Natalie's mother complained as her father signed the check.

"I don't need to know how the technology works, Matilda. Get off my ass, will ya?"

"You just can't admit that you only see what you want to see, that you have zero evidence to back up your argument."

"Why do you even care?" her father whined. "You're going to Chicago."

"I'm thinking about our daughter."

Her father laughed loudly at her mother's comment, forcing Natalie's fantasy to dissipate. "Our daughter," he laughed, tears streaming down his face. "Natalie," he asked, collecting himself. "Do you want to go into business with me?"

The question terrified her. She knew she wanted to go to SCAD far more than she wanted to work for her father. The school had even offered her a full scholarship to study photography; but she couldn't tell him that, not now, not even on her birthday. If she mentioned the scholarship, she'd be forced to admit how she got it. "I…I don't know…"

"Come on, Peanut. It's an easy question."

No it wasn't. No question her father asked was ever easy to answer. She wanted to make him proud, but rejecting his offer would devastate him. There was no escaping that, and she resented being put into such a perilous position. After all, Natalie had always tried to bring joy to his life, not more heartache. While her mother wore somber tones and ran their lives with an iron fist, Natalie wore pinks and delicate blues, dancing and singing around the house, filling it as best she could with her own personal brand of magic. While her mother was always at war, with everyone, she felt that it was her duty as Charles' daughter to bring stability and love into the home, ensuring that everything was perfect before her father walked through the door at the end of the day. And yes, showing horses on the national circuit had been terribly expensive, but hadn't she justified the cost by being the best daughter she could be? What was her happiness worth to him? Did it have to mean imprisonment in a plasma business that made her feel dirty and disgusting? Must she be sentenced to a life unlived?

"Tell me Daddy, why do you want to work *with me?*"

"Well, I want to show you the ropes, the way my father showed me. You have to understand, Peanut, plasma is liquid gold. It's more expensive than oil. And I know you like your pretty dresses and your pretty things, and they all cost a mighty pretty penny. This is an easy way to keep you in those things, and if you want to keep riding horses, well, this helps you do that too. Like I've told you before, plasma has no substitute. You've got no competition, apart from other brokers. And I know that one woman is promising some kind of cure for hemophilia, but there are lots of rare diseases out there, and all those medicines need plasma to work. There's even talk that plasma might be used to cure this new disease that's going around. So, you'd get to save lives and make a difference in the world, help the people who really need it."

"Ha," her mother snapped. "Yeah, it's all about the people."

"Look, everything is already set up for you," her father continued, giving her mother a nasty look. "You'd be sitting nice and pretty. Business is good, this research deal with Blue Lotus is filling the coffers, and donations are always increasing…hell, they've tripled over the past few years. It costs me 150 bucks to collect one liter of plasma, and then I turn around and sell it for 500. Each donor provides about a liter each visit, and we've got a line out the door from open to close, seven days a week. Think of all the bracelets and purses, makeup and dresses, you could buy with that kind of money. You could go to Paris and buy your dresses there if you'd like."

"What a winning argument, Charles," her mother mumbled before drinking the last of her Negroni.

"Stay out this Matilda," he growled in her direction. "The best part is, you'd get to work with me, Peanut. Every day. I'll teach you everything I know. You can even live at home if you'd like. Wouldn't that be nice? I mean, you're gonna inherit it all anyway. Why not learn how it works?"

The hope in her father's eyes filled her with feelings of unworthiness and doubt. He was right, she did love her things. She didn't want to give them up; but life was so much more complicated than that. She couldn't begin to describe her hesitation. There was just something within her screaming "NO." That scream echoed within the four chambers of her heart then rose up the empty column of her throat, never to be vocalized. That "no" would shatter her father's hope, if not his adoration.

"Do I have to answer now?"

"No, Peanut. Take your time. It will still be here waiting for you when you're ready." He grabbed her hand and kissed it again. "Are we ready to go home?"

"Yes, Daddy. Thank you for dinner."

"My pleasure. Matilda?"

"Oh gee, Mister, thank you so much for feeding poor little old me. What would I ever do without you?"

Her father rolled his eyes, then headed towards the valet. As Natalie left the table, she suddenly felt her mother's talons grip her arm as she was spun around to face those haunting golden eyes. "What did you do, Natalie Rose?"

"Nothing," she pleaded.

"Well you're looking awfully guilty."

"I didn't do anything. I swear."

"Uh-huh. Get your ass in the car."

Fear was sticking to the back of Natalie's throat as she fastened her seatbelt. The entire ride home was quiet as the Maserati sped down the main arteries of Lafayette and out into the country. Her father had never known another home and neither had she. As they pulled into the driveway, then drove between the opened wrought iron gates and down the winding road towards the house, Natalie wondered what it was that she truly wanted. Her fantasy was that she and David would ride off into the sunset together, have children, and be wild and free, showing horses and living in the moment. She believed that was possible; but she also looked at her mother, who was bitter, cold, and angry. Surely she must have loved once. How had she become so callous? Natalie never wanted to end up like her. But was that her father's fault, or her mother's? Could anyone truly accept responsibility for another's happiness?

When they reached the house, Natalie told her parents good-night, kissed her father's cheek, then raced towards her room. The dark pink walls came to life as she flipped on the light. She locked her door, turned on the bath, and reached between the mattresses for her portfolio. There she found countless photographs of David she had taken at horse shows around the country. The sight of him made her lips curve into a smile. There was so much comfort to be found in his hazel eyes and gentle grin. His image made her heart beat that much faster, as her longing for him grew. She wanted so desperately to reach out and touch him, just so that her fingertips might feel the warmth of his skin. She hungered for the softness of his lips, the feel of his stubble against her face. He was everything she wanted, and everything she feared she would never have. A twinge of sadness began to stir behind her nose and in her eyes. His profound distance from her filled her with a deep and mournful grief strong enough to split her heart clean in half. Did he feel the same way about her? She didn't know. She had no way of knowing.

Natalie had only taken up photography as a way to get closer to David. He claimed to have been a model in the past, and was always willing to take one more shot. Her portfolio was filled with his image, and not once had Natalie regretted a moment in the darkroom, mixing those chemicals to conjure up the face she most adored. It was only in the darkness that light could be manipulated to expose the truth of the moment, and from moment to moment, she watched David's face emerge: his beautiful face complemented by feathery hair and deep-set eyes, his sullen cheeks forged into a sexy sneer. Never before had she seen such a face. It inspired her to be better, to capture him better, to understand his face better than anyone else ever had. Lighting David was an art unto itself, and only she would master it. He made her a better artist, and he made her feel that she could be a better person too.

Reluctantly, but forcefully, she flipped through her portfolio, reaching the very end. Darker faces began to appear. Tired faces with missing teeth and tattoos around their eyes. These men and women had weathered skin and pores as large as gnats. Their sullen faces and deep-set eyes weren't attractive, they were horrifying. Taking pictures of David was an act of capturing beauty, while these photographs seemed to exhibit a painful and ugly truth she didn't feel strong enough to withstand. Who were these people? What were their stories? Why were they donating their blood plasma for a mere thirty dollars and a cookie? Natalie had only shadowed at the centers a handful of times, but the images remained the same: the poorest of the poor, lining up like cattle, day after day, from seven in the morning until seven in the evening. The couches were always full of donors with track marks broadcasting their only source of income. The smell was wretched, their chatter incessant. She didn't want to be involved with something so ugly, so shocking and raw. Her father was promising money, but money made from this? Money harvested from these poor people?

Her advisor at school, Sister Léger, had once told her that the role of a photographer is to tell the stories of people whose stories would never be told otherwise, a story told through a powerful image that cannot be ignored. She had no doubt that the images of these plassers had played a large role in her acceptance to SCAD, and she was terrified of what these images might mean to the public. She was afraid of what they might reveal about her father, and say about herself. Was she ready to accept the consequences of life as an artist? Both of her parents had failed in that regard: her father with his violin, her mother with her acting. That stench of failure seemed to stink up the house. Did she dare travel down the same road? Her father had promised that this golden door to riches would always be open to her, but he had no idea what dark art she kept in her back pocket. Should she make her work known to the public, that golden door would be closed to her, forever.

No, no. She couldn't think about such things now. She flipped back to the images of David, beautiful David. How virtuous he was! A master of horses and nature, not a vampire feeding on the poor. Her father always said that when it came to business, you didn't need data because you always did best when you bet on the right person. She was betting on David. David would save her from this ugly mess, somehow. She had faith in that. She had faith in love.

WHITNEY DUGAS WAS A NERVOUS WRECK, inhaling her second cigarette of the morning in deep, heavy drags. Vivienne Shaw's article was to be published within the week, and despite her better judgment, Whitney found herself standing in line outside of her local Price Plasma donation center yet again. The sun had been painting the sky for the past thirty minutes, first in hues of grayish-pink, then burning reds slowly blending into shades of yellow and orange. She couldn't help but think that, like the sun, she too often rose high only to fall far. Mere months ago, she had reached the peak of her career back in California. Now she wondered just how far she'd be forced to fall, once everything was said and done.

For as long as she could remember, her parents had pushed her to make something of herself. Her mother had been a house maid for most of her life, as had her mother before her. Her father had experienced a horrible childhood before being sent to Angola, a historically corrupt and brutal hellhole. It took over three decades for him to finally be proven innocent of a most horrendous crime, and he had only been released mere weeks ago. Despite, or because of all this, both of Whitney's parents had always encouraged her to do something significant with her life, to do work that was meaningful, if not important. She quickly learned that the only way to get any attention from either one of them was by doing well in school. So she chose the road oft traveled, with nothing but some loose change rattling in her pockets and a brain loaded to the gills with math and science. That narrow path had been carefully carved out for her and everyone else involved. Hundreds if not thousands of people had walked that exact same ground before, pummeling the once fertile soil beneath their forever marching feet until the dirt path itself resembled hardened stone. This was the path that had led her through a mostly barren landscape, which may have been lush and beautiful once upon a time. It was a path that now bored her to tears.

The problem was that Whitney was curious. She walked the path alright, but she was often distracted by small birds, delicate butterflies, and all sorts of flora and fauna. "Focus, Whitney, focus," almost everyone begged, from her mother to her teachers to her co-workers. She *was* focused, but if you happened to tell her *not* to do something, that only made her more curious. Others could yell, scream, jump up and down, but she'd still go chasing after butterflies and squirrels, blissfully unaware of any impending cliffs. If there were fences or walls designed to keep her out or drive her back towards the path, she became all the more interested in whatever was hidden on the other side. She couldn't help herself. It was simply who she was, in her mind anyway. She was part Empress, part Fool, sometimes channeling both within the span of a minute. It really depended on her audience.

Whitney couldn't deny that some of her best ideas had been uncovered while wandering, as well as some of her worst. That's why she couldn't be bothered to consider the consequences beforehand; she never knew if what she was doing was good or bad until the answer revealed itself, and by then it was often far too late to do anything about it. That's why she was in exile now, back in Opelousas, Louisiana, about thirty minutes from Lafayette, tempted to reach for yet another cigarette from her dwindling box of Natural American Spirits. It wasn't even seven o'clock.

Smoking was one of those nervous habits she couldn't quite kick. She promised her father that she would let him teach her how to meditate, so that she might free herself from the habit, but Whitney wasn't ready to make that kind of commitment quite yet. Maybe when all this was over she'd throw the old man a bone, but not today. Besides, it wasn't that she enjoyed the act of smoking itself, so much as she just couldn't keep still. The repetitive motion of hand from thigh, filter to lips, hand to side and down again gave her something to do, something natural that no one questioned. The buzz didn't hurt either, not that she wasn't already buzzing with anxiety. To make matters worse, she thought she was being followed. A black sedan had been parked outside her house for the past few nights, just across the street. Now a similar car was parked two blocks away from the plasmapheresis center. There was only one reason for a car to be following her, just as there had only been one reason why her apartment outside of San Francisco had been broken into, why only her computers had been stolen, and why a journalist of the caliber of Vivienne Shaw was at all interested in speaking with her. Whitney knew that her mother's name might have gotten Vivienne on the phone, but it was this new story that kept her coming back for more.

She didn't reach for that third cigarette. Instead Whitney brought her bleeding cuticles towards her teeth and tried to find something left to bite. The whites of her fingernails were long gone, bitten down to the quick. She went ahead and used her straight but worn teeth to search for tender bits of meat protruding ever so slightly from beneath her nail beds. It hurt so good to bite. The inside of her mouth was pocked and ravaged, her lips sliced to shreds. She couldn't take the wait much longer. "This week, I promise," Vivienne said over the phone. "We're doing a final polish before we print." Whitney knew that Delilah Russell would do anything to keep the truth from coming out. That woman was going to succeed no matter the cost, and Whitney was little more than a flea on her arm; but sometimes, the smallest nuisance could cause the most trouble. Even a creature as small as a flea could trigger a global awakening.

The premise driving Blue Lotus, as described to Whitney, was simple: just because we haven't seen proof of something doesn't mean it's impossible. In other words, a cure for aging might very well exist, even if the problem has always been viewed as unsolvable. Delilah was a nonconformist by this logic. She believed that she could end aging entirely through the use of highly complex regenerative medicines developed by her company. The name of the game was to turn back the clock by isolating damage caused by time, vices, and pre-existing conditions, then repairing that damage at both the cellular and molecular levels through the help of a "golden elixir." Blue Lotus claimed that this revolutionary treatment would enable a sixty-year-old woman to completely rejuvenate her cells, molecules, tissues and organs back to the robust health experienced in early adulthood. As for anyone aged thirty-five or older, Delilah promised the finest preventative care available.

Where better than Silicon Valley to create such a disruptive company? Located forty-five minutes from San Francisco, this area was considered the fertile crescent of tech innovation, and Blue Lotus had shot to stardom as quickly as a flash in a pan. One day, no one knew who Delilah Russell was; the next, her image was plastered across every newsstand in America, her onyx hair, porcelain skin, and emerald eyes gracing the cover of every major magazine from business affairs to women's fashion. Not only was she a female innovator in a man's high-tech world, but she was also a job creator, with over two hundred employees working around the clock to help her win the war against aging. Whitney was just a humble foot soldier, knee deep in the mud.

Naturally, there were multiple components to the Blue Lotus offer, and Whitney knew about them all. First, there was the rejuvenation therapy, which the press had coined the "golden elixir of life." The dream, as explained in countless profile pieces and articles, was for a customer to purchase this intravenous treatment, which could be customized based on their specific genetic profile, at any one of over five hundred medical spas across the United States for eight thousand dollars per treatment. Fashion and health magazines were calling it the next Botox, drawing parallels between the youthful appearance users acquired and the need for multiple treatments over time. "You didn't cause the damage in one day, so we can't remove it with a single treatment," Delilah explained on daytime talk shows and late night appearances, flashing her billion dollar smile.

In order to monitor their progress across this winding road towards life everlasting, customers could purchase the Blue Lotus patch, a skin-like material to be worn over the course of twenty-four hours on either the shoulder, forearm, or thigh. The patch, using the art of microfluidics, monitored undisclosed biometrics, mostly from data communicated through sweat. All of this information was transmitted wirelessly to the encrypted Blue Lotus app, which of course had been built on a blockchain and worked across all devices.

For heavy users who were desperate for faster results, or those on-the-go, an at-home treatment was also available, with the infamous elixir being sold in powder form. No refrigeration was needed. Users could simply throw the six thousand dollar kit into their suitcase and hit the road, after signing a comprehensive release form. If the biomarkers monitored by the patch indicated that another dose of rejuvenation was needed, as expressed with various color codes and metrics displayed in the app's user interface, all the customer needed to do was blend the powder with the included saline, wrap a baby blue tourniquet with a golden Lotus stamp around their arm, and inject the solution directly into a vein themselves. A four minute video online walked them through this process.

None of this had been approved by the U.S. Food and Drug Administration; but early adopters of these products didn't seem to mind, having lost faith in the system entirely. In preparation for a national launch, which would make these products available to Americans outside of California, Delilah made very persuasive arguments as to why regulation was unnecessary, ranging from a lack of trust in bureaucratic organizations to the suppression of new medical technology by political players who failed to understand the science. To further seal the deal, she campaigned heavily for the expansion of patient rights, demanding that her customers be allowed to make their own informed choices when it came to their health, while preaching the virtues of an open market for medical technology.

"My belief," she said in a recent interview, "is to provide Americans with more choices in healthcare, choices that are often squashed by an oppressive regulatory environment that's costly, slow, and completely outdated. The FDA doesn't even recognize longevity medicine or lifespan extension technologies, let alone understand them. That ignorance is creating an unnecessary barrier for innovation while slowing progress in a deeply important and increasingly competitive field. In my mind, by standing in the way of medical progress, the FDA is basically saying that they are more than willing to hold innocent lives hostage until the scientific communities agree to their pay-to-play structure. That's not why I became a doctor. I'm here to save lives, not play politics as innocent people die, needlessly, when we have a cure."

That said, Delilah Russell had immensely powerful friends in very political places. The Blue Lotus Board of Directors included former U.S. Presidents, military generals, regulators, Secretaries of State, and many of Silicon Valley's most highly respected minds and investors. All had received ample stock options, but this inherent bias didn't stop publications from printing their rave reviews of Delilah's miraculous innovation, or their elaborate explanations concerning how this relatively unknown company was going to increase the human healthspan and drive down the cost of healthcare through preventative measures. All spoke fondly of this beautiful genius who had earned a bachelor's degree in chemical engineering before completing

Stanford Medical School. She'd specialized in dermatology, one of the most difficult fields of medicine for any student to gain entry, mostly due to the competitive desire for a certain lifestyle. All of this Whitney knew backwards and forwards, as this was the narrative that had been force-fed to the public, but she also knew that this was by no means the whole story.

Whitney had been hired by Blue Lotus at the suggestion of her mentor, Eliot Lawrence. Eliot was a world-renowned biochemist who had been serving as a father figure to Whitney for years. When he was hired to head the research lab at the notoriously secretive startup, he insisted that Whitney come along for the ride. She was only twenty-eight, but soon she was tasked with developing a new version of the "golden elixir" that would not only reverse damage but actually guarantee immortality. In short, she and Eliot were hired to finally defeat mankind's oldest foe: Death. But they were only given three years of runway to accomplish this herculean feat, which countless other labs had been working on for decades.

And while Whitney may have been young for a biochemist, she had worked in enough labs to understand that medicines needed a much longer lifecycle to be developed, tested, approved and launched. Even Eliot seemed suspicious, which made her anxious. He'd whisper to her off and on during their shifts that Delilah refused to share the formula of her original elixir, that she demanded they begin from scratch to develop a more effective one, and that, as far as he knew, the original cocktail had never been peer-reviewed. He didn't dare press Delilah on these points, mostly because within their first week of working at Blue Lotus both Eliot and Whitney had come to understand that they were not involved with a normal biotechnology company. In fact, nothing about Blue Lotus could be called normal at all.

For starters, Delilah was a fierce general who believed strongly in absolute loyalty. If anyone questioned her decisions, they stood a serious risk of being fired on the spot, no matter how innocent the suggestion. And if you tried to get information out of her, information that she did not believe you needed, she would immediately accuse you of trying to bring about the downfall of her world-changing initiative by collecting trade secrets on behalf of the competition. Whitney assumed this gross paranoia explained why this particular biotech company was one of the most compartmentalized organizations she had ever experienced.

Delilah maintained tight control over all operations and didn't wish for you to speak unless you were called upon. Collaboration was a word that might as well have been attached to ancient history and failed civilizations as it was absolutely foreign to this work culture. No two teams were allowed to communicate with each other, even when they were working on the exact same project. Management tracked every key card, every keystroke, every entrance and exit. In whispers, colleagues often compared the bare white walls and constant surveillance to a prison, just with hoodies and an endless supply of Twizzlers and Red Bull. All internal communication was monitored, from emails and phone calls to harmless instant message chats. Stacks of paperwork had to be signed by new hires, as well as all new stacks to be signed whenever updates to the software were installed or any changes were issued.

Co-workers didn't dare look each other in the eye. No one spoke. Employees weren't even allowed to tell their families or friends what it was that they did for the company, as if Blue Lotus were a shell for government intelligence and they'd soon be black-bagged if they did. The entire staff worked tirelessly, some even seven days a week, but the only sounds you could hear echoing down the halls were either the muffled shuffles of Converse sneakers or Delilah's fiercest Louboutin pumps storming the gates between one locked territory and the next. It was a company staffed by ghosts, all invisible to each other, serving one god, or rather, one goddess, who demanded constant worship. However, this goddess couldn't seem to accept that there were problems within her organization, and hardly anyone had the gall to tell her. If someone did happen to mention that the company was "a sinking ship running on pure panic," as one incident of Sharpie graffiti expressed, they would be unceremoniously fired, just as that graffiti in the women's restroom has been painted over within the hour. During Whitney's few years of employment with Blue Lotus, she had known of at least twenty co-workers being fired. Whispers in the parking lot suggested that Delilah simply didn't like to be told "no." And for a company offering the "next best thing to immortality," employees sure did look as if Blue Lotus was actively and consistently sucking years off of their lives. Those who were fired simply disappeared. Security would escort them to their cars, often without even giving them the opportunity to collect their personal belongings. No one would ever hear from them again, mostly because of the additional stack of paperwork everyone had to sign on the way out.

It was in this hostile environment that Whitney began to lose faith in innovation altogether. That veil of delusion thinned every time an experiment failed, every time Delilah attacked Eliot for his incompetence, and every time they had to start over from scratch. Eventually, Whitney began to view the "progressive" environment of Silicon Valley as shamefully ego-driven, with so-called innovators declaring personal wars of 'us versus them,' all based purely on some cooked-up ideology designed to lure blind followers to their side of an arbitrary line. As for the zealots of the Valley, such as Delilah, they believed completely in what they were doing, yet were often blind to one very important aspect of their mission: the constraints of reality. It was this blindness that had driven them all wild with passion for their respective causes.

Eliot had once told Whitney that personal passions can be dangerous in science, if such strong emotions could not be brought under control, but everywhere Whitney looked there was unchecked passion. The investors were passionate about Delilah's cause and feared missing out on an enormous return on investment. The board was passionate about being seen by their peers as the wise and respected mentors to the next Archimedes, the one who had finally cracked the code of matter versus time. And employees, mostly the new, young or naive, were passionate about making the world a better place in any way that they could. "Aging is the greatest cause of suffering," Delilah would say. Her blind followers would nod their heads in agreement. "If you don't think bringing an end to suffering is important, then you should leave." Anything or anyone that did not fit within this narrow window of belief, or walk that increasingly constrictive path, would never be welcomed into a world ruled by Delilah Russell, the woman who swore she'd conquer death.

It certainly didn't help that every major publication lifted Delilah to the status of genius without ever wondering if she truly possessed that gift. Even Whitney had completely believed the claims, sight unseen, assuming that being popular or famous somehow meant being correct. She didn't even begin to grow curious about Delilah's secrets until Eliot casually pointed her towards a new butterfly to chase. All he'd done was mumble under his breath, "If we haven't created an elixir that works, then what the hell are they selling?" Neither of them believed that Delilah actually had a working elixir; but something was being packaged, sold, and given positive reviews by "journalists" and early adopters. What was it? No one knew the full answer to that question, apart from Delilah. And now Whitney felt compelled to unmask the great secret behind Blue Lotus, well before their upcoming national launch.

She started at the bars surrounding Palo Alto, followed by the liquor stores and vape shops. Sometimes she'd dress in jeans and a hoodie; other times, in leather pants and halter tops, with her Blue Lotus ID badge always in prominent view. She would sit at a bar for hours, sipping on a Pilsner, just waiting to see if some prized fish might come to jiggle the line. She'd make conversation with just about anyone, name dropping here and there about her job, her employer, her mission to end aging. "I can drink as many beers as I want. I'll just take the medicine we're developing and reverse the damage later." If a man snorted, chuckled, or rolled his eyes, he became her mark. She'd take her time though, look him up and down, read his body language. Should she be tough as leather, or a giggly little fool? Would he respond to some helpless babydoll, or a ruthless scientist looking to make a stir? More importantly, did that man hate Delilah, or was he forever loyal to the ruling goddess of the Valley?

Whitney could go either way, in any conversation, as long as she got what she wanted in the end. She could be as sweet as Chantilly cream, nodding her head through dull, never-ending monologues on cryptocurrency, or as tough as iron arguing for mutiny in the ranks. It all depended on her audience. And because Blue Lotus was so compartmentalized, she could work her way through the men without any detection. None of them knew each other, and none had ever so much as entered the research lab. They probably didn't even know where it was. And so she fished, and she gossiped, and she gathered information. The men would be rewarded for their candor with a kiss, or some hot and heavy make-out session, depending on the personality. If they provided her with documents, which they'd somehow managed to sneak out of their offices, she'd drop to her knees to thank them. And if they provided photographs, especially from the production line, she'd consider doing more than that.

Apart from biochemistry, seduction was Whitney's true gift. From the time she was a teenager at math camp she knew that she could drive a nerdy boy wild with her mouth, hands and honey pot. By her twenties, she could get almost any man to do anything she wanted, and drive them absolutely insane in the process. It was a craft she had been perfecting for almost two decades; and in the case of Blue Lotus, Delilah's troops, eager for a coup, didn't stand a chance. Over the course of six months, Whitney gathered quite the treasure trove of source material that painted a very disturbing picture, one she quickly shared with Vivienne Shaw, along with her own collection of source documents gathered from the research lab. Then, satisfied with her work, Whitney quit Blue Lotus altogether.

But leaving wasn't as easy as just dropping her keycard in the mail slot and walking through the door. At first, Delilah begged her to stay; but when Whitney held strong, stating that it was time she went to work on other projects, Delilah's demeanor changed from friendly to cold to furious. "Well you can't just leave. We need to determine how much you're walking away with."

"I'm not walking away with anything," Whitney stated.

"Oh yes you are. Eliot might trust you, but I don't. It's time for you to tell me exactly what you know."

After five hours of exit interviews, which could easily have been called an interrogation, Whitney continued to play dumb, as if begging them to fire her for incompetence. Then she refused to sign a final stack of non-disclosure agreements. "I've signed plenty of those during my tenure here. I'm not signing another piece of paper. It's time you let me go."

Management threatened her, Delilah mocked her, the human resources department searched for any reason to hold her there; but eventually, they had to let her leave. The next week, her computers were stolen from her apartment. That next day, Whitney drove her Honda Fit to Louisiana, while Vivienne sorted through over two hundred pages of original source documents with photographs included. By then, both women knew the dirty truth behind the secretive startup's product line, and soon the public would know too. Even worse, *everyone* would know that Blue Lotus had something to do with the rare pneumonia spreading like wildfire throughout the state, and that was a crime few would forgive, especially as the death tolls had already started to climb with additional cases popping up across the country.

In response to Eliot's question, the material being sold in shiny packaging wasn't a medical breakthrough at all. It was source plasma, a component of blood often sold to pharmaceutical companies and used to produce medications for autoimmune disorders and hemophilia. It wasn't anything fancy, surprising, or even effective in terms of anti-aging properties. It was just proteins, antibodies, water and salt. The great mystery behind Delilah's genius turned out to be something everyone already had within their bodies. As for the rave reviews from users? Since they were just being infused with pure plasma, any results from this "rejuvenation therapy" were little more than placebo effects.

However, what was more terrifying to Whitney was that Delilah had refused to follow simple protocol widely accepted within the pharmaceutical industry to both purify the material of contaminants and deactivate any viruses within the plasma, which was a known carrier for bloodborne pathogens and other infectious diseases. This meant she was selling this human material raw, with God only knows what viruses tainting the cocktail. Why? The purification process would require the use of additional equipment, and since she didn't want her board to know that she had yet to discover a true "anti-aging elixir," Delilah wasn't willing to take those necessary precautions, or be forced to explain that expense. Instead, she decided to roll the dice on patient health, in the vain hope that Eliot and Whitney would crack the code any day now. No one could know that the company would need to go back to the drawing board before their upcoming national launch. All that mattered to Delilah was that Blue Lotus achieve first-to-market status, regardless of whether or not she was peddling a safe or effective product.

What most people didn't know was that Blue Lotus had quietly formed a partnership with Price Plasma, the equivalent of a mom and pop shop within the world of source plasma, having only fifteen locations scattered across the Gulf Coast. According to internal documents, Price was under the impression that they were selling their material to the biotech firm for purposes related to research and development. Instead, Delilah was secretly using their plasma, along with additional plasma purchased at an even cheaper rate from an array of Chinese and Indian firms, as the elixir's replacement until another solution could be found. Blood plasma was already approved by the FDA as a treatment protocol, so why get regulators involved, especially when this was merely a temporary fix to a short-lived problem? And why let Price know the true reason behind their plasma needs, if that would only inspire them to increase their prices? In fact, why let anyone know anything at all? It would only upset investors and damage the brand at its most vulnerable moment in the marketplace. And wasn't the elixir protected by trade secrets? Of course it was. As far as Delilah was concerned, no one needed to know if they changed the formula. *Her* approval was all that mattered.

The only thing Delilah had not anticipated was that a single biochemist in her employ, one with an insatiable curiosity, had grown up with the name Price ringing in her ears. Whitney's mother, Helen, had practically raised Charles Price. As a result, Whitney had spent afternoons and summers playing in his yard, helping her mother in his kitchen, and folding his underwear in his basement. All while growing up, every evening after school, she'd hear about Charles and his violin, or Charles and his father's company, or Charles and some soul-eating harpy he'd aligned himself with that week. She'd attended his father's funeral, as if that insufferable man had actually been a member of their own family. They even prayed for him at church. And Whitney had driven by Price Plasma donation centers countless times over the years. She'd heard the ads on television boast about how housewives and college students donated there, but you'd never see those kinds of people standing in line. Of course, Whitney never thought that one day she'd be standing in this line too, waiting for the doors to open. She blamed her curiosity, as always.

She listened more than spoke when she visited these donation centers, although her mind was often running at about a million miles a minute as she did. Listening had never been a great talent of hers, but for the first time in her life, Whitney could find stillness in the chatter. She purposefully ventured towards various centers on different days and at different times, always seeking to gain a better understanding of the donor pool. No matter the variables involved, the people in line were often the same type: the homeless, the desperate, the sick, the addicted, the undocumented. Many complained about how difficult it was to raise a family on two dollars per person per day. Advice shared among the plassers often focused on making the best out of a bad. Reassurances of the power of prayer and hustle were often reiterated. Real jobs were considered; but for those on welfare, for every dollar earned outside of the system, a much needed welfare dollar was lost, all while expenses steadily increased. There was childcare to consider, the cost of travel to calculate, and the ever present need for health services. It was more expensive to work a straight job than it was to stay on welfare, cleaning houses and selling drugs on the side for under-the-table cash.

Other donors had recently lost their jobs or had simply been unable to find work in the first place. Some didn't want to ask for financial help from family or friends, so their plasma had become a liquid gold of sorts for their pocketbooks. It was something they could sell, and the money was immediately deposited onto their Price debit cards with a small transaction fee deducted. That kind of money was good anywhere, and for anything, without more successful people "complaining about their tax dollars being wasted on the bums," as one plasser said in line. That may be true, but there was no doubt in Whitney's mind that these people were walking tightropes across the whole of their lives, all while being guaranteed by employees of Price Plasma that donating twice a week to receive two hundred dollars per month was completely safe.

Whitney researched it out of curiosity. It didn't seem like anyone had ever studied the true long-term effects of regular plassing. All she knew was what she saw and heard: the huge sores and needle marks on their arms, along with complaints of extreme fatigue and frequent blackouts. Some people would joke that being at Price was their "me time" or their "little vacation from the kids." Still the truth hung over their heads like a heavy cloud: plassing was making them sick, and once they got sick past a certain point, they couldn't donate anymore. And if they couldn't donate, how would they survive? Those donors were a human resource with a high rate of depreciation, and the obnoxious sign that hung from the ceiling, with its chain collecting dust, made the company's priorities awfully clear. It read: NO PAYMENT UNLESS DONATION COMPLETED.

Every time Whitney visited Price Plasma, the procedure had been the same: go to the touchscreen, check "no" to all the questions on the health questionnaire within sixty seconds (she'd been told on multiple occasions by fellow plassers not to worry about her answers because "everyone lies on that test anyway"), get her iron levels and blood pressure checked, then join one of sixty plassers in the middle of the room to begin the donation process. An attendant in a white coat, despite having no medical degree to speak of, would feel around for a vein, rub some iodine onto her arm, then stick her with a butterfly needle before turning on the fractionation device. Like a cow hooked up to an automated milking machine, Whitney like everyone else would be expected to stay still and let the device do its work, while pumping a small ball in her hand to steady the flow. All in all, the procedure would take ninety minutes, with blood platelets being separated from plasma in real-time and full view. Was this really the path to making the world a better place? To ending the suffering Delilah spoke so strongly about?

This was the plasma being shipped to Palo Alto and sold as part of Delilah's precious elixir. It was the plasma of the poorest of the poor, people trying to trick the system by wearing extra clothes or ankle weights to get past the minimum weight restriction of 110 pounds, or swallowing entire packets of ketchup in line just to trick the iron test. They were an at-risk population for HIV, hepatitis, and worse. Talk of a new drug called K2 was a recent favorite, as it didn't show up in urine tests. Whitney couldn't help but wonder, apart from the plasma collected overseas, could these be the donations hosting a new pathogen, one previously undiscovered? That certainly wasn't the "new" Silicon Valley was chasing; yet the donors providing the only ingredient for a product sold by the hottest new startup in the Valley were living in horrible conditions, such as under the overpass or near the swamps. Whitney once saw a woman in line lend her tennis shoes and address to a homeless man so that he might donate his plasma for $35. And this plasma was being pooled together in enormous vats by Blue Lotus—contaminants, viruses, and all—in order to create novelty treatments sold to the rich and beautiful. It would be poetic if it wasn't so outrageous.

The doors to the plasma center finally opened. The line began to move as the sun glowed a vibrant yellow. Feet were shuffling towards the entrance as Whitney caught sight of something moving across the street. She turned her head to see a man wearing a navy polo shirt and dark wash jeans exit the black sedan, adjust his reflective sunglasses, then approach her in the line. He was carrying a manila envelope.

"Whitney Dugas?" he asked.

"That's me."

He handed her the thin, heavy package. "You've been served."

Whitney watched as the man walked back towards his sedan then drove away. She pulled herself out of the line and opened the envelope. On the first page, the document read, in part:

Ms. Dugas,

It has come to our attention that you have disclosed confidential information and other trade secrets specific to Blue Lotus despite signing multiple contracts not to use or disseminate such information. We also have reason to believe that you have done so in connection with making multiple false and defamatory statements about Blue Lotus, all for the purpose of harming its business. You are hereby instructed to immediately cease and desist from these activities...

A tightness formed in Whitney's chest as she held the paper
and read on. She was anxious, terrified even. She had no money
for lawyer fees, and certainly no reasonable defense. She could
apply for whistleblower status by sharing her information with a
regulatory body, but which one? Aging wasn't even registered as
a disease by the FDA. This was all uncharted territory, and apart
from Vivienne, she had no one else to turn to for advice. Then,
it suddenly dawned on Whitney that being served papers was actually a good thing. First of all, it meant she wasn't crazy. Second,
it meant that when it came to Delilah Russell, the current ruling
goddess of Silicon Valley, she, a mere mortal, had managed to
strike a nerve. For the first time in months, Whitney surrendered
a mischievous smile.

I.V.

SARAH MICHAELS FELT GLUED TO THE COUCH, forced to stomach the silent tension kneading into her bones. Theodore was sitting across the room, perfectly still as usual, his arms glued to his sides. His icy grey eyes were darting around the apartment, occasionally landing on her with the fierce precision of an artificial intelligence programmed to kill. That deeply violent look sent shivers through her body. She knew she was guilty, but she believed that he was too. Sarah focused on her breath, feeling the warm sensations hit the small blonde hairs between her nostrils and upper lip. For years, each and every sensation had been pushed into her subconscious, and there, each suppressed emotion had multiplied—all of her anger, cravings, loneliness and needs. She'd buried each and every swell of feeling within the sand, then covered it all with the coldest water contained behind her hardest shell. She'd never felt strong enough to face those feelings before, or even admit her unhappiness. She'd never been able to vocalize her deep dissatisfaction with her relationship, and now the flood approached.

Over the years, she had become a prisoner to her own habits of suppression, filling her mind with hatred, envy and self-loathing—all forms of venom she dared not share. Theo didn't like to hear negative thoughts expressed, and he didn't seem to approve of depression or anger either. If she voiced her misery, he'd tell her to take a pill. If she suggested that he was hurting her with his emotional and physical distance, he'd tell her that she was insane. If she said that she was lonely, he'd offer to adopt a cat. They'd been together for almost two decades, and more than ever, Theo remained a mystery to her. He seemed to live so deep within his own mind that he could barely be bothered to notice her breathing beside him. Sarah had no choice but to believe that whatever existed on that other plane, that far-off world only Theo could visit, was far more beautiful and interesting than she would ever be.

She had known, going in, that Theo struggled with his feelings. For an up-and-coming playwright, Sarah had always found it strange that he couldn't express himself; but his stillness had made her feel anchored, while his quiet nature seemed to disguise a hidden strength that made her feel safe and protected. His stern gaze could be unsettling at times, but she always felt that there was some form of love behind those silver eyes. As he sat in the armchair across from her now, that gaze seemed purely judgmental, as if he was ashamed of her, or even disgusted by her very existence. He'd never tell her either way, she thought. For as soft-spoken and as gentle as Theo could be, Sarah imagined that he was a bundle of knots on the inside, and that he would never share the truth of those knots with her, whether he was angry or not. No, Theo only expressed himself through cold-blooded detachment.

She didn't know this at first. Initially, their passion for each other had caused their cups to overflow with love and devotion. Each drank greedily from the other's, as a new moon slowly discovered itself to be full. And over that brief period of courtship—too brief, now that Sarah thought on it—she had been more satisfied than she had ever been in any other relationship. Yes, he was reserved, even then, but Sarah had fallen in love with his restrained distance, especially after drowning in her relationship with Matilda. Her identity had been lost completely in that pairing, with them competing against each other, and feeding off of each other, to such a degree that she didn't know who she was if not purely a reaction to Matilda's deep-seated need for control.

Sarah had exhausted herself with their fights, often silently crying her eyes out until early in the morning, hiding under the hanging clothes in their shared closet so as not to wake Matilda. There had been high highs and extremely low lows felt within that small one-bedroom apartment, and when Matilda had miraculously shifted from controlling to distant, Sarah saw her opportunity to run. And run she did, right into the least emotional arms she could find. In fact, she had practically thrown herself into his bed, as if begging for political asylum from her own tormented feelings.

In the beginning, Theo seemed to be perfect for her. And during their conversations, he painted this big, beautiful picture of their lives together, a shared life dedicated to truth expressed through art. He made her believe that she was special for merely being asked to join him on this crusade, as if God Himself had chosen Theo to embark on this grueling mission with Sarah serving as his pre-ordained mate. He promised that he would help her live life as it was meant to be experienced, and that their shared purpose would give fresh meaning to their existence. He swore that as long as they pursued this profound vision for the future, they could overcome anything together. He made her believe that change could occur in this world, and that they might actually be able to carve this vitally important path themselves so that others might eventually follow. And they worshipped each other the same way that they worshipped this idea: daily, strategically, and without distraction.

In her opinion, everything about their bond was focused on Theo's dream for the future. The plays he wrote, the conversations they had, even the way he introduced Sarah to others, all were focused on driving his message forward. It wasn't long before she realized that this dream was the only thing Theo truly cared about, and that he would only extend his affection toward her as long as she devoted herself to that dream too. She had been a blind follower of his dogma as layer after layer was peeled from her idealism, until Sarah began to see the real man behind that silver grey vision.

It seemed increasingly obvious to her that he was far more interested in the appearance of being in a loving relationship than he was in building a real one together. Nothing Theo said was ever open for debate or discussion. His opinions were always to be regarded as the final word, and anything that went against his opinion was considered obscene. And while Sarah had her own opinions, often grounded by her emotions and intuition, her feelings were plainly ignored when shared. It seemed that Theo was either bored out of his mind, rendering him incapable of listening to her, or that he was shielding her from his unrelenting disapproval. He once told Sarah that he found her emotional outbursts to be horribly unattractive, even when she professed her love for him. Comments such as these both wounded and confused her, as Sarah had always been open about her true nature, that she was an emotional being. It was what had drawn her to the theatre in the first place; but even that, Theo had chosen to reject. He seemed to expect her to reject it too.

In the past, theatre critics had called Theo's work "nothing but a lecture with a high production value" and "unwilling to explore the darker truths of human experience." Over the course of nearly twenty years, he'd managed to have twelve plays produced by local theaters. Four had been Jeff Recommended, but not one had ever won a shooting star. Sarah had performed in most of them, in some capacity or another. She'd played a saint, a sinner, a mother, a daughter, a genius, a schizophrenic, and now, in Theo's latest play, she had gotten the opportunity to portray the starlet Rita Hayworth in *Blood and Sand: The Tragic Life of Margarita Cansino*. Sarah didn't look anything like Rita, and the play, as written on the page, seemed like yet another lecture designed to bore audiences into submission. Theo swore this would be his last play, having recently decided that investigative journalism might be his true calling, not the "vapid world of theatre." This was why he didn't protest when Greyson Carter was hired by the theatre company to direct. It didn't hurt that

Theo would also be in Africa, working with a team of journalists finishing a documentary about child slavery in the chocolate industry, for almost the entire rehearsal process and actual run of the show.

Greyson Carter was notorious for his controlling behavior. He didn't collaborate with playwrights, and if hired to direct, he would do whatever it took to make that play both daring and modern. Audiences loved him for his violence on stage, how real he made even the most artificial situations feel, and how deep he was willing to go within the realm of human experience to tell an otherwise simple story. He alone could make a small black box theatre come alive with blood, sweat, screams and sex. Audience members could practically smell the truth of each and every moment. These experiences were visceral, animalistic, and raw. And Sarah had been wanting to play in that sandbox for decades. Ever since Matilda had gotten the opportunity to work with Greyson, Sarah had been chasing after his work. She'd auditioned for nearly every show he'd ever been involved with, and had been rejected time and time again. But Theo had only agreed to the theatre company's contract on the condition that Sarah would get to portray the starlet. He said he didn't trust the role with anyone else, so Greyson's hands were tied.

Before turning his full attention to the global chocolate industry, Theo had lived and breathed Rita Hayworth, and by virtue of living with him, so had Sarah. She watched every one of the starlet's performances, read every one of the biographies on Theo's desk, and reviewed every single draft of the play in progress. More than that, she felt that she inherently understood the actress in a way that no one else could. Rita had allowed herself to be defined by her many relationships, enabling the men in her life to steer her career path and dictate her transitions from love goddess to princess to "whore." Her father sexually abused her, her first husband pimped her out to studio heads, her second cheated on her constantly, her third was a gambler who squandered her earnings,

her fourth physically abused her, as did her fifth. Alzheimer's was
just the cherry on top of a truly tragic existence. Theo was quoted
in the press release as saying that this "is a play about how people
hurt one another." She knew he never imagined he'd get hurt too.

"Whose idea was it to change my play?" he snarled.

He was referring to the dance numbers. Theo had never written a musical number into any of his plays. He hated musical
numbers. Sarah and Greyson had added six. Of course, they both
figured that Theo would never see the play. How was she supposed to know that he'd return from the Ivory Coast three days
early? When the music began for her first dance, she saw Theo in
the audience. She saw the look of confusion, then panic, then absolute rage flash across his face as she began to remove her clothes
to the sound of "Down in Mexico" by The Coasters.

If any moment in their relationship had been a defining one,
this was it. Sarah was portraying a teenaged Margarita Cansino,
dancing for film executives vacationing in Tijuana, slowly removing her clothing as she rubbed up against the men sitting in the
front row of the theatre. This action was darker and grittier than
burlesque, it was damn near fiction, but it felt more real than any
other performance Sarah had ever given. And as she shook her
shoulders, twisted her hips, removed her clothing, and flipped
her long auburn locks to the beat, she felt more vulnerable, wild
and sexual than she had ever felt before. The fact that Theo was
watching in the audience, and could do nothing to stop it, turned
her on all the more.

At the end of the show, when she went backstage to change
after curtain call, Greyson ran his fingers between her legs then
licked each one clean. She kissed him, knowing that the world
she had built with Theo had been destroyed, and that for the first
time, one of Theo's plays had brought an audience to the edge
of their seats—not because of his lofty vision for the future, but
because of her emotional response to the moment. And he'd been
forced to watch.

"I don't know how to answer that," she replied, still frozen on the couch across from him.

"How could you let Greyson change the play?" he asked. "You saw the work I put into that."

"I suppose the standing ovation last night didn't mean anything to you."

"I don't think anyone should applaud incest."

Sarah rolled her eyes. "They weren't applauding incest, Theo. They were applauding me."

His eyes flashed with recognition. "*You* changed it, didn't you?"

"We both did," she said, begging for a fight.

"Did you sleep with him?"

"What do you mean?"

"Did you have sex with Greyson Carter, *Sarah?*"

She held back a laugh, believing that Theo didn't know what sex was. In the beginning, she had spent many an hour on her knees, deeply engaged in their mutual prayers, struggling to swallow all of Theo's hard, swollen truth; but that was as close as he would ever let her get to full-on contact. No, Theo preferred a hands-off approach, with silicone and metal toys doing the work he felt too high and mighty to do himself. Instead, he preferred to watch from the corner of the room with a remote control in his hand. If anything, he made her beg for his attention, only allowing her to softly kiss his throbbing head or barely touch that softest skin. He teased her with the idea of long, passionate thrusts, only to abandon the act entirely a few inches in. He loved his gadgets, but hated the idea of getting wet, as if he might short circuit if he got too close. He hated hugging, personal displays of affection were forbidden, and his robotic body wasn't capable of contortions of any kind. And eye contact during "sex" was completely out of the question.

Greyson was different. Onstage and off, he was a surge of creative energy, willing to explore areas Theo had only read about before dismissing. Kissing Greyson was like melting in the heat of the sun. He made sex feel dangerous and exhilarating, and riding him made Sarah feel powerful. Theo had only served her from his cup of love once, then expected her to survive off of those trace minerals for decades to come. It was as if he had pulled her up from the ocean only to abandon her on the shore, watching from his nearby vessel as she withered and dried out into a powder of who she once was. She had turned to alcohol to numb this nagging pain of dryness and thirst, but it was Greyson who had realized she'd been beached, then guided her back towards the ocean. It was Greyson who had fed her the nutrients she needed, from affectionate touch to intense sexual contact. That's why she loved him. He had fucked her back to life.

"We didn't have sex," she said. "We made love."

Sarah expected Theo to scream, throw something, cry even. He had never once shown his true feelings in the moment. He had never exhibited any emotion, and now, she felt that he must. Not once in two decades had he ever gotten angry or sad in front of her. She wanted to hear him yell. She wanted to see that he was capable of tears. She wanted proof that he loved her as much as she had loved him. Instead, Theo just sighed. "Oh, Sarah, Sarah. How could you be so stupid?"

She knew what he meant. Rumors had circulated around Chicago for years about Greyson Carter. People whispered about his affairs with actresses, as well as his continued abuses against them. Some women worked with him then vanished from the acting scene entirely, deciding instead to become accountants or counselors rather than remain dramatic actresses in the storefront theatre scene. Most assumed they just couldn't handle the demands of the craft; but no one really knew either way. During rehearsals, Greyson joked about his "bad boy reputation," telling her not to believe everything she heard from those "crazy women." Sarah had been called crazy by Theo so many times she had lost count, but when Greyson said that other women were crazy, she felt that she knew what he meant. There would always be women tempted to sleep their way to the top. Even Sarah had been accused of that behavior herself. But there was something about Greyson that felt more powerful than mere ambition: she truly felt that she loved him, and that he loved her.

Over the years, she had come to feel dead inside. She was angry that Matilda had run off to Louisiana and married well, that she didn't have to struggle anymore or fight for anything. She resented that Matilda had recovered from their breakup with such ease. And she was angry at herself for jumping into a relationship with Theo only to be held hostage, emotionally; but even that anger, along with everything else she felt so intensely, had to be submerged and buried. She felt such cravings for physical contact, affection, a kind word or even a kiss; but Theo made her beg for the kitchen scraps of his attention on her hands and knees. He seemed to get off on her desperation for his crumbs. And isolated from what she wanted and who she was, a sort of loneliness had overcome her, as if she were slowly floating deeper into a forbidden darkness. She felt lonely even for her own feelings and sensations. It was as if life with Theo was to be sentenced to solitary confinement, and the only way to feel *anything* at all was to turn to self-mutilation. So she drank vodka in hearty amounts, all while trying to ignore that drinking alcohol to heal her emotional wounds was as ignorant as drinking saltwater to cure her thirst. Even on stage, she felt nothing, despite needing to feel everything.

That sense of coldness and numbness at the center of her being had made Sarah a frail shadow of her former self. She hated that shadow. She envied people who had retained their flesh. And she hated herself all the more because she had sacrificed her Self in the name of a dream that wasn't even hers. She didn't know who she was anymore, only that she needed change, immediately. Her own feelings had been blocked off from her, as if the great depth of her emotions had been covered by a thick sheet of ice. And all Theo was capable of doing was watching her wither away from the opposite side of the room, her cold blood matching his, drop for drop.

Greyson had broken through that ice by providing a sense of honest engagement with her. He rescued her from states of depression and anxiety by helping her channel those feelings of sadness, anger and fear into her work. By getting her on her feet, and forcing her to move through the pain, she was finally able to begin the process of true healing, which always starts with removing the debris of the past. During that rehearsal process, Greyson shattered her illusions so that she might rebuild herself completely. He challenged her to feel every moment, every sensation, and to focus on the change in her breath as she faced those demons buried deep within herself. At times, Greyson could be frightening, screaming at her with absolute rage, telling her that she made mistakes she hadn't even noticed. She would be terrified, but at least it all felt real, at least it felt like progress.

Working with Greyson made Sarah a better artist. She truly believed that. He pushed her to be better; he expected her to be the best. He made her feel that she was special and could become one of the best actresses in the city if she just remained disciplined and honest. "I know you could outwork 'em, baby," he'd say to her. "Just keep pushing forward. You have more talent than you realize." He promised to personally introduce her to the casting directors of the city's finest theaters, from Steppenwolf to the Goodman and even Chicago Shakes. "You're not like those other actresses, baby. *You're interesting.*" With his help, she knew she could transform all of her pain, suffering and doubt into the most beautiful pearl, a priceless treasure that both she and Theo had neglected to build.

It was as if Greyson could see all that Theo could not. He would hang on Sarah's every word in conversation. He asked questions that in nineteen years Theo had never thought to ask. He said he wanted to know her inside and out. He even told her that he loved her, after opening night of the show. They'd walked down the alley behind the theatre, where he pressed her up against the cold, brick wall, kissed her passionately, then whispered those words into her ear. In that moment, Greyson's love became her new drug of choice, and she yearned for that high again and again. Sarah no longer wished to worship at the feet of Theo's insatiable dream. She wanted to create her own vision for the future and to storm the stages of Chicago beneath the watchful gaze of Greyson's sharp blue eyes. He told her she could live with him, if she wanted. "One condition," he said. "You can't bring anything from your past with you. If you want to be with me, baby, you have to start over completely." She wanted to jump into that abyss with eyes closed and arms open.

Back in the moment, she responded to Theo, "Why am I stupid?"

"That man is a shameless fraud, and the sooner the theatre community wakes up to that fact, the better. I just never thought *you'd* fall prey to his charms. I thought you were better than that."

"I guess I'll never be as good as you, Theo."

"Well, I can't be that good," he said. "Clearly I couldn't give you what you need."

"No. You never did."

"I just wish you would have had the decency to take my name off the playbill before you turned my work into the laughingstock of the city."

"The audience *loved* it!"

"Oh Sarah! Even the worst burlesque dancers get applause. That's why it's cheap."

Sarah could feel tears well up against her eyes, as if those words had slapped her across the face. The weight in her cheeks increased tenfold as the sensations throbbed. Her nose was burning, tingling, pounding. Her chin crinkled, despite her attempts to control it. Everything she had suppressed was now pushing through to the surface level from that hidden ocean of feeling. She didn't want to release all that she'd been holding, not now, not in front of Theo, not after what he'd just said. Yet the waves were growing in size as their rhythm clicked up a few knots. She could sense those emotions crashing against the rocks of her physical structure, as her breathing intensified and quickened. It seemed as if every subatomic particle in her being was vibrating with emotion, and the harder she tried to control it, the fiercer those emotions raged.

She tried to calm her mind, to think of a phrase, an image, anything to control what was coming. She looked at Theo's feet, enclosed in his black leather shoes. He always wore black pants and a white Oxford shirt. She hated his clothes, and that hatred made her want to release her emotions all the more. She tried to concentrate on Greyson, on the image of him in her mind, but those raging emotions would not quiet down or subside. It seemed that the very roots of her being were trembling and there was no way to stop the floodgates from opening. Theo didn't so much as flinch in his chair as she began to sob. He merely watched, as if her emotional crisis were just another work of theatre that required him to remain detached.

"Did you ever love me?" Sarah cried, her mouth sticky with spit.

"Yes," he said.

"WHY?"

"Because I thought you were the most amazing actress I'd ever met, and one of the best people. I didn't realize you'd crumble like a pile of dirt without my help, or that you'd fuck up my work just to get some attention. But I did love you."

"You never loved me," she screamed through her tears.

"Yes I did." He paused and looked away. Her eyes may have been blurry from tears flowing at such a rapid rate, but Sarah thought she saw tears welling up in Theo's eyes too. "But as I was watching the play," he continued. "The play I wrote for you, the play you *begged* me to write for you...I certainly didn't have any interest in starlets or Hollywood...I *knew* you were unhappy. I was trying to make you happy. You told me you loved the play. I didn't realize you were lying."

"I wasn't lying," she sobbed.

"That sure didn't stop you from mauling it!"

They were both crying now, Sarah far more intensely than Theo. "I can't be with you now, not after what you've done," he said. "I've tried so hard to make you happy. I know you don't think that, but I did try. And I know you think I'm weak, that I'm running away from my failures in theater, that I'm not brave enough to take artistic risks like Greyson Carter. But the work I'm doing now is more important than getting you to take your clothes off onstage. I've spent the past few months talking to kids as young as six, all forced into fucking slavery so someone like you or me can eat a goddamn chocolate bar. I'm not asking you to love me anymore, but I deserve your respect, even if you've lost mine."

Sarah was sobbing into her hands as Theo rose from his chair. "I have a new story I'm chasing. I'll be back in a week. Please be gone by then. I don't care where you go; I just can't look at you."

He'd never unpacked his bags, so Theo simply picked them up and walked out of the apartment they'd shared for the past seven years, not once looking back at Sarah. As he locked the door behind him, Sarah finally felt free to let everything go, to cry until there was nothing left to purge. She prayed that those tears might wash away her guilt, her anger, all of her shame. She couldn't think of the problems of the world. She could barely save herself. And so she cried and she cried, releasing all that had been suppressed, praying that Theo wouldn't walk right back through that door. It wasn't until she had worn herself out completely that she wondered if the decision she had made had been the correct one. Her eyes were puffy, her nose burned, and her throat felt harsh and dry. Nothing mattered anymore, she thought. That past had already been washed away by the flood. All she could do was breathe, and start again.

Jonathan James Karl, J.J. to some, and his wife Margot had yet to return home from work. Their Bengal cat, known fondly as Isabella, had remained carefully perched on the arm of their leather sofa for the past two hours in anticipation of their arrival. The delicate feline quickly rose to her feet as she heard them enter through the two exterior doors of their apartment building in Logan Square, a mere fifteen minutes from downtown Chicago by rail. Neither Jonathan nor Margot spoke as they entered the apartment, carrying takeout from Crisp, a small Korean fried chicken restaurant in Lakeview. Margot handed over her cellphone to Jonathan, who then wandered towards the bedroom while Isabella followed her mother to the kitchen. The spotted cat watched with great interest as the woman with chestnut hair and dark brown eyes portioned out the pieces of fried chicken, as well as extra servings of Seoul Sassy sauce and kimchi, onto two separate dinner plates. When a tiny scrap of meat was shared, the exotic cat devoured it with fervor before following her mother, and the plates, into the living room. Only once Jonathan had emerged from the bedroom did either human speak.

"All clear," he said, taking a seat beside his wife on the couch and grabbing a piece of fried chicken.

"Thank fucking God!" Margot shouted. "I was ready to explode the second we left the office. First of all, fuck that woman. Fuck her product. Fuck her company. Fuck her fucking marketing plan.

I am sick to death of writing her fucking copy over and *over* and
over again, only for the bitch to cancel the national launch. What
is this? The sixth fucking time! FUCK HER! I'm done."

"Let's just talk to Stuart tomorrow," Jonathan said patiently
between bites of kimchi.

"Fuck Stuart too! Fuck this entire project. I'm not doing it. I'm
not writing another word of copy. Not a headline. Not a tagline.
Not a fucking contact form thank you message. I AM DONE."

"You're not done," her husband sighed, slowly chewing his food.

"We're stuck in some sort of toxic relationship with these people. We should have gone to Stuart months ago demanding we cut
the cord. I'm not writing another word for that woman, I swear
to fucking God. I don't even understand why we agreed to write
this shit in the first place."

Jonathan took another bite out of his chicken, chewed it carefully, then said, "There's this thing called money…maybe you've
heard of it."

"Well fuck money too."

"You, of all people, don't mean that."

"Yes I do."

"It's really not that bad. We'll get through it. We always do."

Margot leaned against her husband as their cat jumped between them to beg for scraps. "But I don't *wanna*," she whined.

Jonathan just kept eating his chicken. "I know, baby. I know."

"You don't wanna do it either."

"That's true."

"Then why are you so calm about this? Don't you want to
scream it from the rooftops?"

"You know what I really want to do…" He made a face she had
seen many times before.

Margot's brown eyes lit up with excitement as her torso
straightened like a puppet on a string. *"Oh, me too!"*

"Unless you went on another one of your 3 a.m. cleaning
expeditions."

"I know there's one somewhere in here, I just don't remember where I put it."

"Do you want me to call Eric?"

"No, fuck Eric."

Jonathan laughed. "Okay. We'll try to find it, but if we can't, I'm calling him."

Margot threw her full weight against the couch. "UGH!!!"

"Let me finish eating, then I'll look for it. You should eat too, you know."

"Yeah, yeah, I'm eating." Margot began to pick at the pieces of fried chicken with her fingernails, grabbing little threads between her teeth and chewing large chunks of crispy skin in the back of her mouth as Seoul Sassy sauce covered her lips and tongue. She mumbled as she chewed, "I swear, this is the best goddamn chicken in Chicago."

"Yup," her husband agreed. "Worth the drive every time. Although, I think you jipped me on the fries."

"*What?!*"

"Don't act all surprised. I'm driving, so I can't count, but it sure seemed like for every fry you fed me, you ate like ten."

"I did not! *They're different lengths.* I gave you the long ones and I ate the short ones. It takes about five to ten short ones to make up for a long one."

"Sure, honey, sure."

"It's true!"

"Okay, hun."

"I didn't jip you."

"Uh-huh."

"I didn't! I swear!"

"Eat your chicken, fool."

Margot smiled then ripped another strip of flesh off a chicken breast. She smacked her lips with joy. "Don't we have beer?"

"Half of the Belgian box is left."

"*YES!*"

"Fetch me a Leffe, would ya?"

Margot bounced off the couch to fetch the beers as Jonathan scrolled through YouTube, using his phone as a remote and his clean pinky finger as a cursor, looking for something to play. At first, Isabella watched his plate with profound interest, then began to slink over to Margot's plate in an attempt to steal away a piece of meat without detection. It was a wise move, as Jonathan didn't notice when she ran off with a chicken wing. He was too busy scrolling, thinking about how he was tired of politics and all of the fear-mongering about that new virus, how they'd watched all of the new comedy specials on Netflix already, and how they'd have to wait a few more days before Screen Junkies released a new Honest Trailer. He clicked on a video ranking Kung Fu movies. As Margot returned with the beers, she laughed. "Oh God, please no."

"Well I'm not watching *Frasier* again."

"WHAT? It's the *best* show ever made. What are you talking about?"

"I swear to God woman, we have watched every episode at least three hundred times. I am not watching *Frasier*."

She released a deep belly laugh as she threw herself back down onto the couch. "If you can't find anything better, *Frasier* it is."

"Fuck. You know I won't."

"Eh, you never know. Surprise me."

"You never like my surprises."

"Sure I do."

Jonathan gave her a knowing smirk. "No you don't."

Margot blushed, then giggled through her nose. "You're right."

"Speaking of surprises," he said with a mouth full of food. "My sister called today."

"Half-sister," Margot corrected.

"She's gonna be in town for two weeks and wants to meet up."

"Ha! That's funny. Haven't heard from her in what? Three years? Four? Now all of a sudden we're supposed to jump when she calls?"

"I told her I could meet up for coffee. Spare you a dinner, at least."

"You're nicer than me. I would have told her to fuck off."

"No you wouldn't. Your bark is way bigger than your bite."

"She deserves a bite. A big old bite, right on the ass."

"You don't have to see her."

"Good. I don't want to see her."

"You know who you will have to see though, right?"

"WHO?!"

"Madeleine LeBlanc. She's coming in to discuss the project in a week."

"Oh, God, baby, I don't want to write about another medical product. Tell her no, please."

"It's not a huge campaign. Just educational stuff, and no one does that better than you."

"Can I think about it? It's just so much research. I don't know if I have it in me."

"You know her story; what she's been through. I think it could be a really powerful message. And I don't think she'll be another Delilah. "

"Ha! Let's hope not. I've had more than enough of the original. Fucking bitch…"

They'd been working for the past year on the national launch campaign for Blue Lotus. Together they were the joint head copy-writers of their agency, having founded their own copywriting firm independently before eventually merging with other like-minded creatives. As a collective, they had done some of the most groundbreaking work across Chicago and Los Angeles with a strict focus on the tech sector. Neither of them really knew why Blue Lotus had chosen to work with them. No one at their firm had any experience with medical devices and the product seemed far too complicated, legally speaking, for their team to manage on their own. Yes, they worked with startups, but not startups with billions in their war chest, dobermans for lawyers on their board, and a product that required being injected into your veins. Regardless, Jonathan and Margot had specifically been requested for the project, with Delilah Russell herself claiming to be a huge fan of their work. Of course, their egos having been properly stroked, they'd signed on almost immediately.

Delilah was charismatic, absolutely beautiful, and amazingly articulate. Most of their clients could barely form a proper sentence, let alone explain why their product was important, but Delilah could speak in full paragraphs on the subject matter. Right away, she captivated both husband and wife. In their early conversations, they discussed the significance of the lotus, how it rose out of dark water to reveal a golden center on a fragile stem, how it represented the womb from which life arises, how the flower itself broke through mud and swamp water to greet the sun at dawn, how it represented the triumph of the soul over its prison of matter. Together, founder and copywriters forged connections between the company and the idea of rebirth, the journey from darkness to light, and the promise of an enlightened jewel being given to mud-born mortals desperate to feel the warm rays of the sun.

Hours upon hours were spent in discussion of the color blue, how it represented wisdom, eternity and spirituality. Jonathan and Margot poured over early customer reviews, highlighting claims that the rejuvenation therapy resulted in a euphoric feeling, as if life itself had become a waking dream. Most users claimed that within fifteen minutes of a treatment they felt tranquil, aware, if not reborn. Board members, during phone interviews with the writing couple, expressed their commitment to Delilah's goal. They all spoke of her purity, sense of ethics, and strength of mind. Almost everyone commented on her ability to break through the male-dominated tech world, as if that were a far more impressive feat than finding a cure for aging.

Long, *long* discussions were had on the idea that aging was not only mankind's oldest enemy, but a horrible humanitarian crisis. Jonathan and Margot were fine with accepting the first statement, but needed some convincing to accept the second. Whenever faced with this doubt, Delilah would raise her voice via speakerphone and begin to preach as if she were a Southern Baptist minister, outlining the suffering involved as thousands died every day from old age or the diseases associated with it. She'd snap her fingers and bark, "Another life gone, because we got stuck in this ridiculous conversation again." She'd fight anyone and everyone on the idea that aging was natural and inevitable, accusing them of being brainwashed by a society that lacked imagination. "Don't you get it?" she'd cry out. "Every two seconds someone is dying and we can stop it. That's 150,000 mothers, sisters, fathers, brothers, lovers, all dying needlessly, every day. Think of the suffering! Have you ever lost someone you loved? Multiply that pain by a hundred *thousand* and then maybe you'll understand how important this work is to humanity."

Once this argument was accepted by the creative team, more or less, they then had to understand how exactly this product was going to save humanity from a form of suffering that was as old as birth itself. Delilah told Jonathan and Margot that her "golden elixir" was designed to not only slow aging but to reverse the damage the aging process had already caused. She boasted that her cure could completely remove any consequences experienced from what some might call a 'negative lifestyle.' For example, she claimed that her elixir could remove any damage caused by being a regular smoker of cigarettes or a life spent as an alcoholic. She promised that even a fifty-year-old man who had lived a life laboring in the sun, smoking a pack a day, and drinking hard liquor to the point of intoxication every night could be returned to the health level of his thirty-year-old self. Several treatments would be required, but she promised such results were "absolutely possible." She even told the copywriters that she had documentation to prove it.

When Delilah repeatedly failed to produce such documentation, that was the first red flag. Time and time again, Jonathan and Margot were promised that a 300-page report would be sent to them "tomorrow." Always tomorrow, never today. Months and months of tomorrows had passed, and the document had not once materialized. Eventually, Jonathan began keeping a printed file of all written correspondence with the biotech company, as well as secret transcripts from their lengthy calls. This was a major risk for them to take as Delilah had forced everyone in the collective to sign extremely complex non-disclosure agreements, and had made it a point in her contract that no one in the agency could discuss Blue Lotus with anyone outside of the pre-approved creative team. Nothing could leave a specific office within the agency's walls. Nothing could be printed without permission, and even then, it had to be shredded at the end of the day. And nothing could be brought home to work on. Conversations were forbidden. Delilah didn't even want individuals from the agency speaking with anyone at her company outside of the board and herself. These constraints were not only intense, but completely foreign to the highly collaborative creative team. Still, they pressed forward, believing that Silicon Valley knew something that they didn't. More than anything, the entire collective feared missing out on the next big thing. And so the phrase "the client is always right" became their daily prayer against overwhelming doubt in preparation for the company's national launch.

The creative team had to quickly produce a new website with fresh brand language and video content, brochures and other written educational material, all new package design, an elevated user interface for the Blue Lotus app, and plenty of additional pieces of content needed to convey the safety of the elixir, the results a customer might expect, and how to use all of the various components, from the patch and corresponding app to the at-home kit. The biggest obstacle to completing this project, however, was Delilah herself. When the creative team brought up a list of likely objections from prospective customers, ranging from fears of the rich being able to live forever to the effect this might have on the planet or the already stressed healthcare system of the United States, Delilah would respond more out of fury than understanding. She simply couldn't see why anyone would object to her offer of life everlasting or true preventative care. She also believed that this was an offer being made to everyone—rich and poor—despite the high cost of her products. The fact that most Americans live on meager incomes and can't afford an eight thousand dollar treatment at a medical spa seemed to roll off of Delilah's mind like water from a duck. That was the second red flag.

Then Margot noticed that the more she questioned Delilah, and even certain board members, about the science behind the product, the faster those conversations were shut down. Eventually, Delilah began to treat Margot as if she were an idiot, completely incapable of understanding the science. When Margot pointed out that Delilah had failed to provide any tangible evidence to support her claims, and that advertising is held to a certain standard of truth, Delilah told her that she wasn't a "Silicon Valley person" and that she should probably "leave the project" if she couldn't understand why certain things were protected by trade secrets. Offended by these remarks, Margot attempted to contact outside experts for greater insight, but Stuart quickly pointed out that she was forbidden to do so, as was outlined in their contract. "We're here to create a consumer brand," he said. "Not validate the product."

Both Jonathan and Margot were ready for the project to be over. It had been a three-month contract that was now venturing into an eleven-month debacle. And while Delilah consistently presented extremely optimistic revenue projections based on impossibly aggressive sales targets, Jonathan overheard someone in accounts complain that Blue Lotus had been fighting them on each and every bill the agency had ever sent. It was becoming more and more difficult to get the company to pay, and billing seemed exhausted from having to go over each invoice point by point. Yet, despite all of these red flags, Stuart, Creative Director of their collective, continued to believe in the beauty of a post-aging world. Maybe it was because he had just turned fifty, maybe it was because he'd lost his father to Alzheimer's, or maybe he was absolutely smitten with Delilah; but as far as Stuart was concerned, all systems were a go, whether the creative teams were skeptical or not. Margot thought they were playing with fire, and she sure as hell didn't want to get burned.

"I thought I had another piece of chicken here," she mumbled.

"What?"

"I split the pieces up evenly. I should have another piece of chicken."

The couple looked around.

"Where's Bella?" Margot asked.

She was in the bathroom, in the clawfoot tub, behind the shower curtain, licking those chicken bones clean. "Goddamn it cat!" her mother hollered.

Jonathan wasn't concerned. He had other things on his mind. "So where do you think you hid it?"

Margot grabbed the chicken bones from Isabella and went to throw them in the nearest trash can with a lid. "Oh, I don't know. It's either in the living room somewhere, or maybe the office."

"How specific."

Margot shot her husband a fierce but playful glance as she walked past him to re-enter the living room, then gather their plates to clean in the kitchen. "Check the bookcase," she hollered from the other room.

Jonathan began to slowly investigate the bookcase. One by one he removed the books to look between them, behind them, even within them. When Margot returned she sighed. "Remember when we used to be excited about this project?"

Jonathan laughed. "It was supposed to be our legacy moment."

"Well that ain't happenin'."

"No, I don't think it will. Oh well."

"I thought it might be nice to be a part of something truly helpful for a change, but if we don't believe in the mission, should we really be writing the copy?"

"You want to abandon the war on aging?" Jonathan asked. "You naughty little deserter."

"UGH! We have become so numb to the idea of endless wars it's seeped into our language. I mean, if I hear the word 'revolution' one more goddamn time…"

"You don't think Delilah's starting a *revolution* in healthcare?" he asked, with a rather sarcastic tone.

"I think it's a dead word. Like, what the fuck does that even mean anymore? If it doesn't mean anything, we should stop using it."

Jonathan was still investigating the bookcase in the living room. "But even if it's not a cure for death, the elixir could be used for preventative care. That's progress, isn't it?"

"Again, progress towards *what* exactly? We're all chasing the future, trying to disrupt the past, and now Delilah's trying to extend the present. Doesn't it seem like we're in this losing battle against time? Talk about a fucking endless war."

"Says the woman who isn't helping me find what *she* hid."

"You're better at finding stuff."

Jonathan looked at her with disapproval. "Go check the office, will ya?"

"Ugh. Fine."

"Maybe all we need is a different framing device," Jacob hollered from the living room. "A new way to present the information."

"Oh, that's an idea," Margot mocked. "Everybody else is doing it. Why not us? Can't afford stuff? My golly, you're not broke, you're a minimalist! Can't afford food? Why, have you tried intermittent fasting?"

"Cute. Real cute."

She poked her head out of the office. "Thank you dear."

Isabella was now crying at the bedroom door, begging to be let inside. "No, Bella," her mother cooed. "You took my chicken so I'm not letting you in, Miss Priss."

Margot quickly looked through the contents of the closet in the office. One by one, she checked all of her coat pockets, inside every one of her handbags, even within her shoes. She then checked all six drawers of the two matching desks before turning her attention back to her husband. She had completed her search before methodical Jonathan had even finished his investigation of the bookshelf in the living room.

"Not in there," Margot hollered as she grabbed another beer.

"What do mean, not in there? You barely looked!"

"I'm telling you, it's not in there."

"Not in there," he mumbled under his breath. "Grab me a beer!"

"Already did," she said, returning with a cold Leffe for him and a Hoegaarden for herself. "No need to shout."

"I don't think it's in here," he said, checking under the couch and between every cushion. Isabella was still mewling at the bedroom door.

"You think she's trying to tell us something?"

"You know what," Margot giggled. "I think I put it in the safe. Did you see it in there?"

"No, but I wasn't looking." Jonathan rose up from his chair, then headed towards the bedroom as his wife and Isabella followed.

As he began to turn the dial, Margot continued to complain. "I just don't want to ask for the sale when we don't understand the product. I don't even know if I trust it. We have no idea what's in this elixir. Our words could lead people to slaughter, and we'd never know until it was too late. This isn't like any other project, and I'm telling you, something is off."

"You say that about every project."

"*I do not.*"

"You do too. You get frustrated when the client rejects our copy, then you think something fishy is going on, then you turn into a little conspiracy theorist, and then—lo and behold—the client loves our next round of copy and suddenly you're their biggest fan."

"*That is not true.*"

"You are all ego, honey. Face it."

"What?!"

"It's true!"

"Well, if I'm all ego, so are you."

Jonathan reached into the safe, pulling their phones out in the process. "Yeah, but I'm the one with the goods," he said, revealing the single joint packaged in a plastic cylinder.

"My hero," she replied, leaning down to kiss him. "Let me see my phone real quick. I just wanna check my email."

"We agreed we'd stop using these fuckers at home."

"*Come on*, just a peek." Margot turned on her phone, which immediately started buzzing with notifications: missed calls, text messages, emails. She asked Jonathan to turn his on too. His did the same. Messages and voicemails flooded their phones, all from coworkers at the agency. They'd gotten word that a story by the famous investigative journalist Vivienne Shaw was to be released tomorrow morning. The subject: Blue Lotus. "I hear it will be devastating for the company, which is why they canceled the launch," Stuart had written in a text to Jonathan. "We can't work with them anymore. I hear it's toxic for all involved. Delilah Russell is a fraud. I can't believe I'm saying this, but there is no magic elixir. Even worse, she may be responsible for that weird flu going around California."

Stuart hadn't reached out to Margot. She knew that he couldn't deal with her response at the moment, especially after fighting her for so long. "Pussy," Margot jabbed, knowing full well that Stuart had called her everything from dramatic to insane over the course of the past six months. She wasn't gonna let that slide either. He was gonna be hearing about this for months, if not years, to come…but not today. She'd let him sweat a little first.

In fact, neither Jonathan nor Margot responded to any of the messages. They didn't want to encourage any bad habits with their coworkers, preferring to maintain their recent decree that when they were home, they were off the clock. Jonathan had even received another message from his sister, letting him know that she was leaving for Chicago tomorrow. They both rolled their eyes at

her request, then put their phones back into the safe. Then they
locked Isabella in the bedroom with a litter box, headed for their
home office, cracked a window, turned on the space heater and
lit the joint. Puff, puff, pass became the rule of the day as they
continued their conversation.

"I feel kind of bad for her," Jonathan said, flicking ashes into a
small Tupperware holding about an inch of water.

"Who? Your sister?"

"God no! Delilah."

"*Delilah?* Why?"

"I think she wanted everything to be true, even though it wasn't."

"If something sounds too good to be true, it is. I've told you
that countless times."

"The idea was perfect. I mean, who wants to get old and die?"

"Well," Margot started. "She fumbled the execution then. But
the thing that still gets me is, are we meant to stop aging in the
first place? Everyone keeps talking about how it's human nature to
pursue progress, but is that progress? I don't think we're meant to
live forever. What if death is a gift? Who are we to say no to that?"

"Science advances funeral by funeral," Jonathan repeated while
releasing a cloud of smoke and a bit of a chuckle. It was a quote by
a physicist named Max Planck that Delilah repeated, often.

"The irony is, if she managed to stop the funerals, Delilah would
also be stopping scientific progress, by that logic anyway. Yet another thing that woman couldn't wrap her damn brain around."

"You don't think she's a genius?"

"I think," Margot said, exhaling a hit, "that when Delilah told
us she admired Steve Jobs and Thomas Edison, she was telling us
exactly who she thought she was. Think about it. What are the qualities of those guys? How did she *embody* those qualities, at least on
the surface level? With that kind of blood in the water, investors
flocked to her like fucking sharks because they knew those qualities
have historically led to high returns. It was all ego, which according
to you, is something I know quite a bit about." She took another hit,

held it, then released. "I can almost hear her investors patting themselves on the back, thinking they were all gonna make a fortune for being so fucking smart. But Delilah never said she admired great healers. Not once. No, she was inspired by modern magicians—the ultimate golden calves. And her believers worshipped her in the hope of financial salvation. It was never about immortality. It was *always* about getting to market first."

"Yeah, you're right," Jonathan laughed. "She's nothing but a failed magician."

"Casting spells for all the wrong reasons, then praying and wishing for luck."

They finished the joint, then went for a walk in the dwindling snow. With stress alleviated by their newfound freedom from Blue Lotus, Jonathan and Margot went to the local cinema, bought tickets for whatever show happened to be playing, then made out like teenagers in the back row. Nobody seemed to understand how two people in their mid-forties could be so blissfully happy and in love, but they'd never worked as copywriters, or experienced the joy of firing a terrible client. Nor did they understand how horny it made Margot to know that she'd been right all along.

Isabella would be sleeping on the couch tonight, if anyone would be sleeping at all.

PART ONE

S ISTER BARBARA LÉGER WAS SITTING in the gardens of the
all-girls Catholic school where she had served as librarian for the past fifty-two years. The vast majority of the
high school student body, as well as the faculty and staff, were
currently attending mass in the small chapel nearby. A few strag-
glers were out and about, preparing a goûter of donuts and orange
juice to be enjoyed after the service. Normally, Barbara would be
in mass with everyone else; but the story in her morning paper
was so disturbing, she had completely failed to hear the bell marking the hour. And maybe that was for the best, she wondered. She
felt that she required some time alone, if only to digest what she
had read in quiet solitude.

As a librarian, she had always taken it upon herself to serve
as an intermediary between her students and the information
they needed; but she wasn't just a clerk or some random nun
armed with a feather duster and an antiquated card catalog
(which she stubbornly refused to move to the attic, despite being
forced to have an electronic system installed fifteen years ago).
No, Barbara considered herself to be a teacher, a guide, and an
advisor. The library itself was simply a center of information, a
place where students might come together to collaborate, experiment, and pursue their higher calling. She merely facilitated

these experiences by teaching them how to study properly, how to seek out the data they most needed, and how to become who they most wanted to be.

She also served as the high school's college advisor. Countless students had journeyed through her office seeking guidance on their futures. She'd helped them work through such complex issues as completing their applications, choosing a major, understanding their curricula, and explaining their choices to their parents. At times she even found herself being asked by students for more personal advice, from how best to handle the struggles faced by their families to understanding themselves at a much deeper level. No matter the question, Barbara took great pride in connecting these young women with the resources they needed to make educated decisions and wise personal choices. And she had never once missed a day of work, because in a world where information is abundant yet truly helpful guidance is scarce, Barbara feared not being available to answer a question.

The seventy-seven-year-old nun would gladly admit that as much as she had influenced the lives of her students, they had equally influenced hers. She firmly believed that anyone could learn a great deal about a vast number of subjects through questions posed by other people. For example, by helping a seventh grader named Jessica with a term paper on the bubonic plague, she had been inspired to read *An Essay on the Principle of Population*, written by Thomas Malthus in 1798. In this influential work, the English clergyman argued that if a human population expanded beyond the limits of their food supply, an inevitable reckoning was bound to take place, whether it be a famine, epidemic, or war. He called these events "positive checks," which often resulted in soaring mortality rates.

Naturally, Barbara also directed the student to the necessary counterarguments to this "Malthusian Principle," as there is little evidence to support a direct link between famine and plague. In fact, research the duo read at the time suggested that malnutrition might actually prevent infection. Barbara explained to the girl, using an event the school had recently overcome as an example, that just as lice prefer clean hair, bacteria require certain nutrients from their human hosts. If the host can't provide the nutrients needed, well, that bacteria simply can't multiply in the same way that a well-fed bacteria might. So a shortage of food might actually be a defense against pestilence, perhaps. Neither of them were experts, so these were simply assumptions to be explored in writing. Yet even after Jessica's paper had been written, proofread, and turned in to her history teacher (she got an A-), Barbara continued to think on the subject. Were plagues truly a reckoning for certain behaviors?

Years later, and in between so many other projects on a wide range of topics, an English paper for a junior named Lainey on the novel *The Plague* by Albert Camus caught Barbara's attention. Camus (and Lainey) argued that epidemics are absurd: a plague is not a reckoning for any behavior, but an indiscriminate force that no one truly understands. However, the student did argue that plagues, as absurd as they may be, do offer substantial benefits by serving as catalysts for social change, in the sense that certain beliefs previously regarded as untouchable could suddenly be threatened by a collective doubt.

Lainey pointed out that, both in the novel and historically, religious orders were forced to admit that they did not know why plagues occurred, or how to stop the senseless chaos of one. Despite her very religious audience, the girl even went so far as to point out that prayer seems absolutely pointless in the face of such a destructive and unstoppable force. And instead of serving as a "reckoning," Lainey argued that these events offer humanity the opportunity to look into a very specific mirror to determine what individuals truly value. The student then argued that actions, not beliefs, demonstrate these values. In other words, once faced with circumstances outside of their control, an individual demonstrates *exactly* who they are and what they really value through their behavior. Do they find meaning by helping others? Do they accept the absurdity of their existence with a smile, or embrace pure, unabashed nihilism? Do they leave those they once claimed to love alone in the streets to die, or do they stay to bravely, selflessly face the moment? In times such as these, beliefs and promises dissolve to reveal the true self, a raw self, with little time to theorize or talk one's way out of action. It was a message that had resonated deeply with Barbara.

By the time Lainey's paper was turned in and graded (she got a C+, for reasons never fully explained by the English teacher in question), the librarian had begun to consider that plagues were not reckonings at all, but absurd events that occurred without warning or reason. She agreed with the student, that society's reaction to such chaos defined humanity in that moment. "We are how we behave," Lainey suggested. She even explained that "a person who rebels against the absurdity of their own despair by smiling through the chaos is very different from the one who gives in to the meaninglessness of it all and surrenders to the hunger of their own misery." This statement, written by someone so young, forced Barbara to think on who she truly was, if defined purely by her actions. She found herself frightened by the possible answer.

Then another student, this time a freshman, working on a paper about global trade for her history class, came across an interesting find. During the Middle Ages, Poland, at least within its borders as they were known at the time, never encountered the bubonic plague because it was so isolated from the rest of the world. Mindy, the student working on this paper, had been researching trade routes from Mongolia in the mid-1300s and had casually discovered that the bubonic plague had likely originated in that region. In fact, certain historians even suggested that the plague had begun as an act of biological warfare, used for the first time in combat during the Siege of Caffa in 1347. From there the plague was carried by merchant ships from Beijing to Constantinople, eventually spreading across the whole of Europe, with the exception of Poland, of course. Mindy wasn't interested in continuing down this rabbit hole, but Barbara wanted to know more.

Through her own independent research, the elderly nun explored the aftermath of the *mors repentina*, or unexpected death, caused by the great plague of the Middle Ages. At first, people blamed the epidemic on "vapors" caused by the planetary alignment of Jupiter, Saturn, and Mars. Then the Flagellants began to beat themselves in a vain and monstrous attempt to appease God through the release of their "sinful" blood. Tensions rose, emotions heated, and the idea of control revealed itself to be nothing more than an illusion. In Milan, if one family member died of the plague, then the community would promptly lock all other family members in the home to die. This cold and brutal tactic managed to contain the disease and protect the vast majority of Milanese, but the thought of such cruelty made Barbara all the more curious. If Lainey was correct about human nature being defined by actions, then what did this act say about human desperation in the face of fatal chaos? Surely such behavior wasn't isolated to the Milanese, and if it was an act all humans were capable of performing, what did that say about humanity as a whole? And what was the solution, if any existed?

Plagues tore down the walls of civility, with neighbors turning against each other in blind panic, desperately looking for someone—*anyone*—to blame. The church had unsatisfactory answers and the physicians were equally unhelpful. Over time, once highly respected customs were completely abandoned. The dead were tossed out into the street without ceremony or respect, only to be thrown into mass graves by absolute strangers without so much as a prayer, flower, or mention of their name. There was little support for the sick, if not outright cruelty towards them. People took to carrying flowers and sweet smelling herbs near their noses, so to purify themselves from the stench of rot; yet no rose or rosemary could save them from falling victim to the pestilence. Both those considered good and evil were equally marked by the kiss of death, as morality revealed itself to be a subjective faith all too easy to abandon, while any sense of ethics was easy to ignore in the cloud of absurdity that was plague.

It was in this environment, filled with anxiety and confusion, without anyone to lead or explain or solve the problem, that a fantasy began to take root in the minds of those alive and panicked. They believed that some new evil had arrived, and that they must cleanse the world of the corruption that had brought down this pestilence upon them. Ideas became movements, and those movements gathered momentum, as fierce yet delusional energies brought emotional relief to those who could no longer handle the chaos. And these same desperate people were more than willing to kill for their dream of control and stability. In short, they searched for a scapegoat, if only to release the tension. And so the Christians accused the Jews of poisoning the wells, and on St. Valentine's Day in 1349, more than nine hundred Jews were burned at the stake in Strasbourg, France. Energies were released; yet despite the horrors of these events, almost invisible fleas continued to spread the fatal pestilence from city to city, port to port. And no one could truly comprehend, in the heat of their continued ignorance, that death cannot be solved by more death and that fear cannot be solved with hate.

Of course, in the aftermath, once everyone had calmed down and felt a renewed sense of equilibrium, a new Europe began to emerge from the death and destruction of the old. Lives lost from such senseless carnage could never be replaced, but the culture shifted because of this experience. For the first time, with a smaller population, the lower classes could afford luxuries previously unavailable to them. New opportunities opened up within the guilds, and even within the more "elite" educational systems. The Gutenberg press eventually emerged as a great technological achievement, making knowledge more easily accessible at a time when higher wages were drastically improving living standards.

Larger tracts of land could support larger families, a more diversified economy could support more unique demands, and Boards of Health were established in the hopes of preventing another pestilence. All of this helped to bring about the cultural nationalism of Europe. These were the survivors of a terrible ordeal that made little sense and caused profound damage, but had somehow generated a cradle for new life.

However, it wasn't until a graduating senior wrote a paper on the AIDS epidemic that Barbara began to understand that all of this knowledge was far more than just a history lesson. All of these bits of information were part of the larger puzzle of human behavior. She had lived through the AIDS crisis. She had read her morning paper as always, watching the protests contract and expand on a seemingly daily basis. The nun had observed the global death toll climb from half a million deaths in 1987 to well over eight million by 1995. Helping that senior, Erin, write her paper, now knowing everything she did about the plagues of the past, Barbara could see her own behavior in the mirror of that epidemic. She had known that hospitals were turning away the sick. She had heard the gay community lament the lack of action by the government. She had seen the pictures of the bright red and purple lesions, of the impossibly thin men protesting for a cure to *at least* be sought, and the obituary portraits of once young, vibrant people who had been snatched in the night by a plague no one understood. And all she had done was pray, even as her own Church condemned condoms—one of the few defenses against the spread of this pestilence—as immoral. A U.S. President even called AIDS a disease "where behavior matters." Everyone seemed to agree—change your behavior and maybe you won't die. Even Barbara was guilty of nodding her head.

Yet by studying the AIDS crisis, the nun learned far more about herself than she might have otherwise. She realized that she had followed a similar pattern outlined by the histories she had studied, all without ever applying those lessons to herself.

At first, she had agreed that AIDS was a reckoning for behavior, feeling all the more justified by the proven correlation between unprotected gay sex and the spread of the disease. She had decided that AIDS was something that happened to other people, to immoral people who made bad decisions. She would pray for them, wish well for them, but she would never see herself as guilty as those suffering. AIDS was something that happened to *other* people, not people like her.

Then Barbara learned of the AIDS crisis within the hemophiliac community—how innocent men, women and children had contracted HIV through the use of a clotting medication known as Factor VIII, which had relied on contaminated blood plasma collected from mostly at-risk prison populations and skid-row communities. As a result, thousands of hemophiliacs died from AIDS, a suffering made all the more complicated by the fact that their blood couldn't clot. Never before had such knowledge made the nun feel more ashamed. She had judged the suffering by their behaviors, their lifestyle, without once looking at her own actions. Had they not also shown her true nature? She had promised to live a life dedicated to God, as the spouse of Christ; yet she had failed to take on the qualities of Christ. Instead, she had succumbed to blind devotion, if only as a way to shield herself from fault.

How many times had she prayed to God, or sang in the chapel out of devotion to Jesus Christ? How many times had she instructed students to pray to God for help with their struggles? And still, the nun had failed to follow the path Jesus had provided, the path of love and compassion for all. At no point had Jesus said, "Only show love and compassion to certain pre-approved people." No! He said we must show love and compassion to *everyone*. Christ was tortured to death, *crucified*. Barbara had a crucifix around her neck to serve as her daily reminder of this, but she had forgotten that even while Christ was being killed in such a brutal, horrible way, He said that those torturing Him should not be punished.

He said that they were ignorant and must be shown compassion. She wasn't harmed in any way during the plague, yet Barbara had shown so little love and compassion for her fellow man. Jesus did not rely on her belief in Him; He wished to serve as an example so that she may be inspired by His qualities and strive to make them her own. And in the face of the AIDS crisis, she knew that she had failed. She also knew that it was all absurd—that she did not know why AIDS existed, or why innocent people needed to suffer, no matter how virtuous she believed herself to be. Those claimed by AIDS had *all* been innocent victims of a modern plague. They deserved compassion, goodwill and love, not her naive and selfish judgment. Barbara had been ignorant. Her actions had been ignorant. And she hung her head in shame at this painful realization.

She now knew how history repeated itself, with the healthy showing disdain and cruelty towards the sick, with the rich wishing to be removed from the presence of the infected poor, and with the religious having little to say that could be of much comfort in a time of crisis and absurdity. She knew now that she had no answers. There was no truth she could impart. All she could do was show love for those affected. But there had been no global plague since a treatment for AIDS had been discovered in the mid-1990s. Barbara had not felt that cold kiss of death so close to home since then, and she feared that it would only be a matter of time, as more and more people preached the benefits of globalism and as foreign wars raged on throughout the decades. So many students had fluttered through the library over the years. There had been so many papers, so much research, on a plethora of issues that had nothing to do with plagues; still plague was all Barbara could think about. She could feel it creeping closer every single day.

When Natalie Price had shown her the images she had taken at her father's plasmapheresis centers, the nun had felt a tug within her heart. Photograph after photograph displayed the weary face of a vulnerable individual, a human being deserving of love. Barbara didn't know much about the blood plasma industry at the time. She knew that Natalie felt pressured to study something that would help the family business, finance or perhaps risk management; but Barbara had helped the student prepare her application for an art school anyway. She knew Natalie had been accepted, and that she'd been offered a full scholarship, which was *extremely* rare for SCAD to offer to anyone. She prayed that Natalie would take the offer. And after reading her morning paper, the nun feared, more than ever, that Natalie would choose her father's path instead.

AIDS had been mentioned in the article. Those four terrifying letters had grabbed the nun's attention right away. HIV was featured with greater frequency, as was hepatitis. But what had truly frightened Sr. Léger was the mention of an unknown pathogen, something researchers had coined "AIDS-like." And this "strange new pathogen" had been discovered in multiple samples taken from a so-called "golden elixir"—a product promising rejuvenation, longevity, and possibly even immortality—sold through a California biotech firm known as Blue Lotus. The company promised that their product relied solely on synthetic materials to minimize health risks; however, a senior employee of the startup's laboratory had provided documentation outlining the company's deception. There was no innovation or miracle cure for aging. It had all been a complete fabrication.

As opposed to synthetic materials developed in-house, this treatment, offering the "next best thing to immortality," was actually source plasma that had been neither purified nor inactivated, meaning that the company had made no effort to remove contaminants or kill viruses within the material harvested from paid donors. Some of these were the same paid donors Natalie had documented: those poor, desperate people lining up outside of Price Plasma centers across the Gulf Coast. And despite regulations and voluntary standards within the plasma industry, each sample acquired from Blue Lotus played host to this AIDS-like pathogen, as all plasma purchased from Price, and even cheaper plasma collected in China and India, had been pooled together. A single contaminated donation could poison the entire batch.

Experts in the industry claimed that plasma-derived products were completely safe, citing the fact that no case of transmission of a viral infection had been confirmed in over two decades; but such complacency made this unpredictable event all the more likely. As noted in the article, if no one knew what this unidentified pathogen was, then no one else had been looking for it, which meant that it could have already infiltrated the global plasma supply. The word "plague" hovered in the air, with Blue Lotus serving as the canary in the coal mine, the first to sing its name.

As the nun considered the implications of this article, students began to exit the chapel and head towards the tables for goûter. Barbara looked around the gardens and waited to see if Natalie Price had attended school today. Surely with such a scandal going on at home, she wouldn't be on campus. The nun waited, just in case. Looking around the garden, Barbara admired the overflowing colors that surrounded her. The calendulas popped in bright orange, the bachelor's buttons bloomed in friendly shades of blue, the bottle brush plants vibrated with sharp reds, and the indigo spires highlighted the grounds with fiery purples. Even the poisonous foxgloves sparkled in subtle shades of creamy yellows and whites. Everywhere else, between the box hedges, were pockets of delicate pinks filled with knockout roses. Barbara admired the beauty of each and every flower as she waited for Natalie. Then she looked across the street towards the alley of oaks that had been growing on that spot for hundreds of years.

The campus was beautiful in the spring, but that beauty also reminded the librarian of a short story by Edgar Allen Poe, "The Masque of the Red Death." Here, they were all cloistered on these two hundred acres featuring the natural splendor of South

Louisiana, decorated by such rich colors and thriving life. Yet within the old woman's gut she could sense that a clock had been ticking, and for the first time in a long time, it was finally able to chime with a dull and heavy clang. The sound of that internal clock caused Barbara to turn clammy and pale, despite the heat of the morning sun and the humidity in the air. Sitting beneath the shadow of a stark white statue of Jesus, the nun imagined the face of that Red Death, with "blood as its Avatar and its seal." She could only sit and think on the horror of that blood, and all that it contained.

Soon, Barbara caught sight of Natalie and flagged her down. The young woman with strawberry blonde hair and china-blue eyes approached her with a bright smile and fresh donut in her hand, still living in the blissful ignorance of the beautiful garden.

"Good morning, Sister," she said enthusiastically.

"Good morning, Natalie. I'm surprised to see you here today."

"Why's that?" she asked, giggling at the question.

"Because of the article about your father's company in the *Journal*. Haven't you read it?"

She looked confused as her nose crinkled at the bridge, causing her freckles to kiss. "What article?"

Barbara sighed. "Come along, dear. Let's get you a copy."

PART TWO

For years, Renée Benoît had wanted to hurt David Hall. She wanted to find the roots of his heart, tear them up from the murky soil in which they had been planted, then slice that beating organ into thin shreds with her fingernails. She wanted to pull each microfiber apart, string by string, thread by thread, until she could beat him to death with those fraying ends. Every time he seemed depressed, despondent, burned out, she wanted to hit him with this whip. For, in her eyes, he did nothing but the easy tasks, the things she could do in her sleep. It was up to her, *always up to her*, to do the heavy lifting. And when his already meager weight of labor increased ever so slightly, he quickly buckled at the knees. But not her—*oh no*—she was forced to endure, overcome, surpass, as he wallowed in self-pity near the floor, playing video games and drinking beer. His behavior was nauseating.

She'd never in her life dreamt of becoming a Wendy, chasing after lost boys to ensure their needs were met. Now that was exactly how she felt as she frantically chased after the emotional clouds hovering over David's head, swatting them away with whatever energy she had left. In vain, she tried to snuff out those smoke signals, but they returned, time and time again, puff by puff by puff. Renée felt trapped within this wicked fog, with guilt keeping her within its dark borders. She couldn't leave David, he lived at her farm. She couldn't tell him to leave, because he had nowhere else to go. And she couldn't express how she truly felt because then there would be nothing left to say.

It had been her idea to join forces, to work together. And day by day, the web surrounding them had only grown more complex. The more she tried to lift them both up, the deeper she found herself within the trap. She'd been foolish to make that deal, unaware of the world still available to her, the world she had yet to explore. Now she felt time slipping into her arteries and bones, thumping at an unusual rate. Was this *all* there really was for her? A sorry repetition that went nowhere and formed nothing? And for what? Emotional comfort or solace in the fact that someone cared enough to be around her for any length of time? What stability was that?

It was as if each day she made her nest of mud and clay, only for it to be torn down in the night. She'd rebuild and rebuild and rebuild every morning, but it was all for naught. Sure, David helped. He brought some clay here and there to do some light patchwork; but really, honestly, *truly*, it was nowhere near enough. He knew it too. That's why he would approach her with that sad little puppy dog face of his, practically begging her to please say, "This is plenty." And she did. *Oh, she did!* Time and time again.

"Good job." "Thank you." "I appreciate it." Those words and sentiments were increasingly empty, like a fundraiser's thermometer that never quite turned red. The shallow amount remained stagnant at the bottom of the pool, allowing fungus to bloom and the oxygen to vanish. There was never any fighting; just cordial, polite decay. She could feel her muscles aching, her spine pinching, her eyes twitching, her fingers breaking, and still she'd smile and say, "Thank you *so much* for trying." The entire world felt firmly attached to her shoulders, and it was bending her backwards, until the very tips of her toes were the only things still touching the ground. She'd never speak of it, but she *resented* David. She wanted to fight, to scream, to yell, to hit, to SNAP! She wanted to break like a glow stick and reveal her colorful fury, squared directly at his pathetic, clueless face.

Years had gone by, *years.* "Things will get better," she told herself, repeatedly. "In time, it won't be so hard." But even in the best of times, she felt that wretched weight crushing her into the grave. She felt her legs sinking, almost to the point where she could hear the grass beneath her gasping for light as she descended into her own painful underworld of repressed truths. "I love you," he'd say, over and over again. Words, just words. Words spoken so many times they'd lost all semblance of meaning. She was tired of being with the boys, those balding boys in such desperate need of mothering. She didn't want to mother anyone anymore. She didn't want to say that things were okay, or that everything was fine. She was dying. Every day. Every moment. Silently screaming for help. But there was no one left to grab onto for dear life, and nowhere else to go but forward, if not up; if only she could find the strength to climb out of this godforsaken pit of her own pathetic design.

A part of her wanted to crawl into the lap of Charles Price and tell him all her pains. She wanted to grab hold of his shoulders and whisper into his ear her deepest, darkest secret: "I'm miserable. Please help me." She could almost smell the cigar on his breath as it merged with hers, feel the rough stubble on his face against her skin, taste his tongue as it twirled around her own. If she could hold on to that man for dear life, she might. She just might. Then again, the temptation itself startled her. It scared her more than the sinking feeling in her chest and spine.

Renée knew the way Charles looked at her. His face was stoic, but his eyes were dirty. The wrinkles around them were kind and friendly; but behind that jovial demeanor, she could see the same melancholia floating just behind his pupils. She could sense a camaraderie of spirit, that same depth of feeling, if not the pain of loss and misunderstandings. And for all of his supposed wisdom and success, he seemed just as lost as she was, and that recognition of a similar form of desperation frightened her, sexually.

She and David rarely had sex. She couldn't even recall the last time they had merged in that way. Physically, there wasn't a spark. Connection felt more like disconnection, with experimentation in bed serving as child's play, complete with kid gloves and safety goggles. Was she truly prepared for what a *man* might bring to the table? A man with that hungry look in his eyes? Sex with David was safe. Sex with Charles promised to be something else entirely, and it sure as hell wasn't going to be sweet. There was still a hint of boyish innocence about that man, but Renée could sense that glimmer of youth had barely survived in spite of everything life had thrown at him. Charles had been chiseled and carved psychically by forces outside of his control, and for all her want of control, Renée knew that he was far more experienced at getting it. And if David was Peter Pan, then maybe Charles was Captain Hook. Did she dare surrender to a man like that? She could barely let go enough to orgasm with David. The very idea of being overwhelmed by any emotion or nervous system response, to be shredded into electric pieces, only to re-form into the shape of her true self in the arms of a comparatively dangerous man—could she surrender to such an experience?

Perhaps she was the one at fault here. Had she been too controlling with David, or too submissive even? Had she somehow, subconsciously, forced him to remain forever aimless as a 35-year-old Peter Pan? Then again, had she ever had control of him in the first place? She couldn't tell David what to do any more than she could rip his heart apart, thread by thread. She'd been working side by side with him for years, sleeping with him, kissing him, riding in the ring under his watchful eye, and yet she didn't really know David Hall. Was his heart hers to tear apart? Could she even find it if she wanted to? Did they truly love each other at all?

Maybe the trap itself was an illusion, nothing but a complicated weave of emotions and promises that didn't truly exist; still, something was holding her back. She could feel it. There was that tightness in her throat again, that chokehold on her future. Were those David's hands suffocating her, or were they truly her own? Even if Charles fucked her into another dimension, if she was killing herself it wouldn't make a bit of difference. It would merely break the bond she'd forged all those years ago. Was that really what she wanted? Freedom? She would never obtain freedom from herself.

Renée looked around the barn she had practically called home for the past twenty years. Her parents had bought the place when she turned thirteen. They saw the property as an investment in her future, being that all she really cared about even then were her horses. She had been the first equestrian from Louisiana to qualify for, and then win, the Maclay Finals, one of the most prestigious competitions for young riders in the United States. She'd been a champion ever since, winning blue and red ribbons left and right, from coast to coast. Her father used to boast that one day she'd ride in the Olympics, but that dream had never materialized.

When she turned twenty-five, both of her parents died in a plane crash. It had been a private plane. They'd run out of fuel, and the engine had stalled. There wasn't even a fire, just shards and spirals of metal and dirt. She'd been at a horse show in River Glen, Tennessee, making out with David Hall in an abandoned shack they'd found during a walk in the rain. As they headed back to the show grounds, Renée could have sworn that she saw two ashen horses, sickly pale and greenish-grey, running through the woods. She found out about her parents that night. David held her as she wept. Then the next morning, he loaded up her horse trailer, drove them both down to Carencro, Louisiana, and by default decided to stay. Renée didn't want to be alone, so she never asked him to leave. That had been eight years ago.

Her farm had been named Pine Grove because of the abundance of pine trees, but also because Renée's mother believed that pine trees absorb negative emotions and guilt, although she never produced any evidence to support this theory. Renée chose to believe it too. Any time she felt disappointed with David, or with her life in general, how it had never panned out the way she had hoped, she would go out to the pine trees barefoot and pray that they'd remove all painful emotions. She'd breathe in their scent and beg the Universe for happiness. But despite all of her secret pain, Renée's life continued to weave into David's until a tight knot had been constructed. Eventually, she came to feel trapped within those interwoven threads, as if that tangle of false promises and shared memories could never be pulled apart. She sensed that the only way to free herself was to cut, deeply and ruthlessly; yet she lacked the courage, mostly because she no longer knew who she was, if not the person joined at the hip with David.

A few weeks ago, Renée had run into her old horse trainer at a show in Covington, Louisiana. Twila Murphy was an Alabama woman who looked old when she was thirty, and doubly so now that she was fifty. "My God," Twila hollered in her direction, even though they were barely six inches apart, standing at the fence of the Grand Prix arena. "Last I saw, you were this wild little thing full of potential. Now this Yank's got you all tacked up and sittin' pretty, waiting on him hand and foot. Shit, your hair's braided and everything."

That comment had stirred something in Renée, and as she pulled her hair out of that French braid, she began to wonder when she'd started styling her light brown hair that way to begin with. She began to wonder how she'd gone from a champion equestrian to a lowly groom and part-time member of the jump crew, setting fences in the schooling ring for David and their students to jump, while her feet remained firmly on the ground. She became acutely aware of the fact that her clothes weren't the kinds of clothes she would normally wear, and that her apartment over the barn had slowly morphed into David's preferred "East Coast" aesthetic. She then realized that even the pictures of her parents had been pushed into a dark corner of the place, and that her ribbons, once on proud display in the clubhouse, had been shoved into random tack trunks around the barn. She was no longer the star equestrian of the two—she was the organizer, the administrator, the trainer for kids under the age of ten, the marketing manager, the shit shoveler, the dry-cleaning fetcher, the mechanic, the cheerleader, and the one who did everything correctly but nothing right. She had completely changed who she was in order to make David happy, never once wondering what might make *her* happy. She had put herself at his service to the detriment of herself, and his dramatic ploys for sympathy infuriated her as a result.

After several handfuls of moonshine-soaked cherries at the Exhibitor's Party that night in Covington, Renée ventured to Twila's table and rambled in emotional distress. What was she to do? She was completely lost. She explained that loving David was like trying to catch air in a jar. As soon as you opened the lid, there was nothing there. The whole thing depended on your belief that you'd caught something real in the first place. "But thinking you have something," she said, "is better than knowing you're alone."

Twila wasn't buying that argument. "You gotta start lookin' at life like you do the show ring, honey. Actually, think of it like a Gambler's Choice. You're the one choosing the obstacles and which way you plan to face 'em. A trainer might be able to show you which way to go, where to turn, when to kick, when to pull, and when to say 'whoa,' but the trainer ain't going in the ring for ya. I can show you the way, but I sure as hell can't carry your ass around the course. You gotta do it yourself, stride by stride, jump by jump. Gotta fight your own battles, honey. Nobody can do it for ya, not me, not David—*you*. So put your goddamn heels down, stop bitchin' and ride on. Whatchu waitin' for? You only got one life and clock's a tickin.'"

That night, Renée knew something had to change, she just didn't know what. Now, weeks later, sitting in the clubhouse of the barn, watching David play an ESPN video game with a Rolling Rock beer in one hand and a Parliament cigarette burning between his fingers in the other, she realized that the person she wanted to beat to death wasn't David—it was her. By being overly malleable to his needs and serving his goals before her own, she had become someone she no longer recognized. She didn't hate David. She hated who she had become in response to him. Maybe lusting after Charles Price was the catalyst for this change, and Twila was merely the one to push her towards the answer; but right now, in this moment, she knew she couldn't move forward until she'd cut that goddamn cord. So she left the clubhouse, went into the feed room, grabbed the pair of scissors hanging from the wall with a frayed piece of twine, then headed back towards David. In one swift motion, she grabbed the cord connecting David to the old Playstation console and cut it clean in half.

"What the fuck?" he screeched.

"David, we're done. I'm done. I don't love you anymore. I don't think I ever did."

It was high time for Renée Benoît to save herself, with or without some fantasy about Charles Price. It wasn't about him. For the first time, in a *long* time, her choices would be all about her.

PART THREE

As Helen Dugas would tell you, she was good at three things: cleaning the Price house, cooking Cajun food, and raising young children alone. She'd been doing all three since she'd been hired by Walter Price at the age of sixteen. And while she never had much education by way of school teachers and books, she knew a thing or two about life, mostly from being in that house nearly every day since 1973. The seven thousand square foot Greek Revival home had been built in the mid-1920s by Edward Price, Charles' grandfather. He'd served as a battlefield surgeon during World War One before returning to his native Louisiana to become a prominent state senator. And when it came to relaxing in his hard-won world of comfort, Edward spared no expense.

The large white house with enormous columns made of cypress had been strategically built on the top of a hill smack dab in the middle of over one hundred acres of paradise. Even today, Helen was dusting old black and white photographs of the family patriarch with his kills of deer and ducks. Hunting seemed to be about the only hobby that old man had, but he'd always returned from his duck blinds and deer stands to a different kind of paradise, one created piece by piece by his Southern Belle of a wife named Rose, whom he had married well before heading off to the war. Everything in the house had been hand selected by the debutante, from the blind stitch embroidered chairs in the living room to the gilded mirrors, all imported from France.

Helen knew the interior of the Price house just about as well as she knew her own body. The floors were pine on the second floor and oak on the first, and from wiping them clean with water and vinegar on her hands and knees, Helen knew every curve, line and knot in that wood. The same applied to the baseboards, the wainscoting, and the decadent grand staircase that seem to pour out in twenty-two steps onto the white marble floors of the foyer. Custom crown molding made of purest plaster seemed to be the icing on the divide between the twelve foot ceilings and the elaborately hand-painted walls. There were seven enormous Belle Epoque chandeliers that needed to be cleaned by hand, one crystal at a time, at least once a month. Each hand-carved medallion above each chandelier's chain also needed a regular dusting.

The entire house was outfitted with handblown glass, and Helen knew every little wrinkle, ripple and deviation in the ninety-six window panes of the kitchen, the thirty-six in the breakfast room, the eighteen in the butler's pantry, and the fifteen on each of the eight French doors on the first floor. The second floor offered even more to clean across seven bedrooms. There were eight wood-burning fireplaces with embellished mantels carved from pine, and just as many needlepoint rugs shipped from France. There was one impossibly large porch in the front, at the entrance of the house, then four smaller, screened-in porches attached to other rooms. Apart from one new artwork—a boudoir painting of Matilda, of all things—each imported painting from Europe had been hand selected by Ms. Rose, as had been the sweet acacia tree she'd planted outside of the kitchen windows overlooking the sink.

That tree was presenting the last of its blooms as Helen washed a few dishes by hand. She had the windows cracked just a bit so she could smell its faint candy scent creep along the breeze to find her curious nose. Helen always wore Egyptian Jasmine to calm her nerves, but there was something about that sweet acacia tree that calmed her even more. The flowers were small yellow pom-poms that seemed to stick to everything when they wilted from the branch, and the tree itself was far smaller in stature than the majestic oaks out front, but the sweet acacia was Helen's favorite, despite its inch long thorns. She loved that tree almost as much as she loved the entire house.

Her momma used to say, if you love a flower, you water it. If you lust after its beauty, that's when you turn all selfish and pluck it. "Lust can feel a lot like love," she'd say. "Until you've got to make a sacrifice, and sometimes leaving that flower right where you found it, to encourage it to grow, well, that's the true cost of love, now ain't it?" Helen believed that you could make the decision to love, unconditionally, same as she had decided to love this old house for all its backbreaking demands, and same as she had decided to love this family, even if she didn't always agree with their way of life. She showed this love through her cooking.

Right now, she was breaking the plastic seal on a large jar of Savoie's Dark Old Fashioned Roux. If she were at her own house, cooking for her own family, she would make the roux from scratch, but Mr. Charlie loved that pre-packaged roux, no matter what Helen said. And so she untwisted that bright red lid, poured out the three inches of oil at the top into thirteen quarts of boiling water, then took a spoon and started to make some room in that heavy glass jar. The smell of grease hit the back of her nose and throat, sticking to the far reaches of her tongue with hints of old chicken bones and dirt. Slowly, she scooped some boiling water into the small-mouthed jar and began to break up that hard roux until spoonfuls of the dark brown paste could be pulled out and stirred into the cast iron pot on the stove. Scoop by scoop, she removed the roux only to add more hot water to the mix. The paste got all over her fingers as she scooped then stirred. If there was one rule while making gumbo, other than keeping cherry tomatoes out of the mix, it was never let the roux burn at the bottom of the pot. So, Helen would scoop, then stir, stir, stir, as a light brown froth appeared. Once the jar was empty, and all had been dissolved, she lowered the fire and moved on to the next step.

That roux would need to cook down for at least an hour, preferably two. In the meantime, Helen chopped her yellow onions, green bell pepper, fresh celery and peeled garlic until about four cups of the stuff were ready to be added to the pot. Then she broke down two whole chickens, keeping the spine intact. (She'd cook with it for a while, then remove the whole thing before serving.) Next, she sliced three full links of mixed smoked sausage and two large pieces of tasso from Country Meat Block in Opelousas—the best place to buy meat in the state, according to Mr. Charlie. Finally, she seasoned all that with a thin layer of Slap Ya Mama from Ville Platte, mindful of the high salt content, then let it rest while she cleaned the kitchen. That gumbo juice made a mess of everything, sticking to the spoon holder with a nasty crust; but the smell of roux cooking down was absolutely divine. She'd add all those other ingredients later, then let them cook for an hour or two. Then she'd add a layer of gumbo filé, or ground sassafras, on top before closing with a curtain of chopped parsley and green onions. By then, it would be much closer to dinner time. It wasn't even noon yet. She'd probably cook some white rice around four, then make the potato salad.

Helen looked at the old clock hanging above the door. She hoped to talk with Natalie today, if the girl managed to come home right after school. Her mother had already left for New Orleans, with a short direct flight to Chicago scheduled for this afternoon. She'd be there for the next two weeks or so. It would be the first of several upcoming trips to Chicago, until that move was permanent, but Natalie didn't know that yet. In fact, out of all the secrets Helen had been forced to keep over the years, this one secret from Natalie had been weighing on her for months. Mr. Charlie himself had told her the news over a bowl of her handmade praline ice cream. "Matilda and I are getting a divorce," he said. "Right after Natalie graduates. I'll make sure she's taken care of, but you were right. She's not the one."

"You should have gone after Ms. Vivi when you had the chance," Helen said. Charlie never replied.

Ms. Vivi was probably the only woman Mr. Charlie had ever loved. Her father had lived on the back of the property in an old Acadian-style home and did some light yard work from time to time in exchange for rent. His wife was a proud little thing from Eunice, who never could quite understand why they never had any money, despite having married a man who only cared about hunting and fishing, that simple life that only requires a shotgun, loaded tackle box, and a bottle of whiskey. She'd been a beauty queen who'd gotten turned around somewhere, or simply tricked into marrying a simple Cajun man with a penchant for chewing tobacco. Their daughter was just about the only thing those two had in common, and you can bet that Mama was plenty hard on the girl too, especially since she took after her Daddy.

That young precocious thing was almost always at the house, and she had joined Helen in the audience for plenty of violin recitals, wearing her simple homemade dresses and bows. She and Charlie had been talking about getting married after college long before either of them even knew what college was; but just as Walter had smashed Charlie's violin after his graduating recital, he seemed to have smashed that budding romance too. Helen still didn't know what had happened. She'd called that girl plenty of times, begging her to come back and talk to Charlie, but there was no changing her mind. That girl had been plain spooked by whatever Walter Price had said, and she ran so far and so fast, nobody knew where she went until she started writing articles for a fancy newspaper out in Washington, D.C.

A few years later she married that paper's owner, who came from some old New Hampshire money, and changed her last name to Shaw. Helen didn't even see her again until Walter's funeral. Of course, she assumed Ms. Vivi would stay after that, being that she was recently divorced; but she didn't. Then Charlie announced, out of the blue, that he was marrying a prominent actress from Chicago. Helen suspected that Charlie had married Matilda partly because she was pregnant, but mostly because he just couldn't bear the pain of loneliness any longer, having lost his only real friend and prospect once and for all.

Helen knew that the Price family had experienced their fair share of pain. Edward had lost both his brother and his childhood friend during World War One. Then he and Rose lost their three older boys to World War Two. Walter was the only survivor, and he came back from duty piss fire mad and ambitious as hell. He started his blood plasma business in the late 1940s with his father's political support and full financial backing, then turned it into some real money by the time he wed a research assistant from Stanford University in 1964. He was late to get married compared to other men of his generation, but Walter had always been married to his work, first and foremost. At least that's the way that Helen heard it.

Obviously, she had never met Eleanor Price, but she'd heard stories from Charlie, who idolized his mother. Her entire family was comprised of musicians, and Eleanor herself played the violin and the piano, with a preference for the Baroque period. For Charlie's fourth birthday, she gave him his own tiny violin. Almost every day thereafter, mother and son were in the music room, sliding those horse hair bows across the strings. Supposedly, Walter was charmed by all this, until Eleanor died in childbirth, along with his daughter, when Charlie was eight. That was when Helen was hired. She moved into the house just as Walter seemed to be moving right on out of it.

She hardly knew anything about raising children at the time, but all of a sudden she was in charge of Charlie Price. She cleaned the house, cooked his meals, read him stories, and watched countless violin lessons and impromptu recitals. She could tell whether that boy was angry or upset simply by the way that tiny violin screeched. And thank goodness for that, because even at a young age Charlie didn't talk much, and especially not about his feelings. He was as sharp as a tack, but kept his wit to himself more often than not. The only one who could lure his opinions out of him was Ms. Vivi, who lived in the shack just across the pond and right along the bayou. She didn't play with dolls, had no interest in beauty pageants, and avoided her mother's hairbrush as one might try to avoid the plague. She was a wild child, better suited to running through the woods barefoot with her bow and arrows than walking around at tea parties in cream colored dresses and matching heels talking about the quality of cucumber sandwiches.

Unlike those proper girls that Walter wanted his son around, Ms. Vivi would ride up to the house on her father's nag, which he'd bought for fifty dollars at the slaughterhouse, using nothing but a halter and lead rope for steering, and Charlie would look at her like she'd put the stars in the sky. Of course, Helen had a hell of a time keeping track of that girl when she came to the house to play. She and Charlie would disappear for hours on end in those woods, exploring the now abandoned hunting spots of his grandfather, only to come back with the wildest stories about the monsters they'd met along the way: poisonous snakes, baby alligators, and vicious mosquitos the size of jacks.

One time she caught Ms. Vivi, still in her underwear from swimming in the pond, with a shovel in her hand. Before Helen could blink, that tiny girl was chopping the head off a water moccasin as Charlie watched from nearby, sipping his soda pop and thinking about things only young boys could understand. When Helen hollered, "What the hell you doing, Ms. Vivi?!" the girl simply responded by holding up the now decapitated snake, which was about as long as her, and smiling with a partially toothless grin, "Protecting Charlie, Ms. Helen. What you think?" That girl's mother would have needed the smelling vapors had she heard the half of these tales; but Charlie loved that girl almost as much as he loved his violin, and Helen wasn't about to split them up. Besides, Walter was almost never home, so really, who were they hurting, other than her nerves?

When Charlie's father did emerge to grace them with his presence, it was often for some sort of fundraiser rather than any form of quality bonding time with his son. He'd come in from his apartment in New Orleans with twenty or so friends in tow, all ready to throw money at politicians to grease the wheels of their big ideas. Helen was grateful that all she had to do was cook breakfast for those fiends. The rest was professionally catered by whatever Creole chef Walter had convinced to make the trek down to Lafayette. During events such as these, Charlie was quick to hide his violin, and if Vivi came over, she was on her very best behavior and in her finest dress. In fact, her mother probably only got the opportunity to wash that girl's hair right before a party. Otherwise, her dirty blonde locks lived up to the full extent of their name.

This went on for a decade, until Charlie was eighteen years old. By then, he'd graduated to an adult violin, which had been sent to him by his grandfather in Connecticut. He hadn't seen his mother's family since her passing, as Walter didn't want them around his son; but Charlie had kept up a secret correspondence with them, and for his fifteenth birthday they'd shipped him a beautiful instrument made in Italy, claiming it had been in their family for generations, one even his mother had played. Helen had never seen a boy so attached to an object. If he hadn't feared breaking it, Charlie might very well have slept with the thing. Naturally, Walter knew none of this. Helen would hear him telling anyone and everyone at parties that Charlie would be joining the family business, just as soon as he got a bachelor's degree in finance. She'd watch as that boy's pale face revealed his dissatisfaction with the path being carved out in front of him. Millions of dollars were filling the family's coffers and Charlie seemed to feel trapped by each and every one.

Still, Helen couldn't watch that boy forever. Once he started college, she moved out of that big house and started keeping regular hours, as opposed to overnight stays. Most of the time, that mansion was hauntingly empty. Walter was seldom there, and Charlie spent all of his time on campus, only venturing home to sleep. He hadn't told his father, but he was majoring in music performance, with only a minor in finance. Helen and Ms. Vivi were the only ones who knew. So many secrets, always piling a mile high for her to keep. Of course Walter found out, and as soon as Charlie graduated, he tried to make damn sure that little hobby wouldn't interfere with his plans for his son. Helen had been in the kitchen when she heard that priceless violin smash. "Do you have any idea the sacrifices that have been made so you can be where you are right now?" Walter screamed. "I'll be damned if you throw it away on that shit. I've worked too hard for you to turn your back on everything we've

built." Charlie started working at Price Plasma that very next morning, bright and early at seven o'clock, *sharp*.

By then, Helen had her own trouble to deal with. As soon as
Charlie had started college and she'd gotten a place of her own, the
women at church started sending her out on dates with available
men. She'd gone on eight before finally meeting Richard, or Richie,
as he preferred to be called. Ironically, he was the one man the
women at church advised her against. "He's full of hot air," they
said. "He'll never be able to support a family." Helen thought she
saw something else, something worth investing in. Richie was a
poet, practically obsessed with equality and democracy. He believed
that power should be spread around, that everyone was his brother
or sister, and that life should be, above all things, beautiful.

During their courtship, he introduced her to a world in which
the art of the Price house, which she had often dusted and scrubbed,
came to life with a sense of movement. He helped her see that beauty
and art was everywhere, not just locked inside fancy houses, from
the perfect symmetry of nature to the glory of righteous ideas. He
brought her into the fold of his artistic community, where the night
came alive with the beating of drums, the lyrics of poetry, and the free,
shameless dancing of the men and women who worshipped each
other beneath the moon. Having been confined to one house, serving a family that wasn't her own, Helen felt liberated and euphoric
in this environment. She thought she'd found a world she could love
just as much as those gilded mirrors and the sounds made by Charlie's
violin, a world that belonged to her and Richie alone.

The problem was that she didn't recognize the dark underbelly
of that beauty. From time to time, she saw some of the dancers
snorting coke, or the drummers smoking pot; but Richie seemed
above all that, with his angelic face and soft spoken voice. He would
talk about running for governor, how he would form committees
to study every parish in the state to figure out what exactly had
gone wrong, and then host public town halls so everyone could
determine the best course of action. He loved Louisiana, he loved

politics, and he loved coming up with ideas. And all this was so different from what she'd heard at those fancy parties held by Walter Price, she dreamed it would all come true. Richie even said he and Helen were soul mates, because she worked at 714 Oak Street, and 714 was his favorite number. She had no idea at the time that 714 was really the number on his favorite drug.

As the years passed, Helen decided that Richie needed quaaludes because he simply knew too much. He knew that all he had were his ideas. He knew that he would struggle to focus on any particular one of them, or to choose one to put into action. And he knew that no matter how hard he tried, there were opposing forces that would always cancel him out. That's why he felt that he needed to dissolve into his addiction, so that his troubles could be forgotten or made completely irrelevant. But she didn't know any of this when she married him. She didn't know that living with Richie would be like chasing after light only to be met by shadow. She didn't realize that if the slightest thing went wrong, he'd go flying off the handle, or that he often chose to ignore the darker aspects of himself entirely. When she realized that she was pregnant with Whitney, she begged him to get a job because she felt she wouldn't be able to clean the Price house forever; but Richie was far more interested in writing his rambling manifestos and increasingly poor poetry than working a common job. Even when he did get one, he'd quit within a matter of weeks.

Soon, but not soon enough, Helen realized that she had married an idea—the one he had knowingly sold to her with the best of intentions, and the one she had bought into without reading the fine print first. She had believed that he was exactly who he claimed to be, not recognizing Richie's true gift back then, which was that he could be just about anybody for short bursts of time, just never fully himself. He seemed to project his light against the world to showcase his beautiful visions for what *could* be, while the truth remained cloaked in shadow behind the projector. He wanted so desperately to be the man he had created in her mind, not the person he had actually become in the process of putting on the show.

But Helen never could stay mad at him, mostly because his love for her made her feel empowered and beautiful, as if she were a living work of art all on her own. In bed, he would touch her as if she were made of precious stardust and clay, using his hands to learn the methods of her divine sculptor. He was slow and gentle, using his mouth to find hidden pockets of pleasure that she hadn't even known to exist. Just as she had cleaned the Price House on her hands and knees, learning every nook and cranny, so did he explore her body, and in a way her soul. He saw Helen in the best possible light, worshipping her rounded shoulders and large breasts as if she were a goddess of abundance. He'd kiss her small feet and hands, as if to heal every callous and scar, then massage her tired muscles with sweet smelling oils until she was relaxed and calm. Their love was deep and poetic in its own right, and even a soft kiss on the end of her plump nose could send shivers racing across her skin. Life with Richie wasn't always easy, but she loved him, more than she had ever loved another human being. Eventually, she even loved the flaws he tried so hard to hide.

Then everything changed. Whitney wasn't even three months old when Helen was woken up in the middle of the night by her neighbor, whose husband was a police officer. A prostitute had been brutally killed in a drug dealer's apartment on the bad side of the tracks and Richie had been arrested for her rape and murder. He claimed that he couldn't have done it, as he had taken three quaaludes and passed out on the couch. None of that mattered. It was a quick trial. The dealer had an alibi and there were no other suspects. Despite Richie's cries of innocence, he was found guilty and sentenced to life in prison at the Louisiana State Penitentiary at Angola, otherwise known as "The Farm." Right up until he was taken away to Baton Rouge, Richie promised Helen that he would make everything right in the end; but that promise, to her, seemed to be the greatest fantasy of them all.

She begged Walter Price for help. He had contacts at Angola, being that he had harvested plasma there, making millions of dollars in the process; but he refused to get involved with the case. "I haven't worked with Angola in five years," he said. "There just aren't any strings left to pull." Reluctantly, she asked Charlie for help, but he didn't want to approach his father with that kind of mess. "You know I want to help you, Ms. Helen, but I'm sure the judge knows more than we do," he said. "We've gotta have faith in the system." All they could do for her was let her move back into the house, so she could at least raise her baby under better conditions.

The first time she went to visit Richie, Helen was shocked. She had always known him as someone who loved to laugh, but it was as if his laugh had been taken away with his personal effects. Even his idealism was gone, seemingly removed with the stamp of his fingerprints. He'd once considered everyone to be his brother, that all people were inherently good; but after letting some men help him move into his cell, everyone became an enemy and he watched their movements with a fearful eye. She didn't think he'd survive in that place, and over the course of those first twenty years or so, her once eternally youthful husband seemed to wither away. His bright complexion became muddy, while his body wasted away to nothing but bone as his joints and knuckles protruded in unnatural ways. With each visit, twice a month, Helen noticed that a little more of Richie's light had gone out, as his hair thinned and teeth went missing. The hint of melancholy in his eyes took over every cell and multiplied with rage. Those rose-colored glasses he had once held onto so desperately had been ripped clean off his face, and there was no hiding from what he was now forced to experience. All Helen could do was raise their daughter and pray for justice. She just never imagined it would take more than three decades to be found.

After her dreams of raising a family with Richie had been shattered, Helen figured that, since she'd learned so much from raising Charlie, she could raise Whitney alone just fine. Only that little shapeshifting pixie didn't make things easy. Just like her father, Whitney was full of ideas, and often swinging from one extreme to the next with the same frequency. The Cajuns would call her *canaille*, or mischievous, and she was always up to some sort of *canaillerie*. One minute she was a sweet, innocent little thing, the next she was beating up boys at school and spitting on them. She was always smart, too smart for her own good, as no one could ever pin any trouble directly on her. She'd just switch gears yet again. "I didn't do nothing," she'd say, with that sweet little voice and big ol' eyes. But Helen knew that her daughter was *never* innocent.

In time, Walter had to ask them to move out again, since Whitney had the attention span of a gnat, was constantly running into priceless antiques, and could never sit still. She was also a constant eavesdropper on conversations. Walter caught her listening in on one of his business calls, then pulled her aside to tell her the story of Chloe, a house slave who liked to eavesdrop too. One day, her master caught her listening in when she shouldn't have, and clean cut off her ear to show her a lesson. "Don't let it happen it you," Walter said. Two days later, after spending plenty of time at the local library, Whitney came back to the house, walked straight up to Mr. Price and said, "I don't believe that story. I went through all the records, and there ain't no proof of no Chloe at the Myrtles. You think people like you don't keep track of your slaves? You sure busy keeping track of me." She was eleven, and they were in a new apartment by the end of the week.

Just thinking of the trouble Whitney caused was enough to give Helen a headache, and that girl was now in her thirties. It was always something. First, she was beating up boys. Then by high school, Helen was chasing them off her porch with a broom. Whitney had a long line of admirers, all sweet and nerdy boys who had fallen head over heels for that careless siren. Whitney was a strange breed of tomboy who went looking for sexual attention, from anyone— old, young, black, white, rich, poor, good and wicked—especially once her bouncy breasts and curvy hips came in around fifteen. The trouble was that Whitney could never sit still long enough to truly get to know any of her admirers. And because she was so gifted in science, and was often the only girl in those groups, she broke heart after heart out of nothing more than a short attention span. She'd get them to do her bidding, sure enough, but then leave them behind in her dust after she'd gotten what she wanted. And knowing all this, Helen was terrified of knowing why exactly Whitney had come running home from California with her tail between her legs, suddenly acting like a saint. If the rumors were bad when Whitney was growing up, how bad would they be this time?

As Helen dumped the meat and chopped trinity of onions, bell pepper, and celery into the gumbo pot, she tried to think of better things, but the fact remained: Natalie was flirting with disaster just as much as Whitney had done at her age. She'd seen that girl's portfolio tucked between her mattresses. Natalie seemed more like a stalker than a wanna-be professional photographer, with countless images of her much older horse trainer filling that flimsy black book. First of all, there was no way that man could ever afford the hundreds of designer lipsticks that girl had in a single drawer in her bathroom, forget her clothes and bangles. He might look like some down-on-his-luck prince, but there was no way that kind of relationship would work. Natalie liked her stuff far too much to go living like some dirty horseback riding gypsy, no matter how Bohemian her sense of style had become lately. Helen didn't go praying for the sweet acacia to turn into a sassafras tree, and no kiss was gonna turn David Hall into Natalie's imaginary Prince Charming, no matter how perfect her cat eye game might be.

It bothered Helen that neither Charlie nor Matilda seemed to notice that their daughter had been blinded by senseless puppy love. Then again, mother and father were pretty blind too. They might have ended up being perfect for one another, had either Charlie or Matilda put down their weapons for half a second. Instead, they brought out the worst in each other, almost as if on purpose. Charlie was constantly dismissing his obviously intelligent wife's ideas, and she in turn spent his money as if shopping were an act of war. That woman practically wore the same thing every day, but her closet was overflowing with luxurious clothing, most with the tags still attached. And while some people saw the Virgin Mary in their toast, Helen couldn't help but see the failures of that marriage grow like poison ivy along the walls, and now everyone was itchy.

Both husband and wife feared venturing into the dark recesses of their deeper needs because they both seemed absolutely petrified of what those needs really were. And since they couldn't digest their own venom, they spread it all around with pleasure. That's why Natalie was anxious to escape with whatever decent looking buffoon made the first offer. Both of her parents were holding onto the past like some kind of life raft, completely oblivious to the fact that they were really holding onto a concrete block. And the more they fought to hold on, the more their marriage drowned beneath the rocky waves of life. Helen knew they were both stubborn survivors who were trying to save themselves, but she wanted to beat them both over the head with her cast iron skillet. Anything to make them realize that the only thing that destroys iron is its own goddamn rust.

Helen stirred the gumbo bubbling in the cast iron pot, feeling the heat of the flame beneath it. She had prayed, time and time again, that Charlie would let the past go, let it burn away. And she prayed that Matilda would stop fighting so hard. No one was at war with her; yet she seemed to be fighting for her life, until she had no more fight left in her. Helen tried to help the woman. In fact, she'd always liked Matilda. Charlie's wife was organized and professional, just emotionally absent. Helen tried to connect with her, but there was no overcoming that barrier she'd built between herself and others. Charlie was the same way, hiding behind his business, same as Walter had done till the day he died. There was no use fighting either one of them. If anything, they were looking for a fight. And because they hated themselves, they couldn't possibly love each other, or even recognize the naive hopes of their lusty teenaged daughter.

But just because Helen knew the cure didn't mean she could fix either one of them. After all, she was only good at raising young children, or at least getting them to adulthood. Once they were adults, they were on their own. Charlie and Matilda needed to find their own salvation, and it wasn't going to be found in work or alcohol either. Eventually, they were going to have to look inside themselves for answers, and Helen sure as hell couldn't do that kind of soul searching for them. It took Angola to kill Richie's ego. She felt it might take worse than that to tackle the internal barriers built by Charlie and his wife. However, now that Natalie was eighteen, the clock was ticking. She needed to have a good stern talk with that girl before she did something stupid. Helen feared it might already be too late. The only saving grace, she thought, was that David Hall had a girlfriend, so he might not make a move; but even Helen knew that was an awfully flimsy barrier to that teenager's hopeless romantic stupidity.

Suddenly, the television set across the room caught Helen's attention. The name Delilah Russell had been mentioned plenty in this house, and now it was echoing throughout the kitchen. In a sit-down interview, a newsreader asked the woman, "In your mind, how long should we want to live?" The stunning dark-haired, green-eyed beauty replied, "Let's face it, it's fun to talk about the prospect of immortality. And I'd be lying if I said we aren't aiming for that in the future; but really, Blue Lotus is about preventative care with longevity being a mere side effect of our treatment. Maybe, in time, immortality will be one too. But right now our company is focused purely on preventing illness in a new, if not more effective way."

Another newsreader interrupted the feed. "That was Delilah Russell three weeks ago, describing her rejuvenation therapies as meant to prevent illness. However, documents provided by an anonymous whistleblower have revealed that her therapies may do quite the opposite. We'll have more on this story at five."

"Oh dear," Helen said. "Speaking of stupidity…"

What had Whitney done now?

PART FOUR

David Hall was sitting in the apartment above the barn in a state of stunned silence. He'd opened a Rolling Rock hours ago, only to watch the condensation stream down the bottle until the now warm beer sat in a pool of its own sweat. Renée had left around noon for New Orleans with the directive that David should be gone by the time she returned tomorrow evening. It was now a little past three o'clock and he had yet to pack. He had nowhere else to go.

The thirty-five-year-old horse trainer wasn't sure if he had ever really loved Renée. It was as if they'd simply fallen into a relationship together, and had, in a sense, become addicted to one another in the process. Originally, she had been dead set on qualifying for the Olympic team, and he had been absolutely determined to prove that he could get her there, if only to rub it in Conrad's face. But those goals had morphed into something else over time, until their relationship had become completely dysfunctional, with each pretending to be someone else entirely.

Renée never really knew about the kind of relationship he had with Conrad. Hardly anyone did. Neither of them were especially eager to broadcast the true nature of their partnership. It was no one's business but theirs. Still, even after eight years apart, David felt that he belonged with Conrad, far more than he ever belonged with Renée. That's also why he had run away from New Jersey. David wanted to prove that he could make it on his own, that he didn't need the support of the "great Conrad Hastings" in order to be a success. He wanted to prove that he was a great equestrian and trainer independent of the former Olympian. And he'd tried to raise himself up all by his lonesome, but it simply hadn't worked.

Six months ago he'd run into Conrad at the Pennsylvania National Horse Show in Harrisburg. He and Renée were there because Natalie had qualified for the Children's Jumper Finals, a sort of national championship for the kids. Initially, David had been excited to show off his girlfriend and wealthy student to all of his East Coast friends, if only to prove that he'd finally made something of himself far away from home. Then Natalie knocked down two rails, went off-course, and didn't even place in the ribbons. Conrad walked up behind David at the gate, squeezed his shoulder, and whispered in his ear, "Ready to come back and play with the big boys?"

The question burned in his mind as David sat on a tack trunk and held Natalie while she wept. "I'm so sorry, I'm so sorry," she kept repeating. "I embarrassed you."

"Don't be silly," David said. "You were great."

She didn't seem to believe him any more than he believed himself. That night, he went to a nearby hotel with the intention of getting blackout drunk at the bar. Instead he found himself in Conrad's hotel room, getting the first blowjob he'd had in years.

"Ready to come home?" Conrad asked, later in the night.

"Now why would I want to do that?" David replied, buttoning up his shirt.

"Because you look miserable," Conrad said, still naked in bed.

"I'm not," David argued. "I'm just...tired."

"Tired of fighting the truth. You belong in New Jersey."

"Nobody belongs in New Jersey. They just end up there."

Conrad reached for David, then kissed him on the forehead. "You're always welcome to come home," he said, those deep blue eyes still beaming with love, even after all this time.

"Maybe I've found a new home. Maybe I'm happy where I am."

"If you're so happy, why are you here with me?" David didn't have an answer.

He would never forget the way Renée's eyes lit up when he told her about working with Conrad and serving as the famous trainer's demonstration rider at clinics. When they first met, he regaled her with story after story of adventures shared with the show jumping legend, from horse shopping in Argentina to competing at major competitions on the grounds of Spruce Meadows, Hickstead, and Aachen. He told her about his experiences at the World Cup, World Equestrian Games, and even the Olympics. Renée would beg to hear stories about the great riders she most admired, from Ian Miller of Canada and Nick Skelton of Great Britain to Ludger Beerbaum of Germany and Eric Navet of France. He had even more to say about the great female riders of the U.S., such as Beezie Madden, Laura Kraut, and Margie Goldstein-Engle. Renée had followed their careers throughout her own and hung on David's every word. If he happened to be hyperbolic in certain cases, well, that was just because he wanted to keep her happy, and in the process make her admire him all the more.

David had never been a great equestrian. He knew that. He'd always been in the proximity of greatness, having never achieved any notoriety himself. More often than not, he stayed on the ground, grooming the horses and setting the fences. If he was in the tack, it was often to warm up a horse, not compete in a Grand Prix. In reality, Renée had far more experience in the show ring than he did; but she seemed to look at him like he was the true champion of the two, and he desperately wanted to believe it. The fact that she was more than eager to become his groom, his jump crew, his eyes on the ground, so that he might find glory in the ring, was exhilarating if not validating. It was as if she had seen something in him that no one else had ever bothered to see before. So how could he be to blame for her unhappiness? She had volunteered to demote herself!

In his opinion, Renée was a control freak. She had to do everything just so, and if David suggested a better or more effective way of doing things, she'd practically bite his head off, or worse, give him that pained look of disappointment. If she wanted to run the barn, fine. It was her barn. If she wanted to organize the tack trunks, the wash rack, the feed room, okay. He was tired of doing that kind of grunt work anyway. And if she didn't want to compete in a Grand Prix, he certainly wasn't going to force her to spend five hundred dollars to enter. Besides, the more he did try to help—with *anything*—the more she told him to go practice, train, focus on himself. But in that Louisiana heat, you can only ride so many horses each day. He wasn't about to get up at four in the morning just to go jump a few sticks. That's why he waited until the evening to train, once the air had cooled. And if he didn't have anything else to do in the middle of the day, why couldn't he play video games? Why did she have to nitpick every little thing to death? She wanted the responsibility—*the power*—of running things. Why would he fight her on that? He thought he was giving her exactly what she wanted. Now it turned out he was "killing her with his laziness." That was certainly news to him.

With the flip of a switch, suddenly David was out on his ass with nowhere to go, no money saved, and no new prospects either. And he wasn't about to call Conrad, only to beg for a one-way ticket home, citing his painful failures as a trainer and competitor. That was not happening. He was not about to run back to New Jersey with his tail between his legs, no matter how much he loved that man. David wasn't going to give Conrad the satisfaction of having been right all along. He wasn't going to cave. No, he was going to figure this thing out all on his own. *Fuck Renée*, he thought.

David was convinced that she only worked as hard as she did, not because of her overwhelming virtue, but because she would be beyond reproach if she single-handedly carried the entire world on her shoulders. No one could critique her if she was the martyr of their relationship. So she built herself up as the victim out of blind arrogance and ego, only to make David the villain, no matter what the truth had actually been between them. Why had she given up riding to begin with? It certainly hadn't been his idea. But as long as she stayed out of the tack, she could somehow remain the champion she had been before meeting David. If there was no chance for failure or embarrassment, then there was no opportunity for her past success to be tarnished by the reality of the present. She could remain perfect that way, as the champion merely taking a hiatus to serve as cheerleader on the sidelines, only to blame everyone else when they inevitably disappointed her.

Then again, Renée had made it possible for him to be head trainer of an equestrian facility. She was the one who had completely streamlined his existence so that all he had to focus on was his craft. And she begged for his advice, relied on it even, believing that David was actually Conrad himself, as if the brilliant trainer had somehow transferred his wisdom to David through mere proximity. Unfortunately, it didn't work that way. Still, Renée promised that she loved him unconditionally, never realizing that he was living a lie. She even seemed to get off on being subservient to him, telling others that he was headed for greatness. He'd be in the tack, looking down at her on the ground as she wiped the slobber off a horse's mouth or cleaned the schooling ring sand off his boots, and she seemed thrilled to be there. She'd look up at him with a huge smile on her face and say, "You got this, champ."

Only, David never felt he could live up to the hype. He couldn't sleep half the time, his mind racing with doubts and fears. He felt like an imposter, that he should be on the ground and she should be in the tack. All of his stories of supposed greatness seemed to wrap around him with their gross exaggerations until he felt he couldn't breathe. So he bought new show shirts and jackets, custom boots and spurs—all with Renée's money—just so that he could at least *look* the part, even if he felt that he could never meet his own impossibly high standards, the exact same standards to which Renée held him accountable. But that only put more stress on their already strained relationship, as neither of them had any money and achieving cash flow was a constant struggle. Students paid fifty dollars an hour for lessons, but that was never enough to cover expenses. It was becoming difficult to feed the horses, let alone themselves.

There was never enough money. The bills were always piling up like a mound of pine shavings, filling their self-inflicted prison with a confetti of obligations that could never be fully met. Fresh shavings were added every day, as paying students became harder and harder to find. Natalie was their lifesaver, as the only student able to afford traveling around the country to chase after points and ribbons. They both relied on her to pay their electric bill, keep their phones working and their cupboards full. And David saw the way Renée looked at Charles Price, the way she devoured him with her eyes. He even suspected she'd fucked that man into buying her a new three-thousand-dollar saddle. It certainly seemed like she wanted to. But David was tired of kissing ass and playing surrogate father to that selfish teenager who never listened. The only reason he posed for photograph after photograph was because he knew he couldn't afford to rock the boat that was their financial security. He'd wanted to jump ship for months, anything to escape Natalie Price, who had greedily glued herself to him over the past four years.

David pulled a pack of Parliament cigarettes out from his pocket and selected one. With a nervous tremor in his hand, he lit the end and inhaled. Soon toxic smoke rings circled his head, descended upon his ears, and sank into his skin. Maybe he was never meant to be the front man of any relationship. He was far more comfortable being a sort of house husband, ensuring that others had whatever they needed rather than pursuing his own ambitions. Actually, if pressed, he couldn't even list what his ambitions were. It all seemed like a fog. Renée's goals had become his own, without warning or mutual agreement. She seemed to expect *him* to qualify for the Olympic team somehow. David knew the kind of talent and determination a role like that required, and he also knew that he didn't have it. Renée had the talent; but she seemed to have abandoned all determination towards the goal, feeling that it was safer for him to have it instead.

But David didn't want anything. There was nothing he truly hungered for. He was fine with just going to shows, drinking beer and smoking cigarettes. Why was that so wrong? There were many ways to live a meaningful life. Not everyone had to be driven and ambitious, fighting battles or pushing for progress. Some people could just choose to exist in the moment without expectation. However, if that was true, if that was what he truly wanted, why did he lie to Renée in the first place? Why had he allowed her dreams to become his own when they clearly didn't want the same things? David didn't have any dreams. He didn't even dream in his sleep.

He did miss Conrad though. He missed their conversations, their gossip, their inside jokes. He missed the luxurious life that Conrad provided for him, jet-setting to horse shows around the world, eating at the finest restaurants in each country, having drinks with nobility and celebrities at late-night exhibitor parties. People practically threw money at Conrad, and David missed, more than anything, being able to reach into those deep, perpetually full pockets. But David had been young and beautiful when he'd lived with Conrad. Now his hair was thinning, and as much as he hated to admit it, he was starting to go bald in the back. His hazel eyes were tired, and his face was beginning to wrinkle. He'd gained at least fifteen pounds over the last few years, and he was already a hulking giant to begin with. Conrad would certainly put him on a diet, if not force him on an entire health regime. He'd hold him to a different standard than Renée had, and David wasn't sure he wanted to try meeting that goal post again. He was tired of changing to please everyone else, but he had no idea who he was without external influence. He'd never gone looking that deeply, preferring to merely change on the surface, if only to minimize conflict and make everyone around him happy. And all that had done was increase his anxiety and nurture the fear that he'd eventually be found out. Someone had to notice, at some point, that he was empty.

David heard a car pull up to the barn. For a split second, he assumed it was Renée, that she'd changed her mind and turned around to seek reunion. The thought struck a chord of fear in his heart. Then he looked out the window to see Natalie's white BMW 7-Series parked out front. He watched the teenager bolt out of the driver's seat in her school uniform of white Oxford shirt, green plaid skirt, white knee high socks, and black Mary Janes. She raced into the barn, determined to reach the clubhouse. Any minute now, she'd come running up the stairs to the apartment to find him. She certainly didn't give up easily, that one. He headed towards the fridge and opened another beer. By the time the girl came bursting through the door, he'd chugged the entire bottle.

"Oh David," she cried. "Thank God you're here!" Her face was puffy and red, her nose completely raw. She ran across the small apartment and threw herself into his arms. David was too tired to conjure an emotional response, so he simply held her, lightly. "I've had the worst day," she said. "I've been waiting to get to you since this morning."

Her face was pressed against his chest, as if she were trying to hide in the nook of his arm. David could feel dampness forming on his skin. The girl was certainly crying. "What's the matter?" he asked, trying as hard as he could to be kind and gentle, despite wanting to run in the opposite direction of her suffocating embrace.

"My father was in the paper today. Oh, David, it's just awful. I don't want to go home. Can I stay here tonight?"

"What was he in the paper for?"

"They're saying he gave people all sorts of diseases, some disease like AIDS. I didn't really read the article. I was crying too hard to read. Please don't make me go home."

David rubbed the back of her head as she sobbed into him. "Oh, Natalie, of course you *could* stay here, but I'm afraid tonight's a bad night."

She pulled away frantically, looking up at him with her puffy blue eyes, red from crying. "Why? Don't you want me here?"

"You know I do," he lied, fully aware that Natalie Price never took 'no' for an answer. "It's just a bad time. You see, I'm getting ready to leave."

"Leave?" Panic flashed across her face. She gripped tighter onto his dark green polo shirt and pulled him closer. "Where are you going? We don't have any shows till next month."

David didn't want to tell her. He didn't want anyone to know just yet. He planned to slip away in the dark of the night, never to be heard from again, with this entire period of his life eventually becoming nothing more than a bad dream. "Renée asked me to leave, so I've got to go."

Natalie pulled away again, this time staggering back a few steps until the island in the kitchen met her back. "She broke up with you?"

"I'm afraid so," he said, reaching for another beer and opening it with his lighter.

"Aren't you sad?"

David did feel sad. He could feel sadness lurking in his bones and blood, weighing him down while simultaneously holding him upright, like a puppet held up by a thumb. He just wasn't going to cry about it. If anything, this break-up had been a long time coming. There was no use shedding tears over the demise of this strange relationship. "Yes, but it's for the best."

"Where will you go?"

"I don't know yet. I just know that I'm going."

The girl was staring at him now. He could almost see ideas forming in the back of her mind, and that sort of calculating worried him. He thought to say "goodbye" or "it's been nice knowing you" or "good luck kid." Any of those would have been decent answers, but he knew that none of them were going to be accepted by Natalie. He sipped his beer and waited, suppressing his impulse to run.

"Take me with you," she said, drying her eyes and trying to appear strong.

David laughed. "You can't come with me. You've got to finish high school and go to college. You've got a bright future ahead of you. I'm not going to ruin your life. Don't worry about me. It's all going to work out in the end."

"David, please, take me with you! I...I love you."

"Natalie," he sighed, looking down at his feet and shaking his head.

She walked up to him, raised his chin, looked him in the eye and said it again. "I love you, David."

He pulled his chin away from her perfectly manicured nails. "That's very sweet, really…"

"I've loved you since the moment I saw you at that horse show in Covington. I've loved you every minute of every day since. I know you, better than anyone. Please, don't leave me behind. I promise that no one will ever love you the way that I love you. Please. Don't turn your back on me. Don't turn away from what we could have together."

David closed his eyes, silently praying that this was all some sort of sick nightmare that would soon end. "Natalie," he sighed again, unable to find the words.

She kissed him. His nose caught the scent of her lip gloss. Something fruity, almost sickly sweet. "I love you," she repeated, tears slowly inching across her face, dragging remnants of her mascara with them. "I'll do whatever it takes to make you happy. I'll do anything. You can have me, all of me, any way you like. Please, don't leave me behind."

David looked at the beautiful girl in front of him. Even with her makeup smudged and her eyes swollen, she presented a treasure trove of pleasure. He had no doubt that making love to Natalie would be an event most men would fight for, if not beg to relish. That is, before they got to know her. Sadly, most people would never experience someone looking at them with eyes filled from lash to lash with overflowing love bordering on obsession. He knew that he could take her, right now, right here in the kitchen of Renée's apartment. He could deflower this bewitching virgin, claiming sex with Natalie as his hard won reward for patience and good behavior; but like someone who's eaten too much dessert, he just couldn't bear the thought of another sugary bite. She was simply too much, and he couldn't stomach sharing any more energy with this horny, desperate teenager.

If anything, her outpouring of love made David miss Conrad all the more, and his heart stung with bitterness and regret that he had let his own ego hold him back. He'd been too proud to call Conrad, to tell him exactly how he felt; now he wished to be as brave as Natalie, hopefully with better results. He wanted to grab hold of Conrad and profess his undying love, once and for all. He wanted to explain how much he missed him in the morning, and how he reached out for him in his sleep. He wanted to explain the heavy pain in his heart that came from knowing Conrad was so far away, and that he could no longer share his thoughts, ideas and pains.

David wanted to pull Conrad close to him, feel his beating heart against his chest, and fall asleep to the rhythm of that sacred drum as it spoke the secrets of their love for each other. He didn't want to have sex with Natalie. He wanted to kiss every inch of flesh along Conrad's body to feel the warmth of him against his lips. He wanted to wrap his arms around that man and never again let go. If he could have Conrad back, he would never run away from home again, the only home he had ever truly known. David knew, now more than ever, that he would love Conrad until the day he died, because they were meant to be together, no matter what anyone said. And in David's mind, there was no denying that it was finally time to return to New Jersey.

"Goddamn it," he whispered.

"What?"

"Natalie..."

"You can't leave me here."

David didn't see any other option. He had to convince this girl, somehow, that running away with him was a terrible idea. If that didn't work, he'd have to lie. "Natalie, I would take you with me, gladly; but I have no money. I can't afford to take you. I can barely afford myself."

"I can get money," she offered.

"You can't ask your parents."

"NO! I can get money on my own. I have an idea! Just promise you won't leave. Give me a few days. I'll get some money. I have something I can sell. Something I *know* someone will want. Please, just wait," she begged.

As usual, Natalie wasn't going to take no for an answer. "I can wait until tomorrow evening," he warned, with no intention of waiting. "But then I have to leave."

"How much do I need?"

"How much do *you* think you need?"

"I'll figure it out," she said. "I promise." Natalie ran into his arms again and kissed him. "I love you so much, David. Please, just wait."

"I'm leaving tomorrow evening, Natalie. I have to."

"I'll be ready, I promise." She kissed him again, not once noticing that he had yet to kiss her back. "Thank you so much, David. You have no idea how much this means to me. I can't be with my family anymore. I'm so grateful to have you!" Within minutes, the teenager was running towards the door. "I'll be here tomorrow, by four at the latest."

"Until we meet again," he replied, lifting his beer in the air.

Natalie giggled with hope, then left the apartment.

David waited until the girl had raced back down the stairs, into her car, and down the driveway before he reached for his cellphone. For a moment, he held his head in his hand, regretting the lies he had just told his student. Eventually she'd have to learn this lesson, he thought. If anything, he'd just served her with a coup de grâce for whatever plans she had concocted in her head. She would land on her feet though. Based on his experience, rich kids were used to people disappointing them.

David found Conrad's number and called.

"*David*," he answered. "I was just thinking about you."

"I love you Conrad."

"I love you too, David. You know that."

David could feel tears beginning to form as his throat tightened. "I want to come home. Right now. For good this time."

"My dear boy, I'll call some friends. We'll get you home tonight. Don't you worry about a thing."

David sighed with relief. He was ready to go home to Daddy.

RICHARD DUGAS WAS NO FOOL. After spending thirty-two years at The Farm, surrounded by murderers, rapists and violent criminals full of hatred and animosity, he still knew that the worst thing he could do was to get in between two women while they were fighting. So he stayed outside on the porch while Helen and Whitney screamed at each other in the kitchen, minding his own business, watching the sun set on Bayou Carron. A common rose chafer landed on the armrest of his rocking chair, and he admired the little bug's golden wings. It looked a bit like a scarab to him, so he figured it was just as likely to be a symbol of rebirth as anything else. Then again, he was biased, having only been reborn nine years ago.

Richie didn't like to focus on "life's sores," as he called them, but something about those women fighting reminded him of prison, and he didn't like to think on that much, now that he was out. He didn't want to remember the sound of harmonicas or the constant chatter in the fields. He didn't want the smell of that stinking mud to come to mind, or how hard it was to harvest cotton by hand or cut down sugarcane beneath the hot Louisiana sun. "More lash, more cash," the guards would say, a good number of them just one temper flare away from becoming inmates themselves. Certain prisoners were even given guns and paid for every runaway they killed. As for Richie, he was only paid about four cents an hour for hard labor in them fields, and spent almost every penny of that on cigarettes, not so that he could smoke but to buy protection from them boys with them guns, as well as those with more creative weapons. He hated the idea of cigarettes, to tell you the truth. He'd been bought and sold for two packs of 'em within his first month there. And those were memories he certainly didn't care to revisit, despite having made peace with it all.

It had been three weeks since he'd been released, about a year after the police had finally caught the man who had raped and killed that poor woman. Turns out that man had been killing prostitutes from Florida to Texas since he'd turned eighteen. He was seventy-two by the time they caught him, with over one hundred notches on his repulsive belt, marked by a collection of faded IDs and locks of hair he kept in a crumbling fanny pack. By then, Richie had been brutally violated countless times, beat unconscious, had three teeth punched clean out his mouth, and was even stabbed in a kidney, which ended up having to be removed. He knew The Farm produced about four million pounds of produce each year, and during his time there he'd probably harvested one million of that on his own. He'd probably sweat enough to equal that weight too, drop for drop. And the only thing he'd truly been guilty of was being selfish, stupid, and addicted to "disco biscuits." It had been an impossibly heavy price to pay for being in the wrong place, at the wrong time, and for such a frivolous reason.

The Louisiana State Penitentiary at Angola was a place you couldn't escape, even in your imagination. He'd heard the stories of people who had tried, but that didn't make much sense to him. Those 18,000 acres were surrounded on three sides by the Mississippi River, which could pull you under faster than you could scream for help. It was also home to bull sharks and gators, which were just as quick. The fourth side was bordered by a large swamp, the unwelcoming home of even more gators, water moccasins that could kill you in ten seconds flat if they hit an artery, and God knows what else. Richie knew he was better off staying put, even if Angola was its own type of hell, one specifically designed to destroy a human being.

He could still remember his first day, even though he tried not to think on it. He'd been warned not to let other people help him, that it was a trap; but Richie had always assumed that people were good. He didn't want to believe that his fellow man would hurt him, not the way that he was hurt. Only, Angola never let you forget your first day because there were always "fresh fish" being introduced into that putrid pond of sin. They'd be taken to a bullpen of sorts, where all the other inmates could circle round those boys and men, as bidders might see livestock for sale before the big auction. Richie never attended, but he'd hear the gossip at lunch as fellow inmates quarreled over the pretty boys and the tough guys that needed to be "broken in." Richie hated knowing that he'd been a pretty boy, back in the day. He knew all too well what that meant, as well as the consequences.

A little later on, those same fish would go to the laundry to get their blankets and mattresses. About eighty inmates out of the five thousand would be waiting for them to come down the walk. They'd have already picked their marks, so they'd wait, then offer to carry their mattress or whatever else. Richie knew them fish had been warned about this; but still, he'd see those clueless boys glad to have the help. And he knew that around nine o'clock that night, those same boys would be wishing that they hadn't accepted a thing. Although, there were some who willingly gave themselves over to the pack, if only for protection. Richie wasn't there to judge. Ain't nobody could tell nobody how to do their time. If they wanted to serve as a "kid" to some gang boss, just to get through it, that was for them to decide. But Richie couldn't help but be disgusted at the idea that you could buy someone's remaining morsels of dignity for two packs of cigarettes and a stick of stale gum.

That was before he understood "the System." You could scream until you went hoarse about your innocence; but to the

System, it was irrelevant whether you were guilty or not. The fact was, you were there, in that closed-off city of punishment and pain. It wasn't about what had happened on the "outside;" all that mattered was how you planned to survive the "inside." Nobody listens because nobody cares. Eventually, you even stop listening to yourself. All forms of individuality are stripped away, from your name to your style to your sexual preferences. None of that matters. You are just another number in a concrete machine that feeds on numbers, and if you've always relied on the trappings of the world to define who you are, then you are that much easier to swallow up in darkness. You have no freedom, no privacy, and no way out. And despite being under constant surveillance, no one so much as blinks as your soul is slowly devoured by a type of spiritual gangrene, which causes whole parts of you to rot in the night and fall off in the morning. There's nothing you can do but let those pieces go, until all that's left is an empty shell walking through the motions. And then, one day, sometimes unexpectedly, that shell mercifully dies.

Everything becomes a prison. Your attachments to the outside world make you miserable with longing. Your hatred for the people around you and the pain they inflict increase your misery even more. Your addictions become a prison, from cigarettes to alcohol to quaaludes, as you find yourself driven mad with desire for the sensations they bring. Craving turns into clinging which turns into deep attachment, and all three generate even more misery. Then there is the misery of aging, the misery of illness, the misery of suffering a situation you never believed you should've had to experience in the first place, compounded by the misery of thinking you'll die in this concrete box, only to be buried in that same stinking mud along with all the other numbers that time forgot. These horrible miseries multiply, day after day, through the same mindless routine enforced by the System, until all you end up craving for is death, if only to stop this vicious chain of miseries from dragging you down into a deeper, darker hell than you ever imagined. That's how Richie met James. He was trying to commit suicide while his new cellmate was asleep, if only to make the pain, the guilt, the self-loathing die, once and for all. Not only had James stopped this action, he ended up saving his life.

James had been a transfer from Donaldson Correctional Facility near Bessemer, Alabama. He'd served out his sentence there and now had to do his time as dictated by the State of Louisiana for a separate crime he'd committed in Slidell. Turns out, he wasn't asleep. He was meditating. He'd learned how to do it during a ten-day course taught at Donaldson. The technique was called Vipassana, and James had been practicing it for over five years: one hour in the morning and one hour at night. He explained to Richie that suicide wouldn't solve his problem, that his agony would just continue indefinitely. He begged Richie to give him three months, and if he still wanted to kill himself after that, he wouldn't interrupt. "You are your own master," he said. "But know, if you want to be free of this misery, I can help you, if you want to work. I can't help you if you don't do the work." That was the first time Richie had cried since he'd gotten to Angola— not because he wanted to die, but because someone in that pit of vipers wanted him to live. And James didn't expect nothing in return neither.

James was a strange cat. Everybody said so; but only Richie got to know him up close. He didn't tell everybody what he believed, but in the process of teaching Richie how to meditate, he sure did share some crazy stuff. First off, he'd made peace with being in prison for the rest of his life. He'd decided that being locked up was similar to becoming a monk, forcing him to live on the charity of others. Of course, James also said that before he was taught Vipassana at Donaldson, he was real bitter. He thought the taxpayers were better off burning their money because the prison system was just causing a whole lotta waste. Half the people there were either sick in the head or had been raised by someone who was; the rest were just victims of circumstance. He said that "as long as prisons only work on the body, without working on the head, it ain't gonna work." He said he was actually sad to leave Donaldson, where all the meditators had group sittings twice a day with more and more people taking courses. "The difference between that place and here, well, it's harsher than day and night." He hadn't wanted to come to Angola at all; but he had to work through "bad karmas of the past," he said. "And if I help you, even just a little, well, it'll be worth it to me."

Lessons started an hour before the guards would wake everyone up in the morning, and progress was real, real slow. "We ain't got the luxury of a ten-day course," James said. "So we gonna have to make it up as we go." He made Richie promise that no matter what—no matter how bored he got, how painful it became, how tired he was, how dark the situation—he wouldn't give up. He would stay committed for the full three months, no matter what. He would meditate for one hour in the morning and one hour in the evening, and James would teach him more about the technique at meals. He explained the process just so:

"We're gonna be doing a deep surgical operation of your mind. Right now, your mind is full of pus. It's real sick with anger, resentment, frustration, fear, you name it. So we're gonna spend this first month sharpening our blade. We gonna make your mind super sharp. That way, when we start cutting, all that pus is gonna come out. And it ain't gonna be pleasant. This operation don't come with no anesthesia or nothing. You gotta be tough. Have strong determination. Stick with it. Don't quit. Thoughts are gonna be flying through your mind because your mind don't wanna be tamed. The teacher called it a 'monkey mind,' constantly grabbing for this branch or that branch. These are just tricks. Distractions. Little shiny things your mind is gonna use to try to avoid this operation. But once we start, I can't make sure you're doing it right. You've got the freedom to participate and the freedom to fuck around and lie to me; but only you can work out your own liberation. I can't do it for ya. You get me?"

"But what's the goal?" Richie asked. "All the pus comes out and then what? I'm still locked up in this shithole."

James paused for a moment. "You know what all the religions and the saints had in common?"

Richie shook his head.

"They all said, 'Know thyself.' Not just on an intellectual level. We can all say we've read this book or that book, studied this in school, or whatever. I'm not talking about that. You need to know yourself at the experiential level. You need to experience the truth of who you are. Nobody else can teach you that. You've gotta go deep within yourself, because that's where the answer is hidden. It's not in your clothes, your house, your people. Hell, it's not even in this prison. Your Self, who you really are, *what* you really are, well, that truth is at the very core of you, and you've gotta go deep to find it. And that's what this technique does—it helps you walk through the darkness of yourself, those things you fear. It makes you face everything you've used to try to destroy yourself. And the greater the discomfort, the closer you are to the truth. Right now, yeah, you're a prisoner at Angola. But you've always been a prisoner of your mind, your ego, the lies you tell yourself about who you are. I'm gonna help you cut through the bullshit, right on down to the very source of your misery, and then you're gonna free yourself."

"I get what you're saying," Richie argued. "But still, what's the point? I'm here for life."

"*What's the point?*" James mocked. "You're alive, aren't ya? You're gonna die eventually, maybe in three months time. I'm gonna teach you how to live, and in the process, you're gonna learn how to die. Who cares if you're here for the rest of your life if you're actually living your life free for the first time ever? This outside world—none of this matters. You'll see that soon. And if you die with a smile on your face instead of misery weighing down your heart with stones, ain't that worth it?"

"I don't know," Richie mumbled.

"You're just scared. I get it. But hear me out. You're only scared of yourself. Once you face that fear, it won't matter whether you're inside or outside. You'll be free either way."

That whole first month, all Richie was allowed to do was focus on his natural breathing. "Don't change it. Don't force it. Don't do nothing. Just breathe like you normally do. Observe it. That's all. *Observe the breath.*" He told Richie to focus on the triangle of flesh on the underside of his nose and above his upper lip. "We're sharpening our blade now, so focus on the sensations—a tingle, an itch, a vibration. *Don't move your body at all.* Just sit there. Don't scratch. Don't twitch. Just feel those sensations and observe them. See how long they last. And don't worry," he said with a smirk. "No itch is eternal."

It sounded simple enough, but it was hardly simple. Richie struggled that entire first month. He hadn't realized how hard it was not to move his body at all. He had to sit there, legs crossed, eyes closed, back straight for a full hour, with only James serving as the clock. For a while, Richie even thought that son of a bitch was lying and making each session longer than it should be; but then the guards were always starting their rounds at the same time every day, and miraculously, their meditations ended just five minutes before, every single time.

At lunch, Richie would beg to know what he should be experiencing; but James wouldn't tell him anything specific. "You're searching for universal truth, but your path there is unique. If I tell you how I got there, you're gonna go searching for my path and that won't get you to the final goal 'cause that ain't your path. You've got to work it out for yourself."

"Well, then tell me what you got out of it then."

"Naw, man, if I tell you that, you're gonna get attached to it. There's a reason why them ten days require a vow of silence. I can't tell you what you should be experiencing or what you should be looking for. Trust the technique. *Observe.*"

Day and night they meditated, with Richie never really understanding what it was he should be looking for or trying to accomplish. "Don't try anything," James kept saying. "Just focus on the area around the nostrils, above the upper lip. That's all you need to do right now. *Observe.*" But ideas, thoughts, memories, and plans all seemed to twirl about in Richie's head like a Rolodex spinning out of control. Faces, images, jokes, foods, smells, pleasures all haunted him during those sixty minutes. He kept returning to his breath, but then he'd get bored again and start following his crazy mind down another path of nonsense.

Within the span of an hour he could think about the joy of fried eggs with a runny yoke, the way Helen's ass looked in her jeans, the letter Whitney had sent him about her first job in California, how his spider model for a fifth grade science class had fallen apart during the presentation and everyone laughed at him, the pleasure of cracking the shells of sunflower seeds between his teeth and licking the salt off his lips, how delicious peanut butter tasted as it slid right off the spoon, how long it had been since he'd had sex with his wife, how she tasted and how her body spasmed during orgasms, how his father used to drink cheap vodka out of a crinkled brown paper bag and fall asleep beneath the cypress tree near their run-down shack, how his mama would brown cheap cuts of meat for dinner in her cast iron pan, how his father beat his mother mercilessly during his drunken fits, how his mother would try to hide her black eye and bruises before church, what her flowery perfume smelled like, how it felt the first time he took a quaalude, how it felt to have sex on 'ludes, how it felt to feel nothing at all, how he planned to get out of here, how he'd get fried chicken from Mama's in Opelousas, along with rice dressing, cole slaw, fried gizzards, fried livers, onions rings, fried okra, and them buttery biscuits. His mouth would start to water at the thought of them gizzards melting on his tongue, then he'd remember to go back to his breath and refocus his mind on those damn sensations. Again and again, he'd journey down this rollercoaster ride taking him to the past, then the future, before he'd force himself to return, once more, to the monotony of the present moment currently being experienced in that humid cell.

But near the end of thirty days, Richie still didn't see the point of all this breathing and searching for sensation. It was also becoming more and more difficult to keep this all a secret from the guards and fellow inmates. He became frustrated with James and demanded to know more.

"Richie, if someone is sick and I take their medicine, will they get better?"

"No."

"Exactly. You've gotta take your medicine. Trust the process, Rich. You're still convinced that something outside yourself knows better than you do, or that there is some supernatural force that will save your ass or suddenly choose to make you enlightened. Stop expecting fireworks or some bright light of virtue to come shining through the ceiling. Just do the work and the answer will reveal itself. *Observe.* We'll be cutting soon enough."

When 'soon enough' arrived, James instructed Richie to start observing sensations as they existed on his entire body. "Now we're going somewhere. Be strong, my friend. Be strong." He taught Richie how to scan for sensations, same as he had on the tip of his nose, around his nostrils, and just above his upper lip; but this time, he scanned from the top of the head to the tips of the toes, then eventually from the tips of the toes to the top of the head. "Whatever the sensation," James warned, "don't react to it. Just observe. If you don't react, the wisdom you seek will arise."

For the next sixty days, Richie felt all sorts of sensations. He experienced tingling, heat, cold, burning, stiffness, aches and pains all over his entire body; and the deeper he meditated, the more of those sensations he found. "Those are *sankharas*," James explained. "Every time you react to a sensation, one is created. You've been collecting these things all your life. They reside deep, deep inside. If you stop reacting, you won't create no more. Then the old stock will rise to the surface and disappear. This is the road towards liberation, my friend. This is the way of the Noble Path."

"What's the deal with this Noble Path?" Richie asked. "What's that even mean?"

"Well," James began. "You've gotta develop equanimity at the deepest level. You gotta have a calm, balanced mind that don't react to no craving for pleasure or aversion to pain. And you gotta be strong not to react. And that strength is how you generate love and compassion for others, not negativity or hate. By purifying the mind like that, you're able to live a good life, without any ego whatsoever. You're able to love yourself, and others too. It's as simple as following the Golden Rule."

"Do unto others as you would have them do unto you?"

"Yeah, that!" James exclaimed. "Don't have nothing against nobody."

"Don't sin against your neighbors."

"Well, think about it. What's sin? It's an unwholesome action with a bad motivation. It's any action, with your body or your words, that harms other people. Anything that throws off their flow. And then its opposite—a wholesome, pious action—that's anything that helps them keep that flow. That's a moral life, when you don't hurt nobody. When you don't wanna hurt nobody. But to live like that, you gotta master your mind."

"You can't live like that here, James. You wouldn't survive!"

"Think about it, Rich. If you wanna hurt somebody, you gotta have a whole lot of negativity burning you up inside. It's practically melting your mind. If you're burning up with greed, you steal someone's shit. You full of hate? You kill some poor fool. You filled with some sort of rage or passion fueled by your ego and jealousy? That's when you cheat on your woman or rape. It all starts in your mind first, with all them sleeping volcanoes. And right now, we're waking those fuckers up so we can root them out. They ain't got no place in a calm, balanced mind. Because if your mind's burning like that, before you hurt someone else, you've already hurt yourself. You've already caught yourself on fire. That's the hell you've been living in. So we're gonna put them fires out."

And so Richie sat in meditation, morning and night, as he observed his *sankharas* from the top of his head to the tips of his toes, then from the tips of his toes to the top of his head. Those sensations were always, always changing, from session to session, from moment to moment. No two meditations were ever the same. His pains and tensions would arise, then pass away, only to arise in a new location with a new sensation, then pass away again. Occasionally, he would find a clear, pleasant flow of sensations, without pain or discomfort. He would scan his entire body, feeling the hum of those gentle vibes in complete and utter bliss; but even bliss would pass away, never proving to be constant. That too would divide, dissolve, separate, only to reveal even deeper, heavier, more painful *sankharas* of the past.

He could sense his hatred for his predicament, his anger at the justice system, his frustration with his own stupidity. He had been furious with Walter Price for not coming to his aid, after everything Helen had done for him. He was bitter towards the drug dealer who had run off and left him alone in that apartment to ride out his high while a complete stranger was there as well, with a woman he'd brought in off the streets. He was angry at that villain, disgusted by his actions, horrified by the ignorance of it all. The smell of that room returned to him. The smell of iron and rot. He remembered the inch-deep puddles of blood on the floor, the smears of the stuff along the walls, how it soaked into the mattress in that horrible room. The flies were already feasting on the stench by the time Richie had come to his senses, and by then the cops had arrived too. He felt the horror of that place vibrating throughout his body. He felt the shame he had experienced when Helen walked into that police station, only to find his hands and shirt caked with dried blood that had mixed with dirt and sweat. He remembered the filth under his fingernails, the buzzing in his mind, the look on that dead woman's face. All of this tortured him, only for deeper *sankharas* to torment him more.

As he observed those sensations, those knots in his jaw and around his eyes, that heavy weight in his shoulders and chest, the shocks along his fingertips and palms, the aches in his hips and thighs, the numbness of his feet, he remembered and he observed the sensations that he had collected over time. A burning sensation across his cheek made him remember the way his father had slapped him, hard, across the face when he was ten, and the pounding that it had caused. The tightness around his heart, like a thicket of thorns, reminded him of the hatred he felt for everyone around him, all while preaching brotherly love. He felt his lies and defense mechanisms reveal themselves as knots tied so tightly, they might as well have been carved out of stone. He wanted to stop. He didn't dare go further, but James encouraged him to stay strong. "Scan deeper," he said. "No sensation is eternal. You must work through them. Observe the source of this misery and come out of it."

The operation of his mind wasn't even halfway finished, yet Richie felt the pus pouring out of him in a heavy flow that he could not escape. Even when he wasn't meditating in his cell, he felt a conscious awareness at all times. As he ate his food, as he worked in the fields, as he showered, as he spoke with fellow inmates, and even as he rested. He felt the sensations of his food from first contact with his tongue to the way his body digested each meal. He was aware of the mud in the fields, the delicate sprouts as they grew, the roots of the weeds that he pulled. When harvesting a crop, he was aware of his movements, of the gestures he had come to take for granted. He was aware of the sun, aware of the breeze, aware of his sweat and its taste. He listened to the songs his fellow inmates sang to pass the time during this hard labor, and was surprised to find them beautiful. While he showered, he felt awareness of his surroundings with a newfound calm. His fellow inmates no longer generated fear or animosity within him.

He began to see them as people who were still blinded and bound by their misery, and he no longer sought to increase their load. He tried to only generate kindness, compassion, and goodwill for all involved, even the guards he had once hated as sworn enemies. He now saw them as fellow prisoners, just wearing a different mask.

More importantly, Richie began to see the patterns of his mind, how certain reactions had caused certain sensations which had driven certain behaviors. He was determined to break the chain. He felt as if he had been running in place, all his life, never realizing that he was tethered to a wall. Now he could see the rope holding him in that spot, and he knew how to cut it. That rope was made up of his own negativity, and it had bound him to his own suffering. Through each meditation, Richie gained a deeper understanding of each thread, each bit of material, which had been braided into this rope for as long as he had lived. He now understood that he could no longer focus on changing his outside environment as a means to happiness. He recognized that happiness was a state of mind, and the only thing holding him back from achieving that state was himself.

Slowly, the heavy black clouds of his misery began to form into distinguishable shapes. By observing his sensations, and only observing those sensations, Richie was able to identify the patterns of his worry, fear, anxiety and anger. He was able to make peace with his suffering, and all of the pain he had endured within those concrete walls of Angola. He no longer hated those who had harmed him, but recognized their ignorance and forgave them. They had reacted out of their own misery, and by hurting him they had only hurt themselves. The darkness that had once encased him began to slowly break away into defined chunks, as slivers of light began to emerge. He was purifying himself of all destructive habits, needless friction, and harmful emotions from moment to moment, breath to breath. And because he was dedicated to finding the universal truth of his deepest Self, he observed all the pain of that mental operation as the pus of his past slowly oozed out, trusting that the great wound of his existence would finally heal.

As Richie released all of that poison from his subconscious, those knots began to soften then unwind. Slowly, those threads which had been binding him to his misery untied and fell away. The dark clouds that had once shrouded his true nature began to thin as well. With each meditation, as he scanned deeper for *sankharas*, he began to see more and more light through what had once been a heavy veil of darkness. Those storms of anger, depression and self-loathing cleared, and for the first time in his life he felt the warm rays of an inner sun. And in the light of that sun, he recognized himself as the patterns of sensations, that he was nothing more than subatomic particles—tiny, microscopic bubbles—arising and passing away. He dissolved into a universe of bubbles, in which there was no "I" or "mine" but All. That All was constantly dividing, separating, dissolving in a continuous flow. There was no pain or misery. There was no attachment or craving. There was only the source from which all things flowed. And in that moment, Richie experienced the true nature of himself, as he discovered the universal truth of change.

For nine years he continued to meditate in his cell, observing *sankharas* as they would arise and pass away. He and James continued their discussions, and both dedicated themselves to a life full of *metta*, unconditional love and compassion for all beings. As a result, Richie remained forever aware of the true law of nature: that at every moment, change is taking place. Every moment everything is growing and decaying, growing and decaying, in a never-ending cycle fueled by love. He had experienced the truth behind the illusion, delusion, and confusion of his own ignorance, and he was free because he possessed this wisdom. He had experienced it for himself, and no person or place could ever take that knowledge away.

The morning of his release from Angola, James hugged him goodbye and said, "Remember, my friend, this will also change."

They were both sixty-five years old and had been charged with similar crimes. One continued to live on the "inside," while the other had been allowed to venture out. Both were completely free. Now, Richie wondered who James might teach next, while he sought a student for himself. He wanted to help all those he loved escape their misery too, just as James had done for him. Sitting on the porch now, Richie rocked back and forth in his chair and listened as Whitney and Helen fought. The murky brown water of the bayou flowed nearby and he observed as a silent witness.

The flow of that bayou was natural, same as the rhythm of life, in which all things flow into all other things as part of the same great pattern. In Richie's mind, he was reminded that all energy exists in perpetual transformation, in which there is no death, only a change of state. The illusion of motion creates the illusion of dimension, while age is nothing more than a dimension, appearing to exist because of the effect of motion. The substance always remains the same, while arising, passing, growing, decaying, dissolving, and beginning again. That stream of consciousness is always flowing, he thought, manifesting through an infinite diversity of forms. Richie knew that if he entered the bayou, the Richie who dived in would not be the same Richie who came up for air. He would be different. The bayou would be different. And life would continue indefinitely.

Whitney kicked open the screen door and came marching onto the porch, tapping her teal pack of cigarettes against the palm of her hand before bringing a single stick up to her lips. "I hate that woman sometimes!"

"Whitney, my dear," Richie said. "Please. Don't smoke."

"Why do you care?"

"Come, meditate with me. One hour. Let me teach you what I know."

"I know I said I would, but I don't feel up to it right now."

"You're angry. Come, sit with me. Observe your anger. What do you have to lose?"

"My anger," she laughed.

"And wouldn't you like to know what's on the other side of that?"

She paused.

"Don't smoke. Please. Come and sit with me. Today's the day. You promised."

Reluctantly, his daughter put her cigarettes away and wandered towards him as Richie moved to the floor of the porch and sat cross-legged with his back to the bayou. She mirrored him.

"Close your eyes," he said. "And keep 'em closed."

She did as he instructed.

"Now, I want you to breathe, naturally. Don't change the breath. Just observe it. Focus on the sensations your breath brings on the tip of your nose, around your nostrils, and on the skin above your upper lip. Focus in on that area, that triangle of flesh. Just breathe and observe. Don't change a thing."

ANTOINE BERGERON COULDN'T SLEEP, and he was bored with pretending to try. He put the leash on Lorelei, a four-year-old Maltese he had adopted a year ago, and led her out into the night. The French Quarter was relatively quiet at three in the morning, and almost all Antoine could hear were the soles of his shoes against the cobblestones and pavement, as well as Lorelei's collar tag jingling against the hook. A slight fog had begun to settle between the old houses and bars, the shuttered shops and empty restaurants. Occasionally they'd pass a stranger smoking a cigarette, some waiter or dishwasher ending their late night shift. A straggling tarot card reader was packing up her table and sign in Jackson Square, and the smell of urine and vomit had yet to be carried away by the morning.

The Quarter seemed to be filled with whispers, which raced against his shoes, rising between the echoes of his stiff, twisted gate. As Antoine walked past various locations he could almost hear the ghosts of past centuries murmur in his ear, begging for his attention so that their souls might finally rest. He reached out his fingertips and felt the stucco of rough exterior walls slide against his skin in a painfully pleasurable way. He could almost sense the energy vibrating off the bright Creole paint, even in the darkest moments of night. The history of this space had been blown into the glass, jammed into the mortar, and painted onto the wrought iron, held in place by a blanket of never-ending humidity. Shadows were everywhere, each offering to tell a different story that no one had heard before, all for a sliver of silver that had fallen from the pockets of the moon.

For Antoine, the past was alive. Not even the idea of death could snuff out that eternal energy, which haunted the French Quarter in waves of memories that rolled in and out like the tide. Darkness here was conscious, forever trying to warn the living of the mistakes of the past. Antoine looked into the glass window of a competitor's shop and saw his image in the shadow. He recognized the bald head, the big eyes, the tight mouth and jaw; yet he felt that he had no reflection. He was no more than a ghost himself, wandering the streets as if he ruled over this graveyard of old ideas and long lost loves.

Lorelei was the brightest creature on those dark grey streets, her white, curly fur almost dancing with every step. Together, she and Antoine walked past the homeless, curled up and asleep in front of locked doors, as well as piles of garbage, oozing out of cans like open sores curated along the streets. Neither man nor little dog stopped to investigate. Instead they wandered back to Royal Street and entered the hundred-year-old antique shop that was their home.

The building had changed hands many times over the years, but the business remained the same. The only goal was to collect the finest of European antiques and sell them to qualified buyers. At some point, a prominent Sicilian named Sebastiano Mistretta had purchased the shop, using money acquired through a growing grocery business on his mother's side of the family, as well as income from his father's investments in Louisiana strawberries in Tangipahoa Parish. Then Sebastiano gave the place to his nephew, Giuseppe, in his will, as the boy had a severe type of hemophilia, making sitting in an antique shop just about the only work he could do. And when Giuseppe died, he left the shop and all of its contents to Antoine. For the past thirty years, Antoine had lived there alone, along with all of the other ghosts.

As he achingly climbed from the first floor to the fourth, he wandered around each room, if only to spend time alone within his jewelry box of gilded ornaments and polished woods, those shadows of past pleasures. Within mere moments, the histories of France, Britain, and the Netherlands seemed to pass before his eyes by way of mirrors, chairs, tables and cabinets. He saw ideas that had taken shape, lovingly designed by nameless craftsmen, and painstakingly constructed over thousands of hours that had never been counted. Time was irrelevant to these pieces. They seemed to supersede the ticking of their own clocks and the passage of aimless days. Instead, each piece of furniture, each embroidered cushion, each crystal chandelier was a representation of timeless study. Such beautiful thought forms chronicled what a fragment of mankind had valued during a specific window of history, providing Antoine with a narrow view of what humanity had once treasured, and who we could be if we so chose.

His dark eyes wandered around the room, paying loving attention to each and every item, as he might to a child demanding eye contact along with a nod of approval. Even these pieces of furniture and ornaments seemed to whisper to him, still holding on to the energies of their sculptors, woodworkers and painters. Each wanted to share how their material forms had started, from the tree they once were to the workshop in which they were carved. They longed to tell stories of glittering parties with petticoats and silk, of card games gone wrong, of political intrigues devised. They wanted to describe journeys by carriage and coach, ships and trains, while longing for new adventures. This shop was merely purgatory for these pieces, a holding cell, until their next lives could begin. They all gossiped together as they waited.

The fourth floor had once been a workshop for repairing pieces. Giuseppe had transformed it into an apartment. However, the lavish furnishings of the lower floors had never been moved into the living quarters. Being that Giuseppe's grandfather had died from slipping on a rug and hitting his head on the bed frame, as well as the continued risk of triggering an internal bleed when clotting factor was costly, they rejected the idea of having "real" furniture on the fourth floor. Instead the entire apartment was filled with plastic lawn furniture, apart from the mattress which rested on the ground. Antoine had never changed this interior design, apart from one exception.

He fed Lorelei the remnants of her wet food, then wandered into his studio, listening as her name tag chimed against the metal bowl. A red fainting couch was the only piece of heavy furniture in the entire apartment, used mostly as a prop for Antoine's side business, creating boudoir paintings for women who wished to preserve their sexual essence in oil on canvas. At the moment, a mannequin was posed on the couch, which had come into his possession only recently. He had gotten a call from Harper, his long-time friend who had donated half of her liver to him some fifteen years ago. She was in a state of emotional distress, mumbling her words and begging him to drive to Baton Rouge to help her solve a problem. "You're the only person I can trust," she said. And so Antoine loaded Lorelei up in his truck and drove the hour to the state capital, where Harper worked as an assistant for a very tight laced state senator. His family lived out in the country, back in Evangeline Parish, while he kept an apartment in Baton Rouge. Turns out, that wasn't all he kept there.

Harper had been cleaning the apartment when she came across a strange cylinder drying on the dish rack in the kitchen. The senator had died suddenly of a heart attack, so everything was exactly how he left it, including his sex toys. The top of the cylinder had an opening for penetration, complete with a rather long, dark labia, and it looked as if it had been used many times. In order to protect her former employer's legacy and reputation, Harper disposed of the cylinder immediately, unaware that there were other treasures in the apartment that she had yet to find. She called Antoine in a panic after opening a closet door in the guest room, where she found a five-foot-five, eighty-five pound life-like doll hanging from a stand affixed to the wall. By the time Antoine arrived to help dispose of the problem, Harper had unpacked all of the additional accessories the senator had purchased for Cora, the doll's name according to handmade labels affixed to countless plastic containers.

There were wig combs and bottles of wig shampoo, as well as five other wig options. At least three bottles of perfume were stored in the closet, along with an array of makeup for when the senator had felt compelled to touch up his doll's dramatic blue eyeshadow with sapphire liner or reapply her red currant lipstick. There were bottles of Static Guard, hand sanitizer and water-based lubes, at least twenty different outfits, an assortment of detachable tongues, six additional inserts for her "honey pot," and a tiny bag of anuses to deal with her "gap." Then there were two other bald heads sitting on a shelf, both designed for "deep throat" action, with the same black brown eyes that were looking so real, Antoine feared those mouths would suddenly take first breath.

"What do you want me to do with her?" he asked.

"*I don't know*," Harper screeched. "Just get rid of it! What if it has a microchip or something. I can't let this thing be traced back to my boss."

"Well I can't just throw her in the dumpster out back."

"*NO!* Take it *far* away from here. Throw it in the Basin for all I care. It just can't stay in this apartment." Harper's voice lowered to a whisper, as if to prevent Cora from overhearing. "His wife will be here in the morning."

Antoine studied the doll more carefully. Her face was wide, with a slightly seductive expression. Her breasts were quite large, but well-crafted. She was relatively short, but fleshy in all the right spots. He studied the little details of her making: the tiny bumps around her nipples, the two-toned coloring of her skin along her hands and feet, her French manicured nails, the human hair carefully punched into two arched eyebrows, the extra full bush of pubic hair, the length of her intricate labia, and the finely painted veins on the whites of her eyes. As an artist himself, he could see that no detail had been overlooked in the construction of this doll. Like the antiques in his shop, every aspect of its creation had been painstakingly considered. He couldn't bring himself to throw this thing into the Atchafalaya swamp, or even bury it in the woods.

"I'll take care of it," he said.

"How?" Harper asked, skepticism riding the waves of her voice.

"I'll take care of it," he repeated, as if warning against continued questions.

"Well take all this stuff too!"

That's how Antoine found himself driving back to New Orleans with an exotic mannequin buckled up in the backseat of his truck, along with three large trash bags full of her accessories. He had every intention of getting rid of the doll. He thought of practically every available option. He could stop his car one night on a nearby bridge and throw her over the railing, or leave her sitting outside of a local bar he hated in the Quarter, just to fuck with the owner. He could put her in their warehouse on the other side of town, or bring her somewhere in the country, deeper into the state, and dump her in a field of sugarcane. He even considered digging the senator up and throwing her into his coffin. At least that way they'd be together; but disturbing remains was a crime and required far too much effort. All of these ideas fluttered within Antoine's mind. He just couldn't pull the trigger on any of them. That's why Cora had been lounging on the fainting couch for the past two weeks as he painted her image onto canvas.

From the moment he first saw the mannequin, Antoine's mind had become insatiably curious about her origins and past. Why had the senator purchased *this* doll, out of all the available options? Had he unwittingly become a modern Hephaestus, fashioning this creature after a lost love, or choosing all of his favorite parts from other women to enjoy alone? If this doll was his

Pandora, what jar of psychological issues had she helped to un-
leash—or better yet, suppress? Antoine had always considered sex
to be a tool for understanding oneself, if not for discovering pain
points of vulnerability. With Cora, had the senator simply opted
out of the learning experience entirely, choosing instead to cloister
himself within a prison of his own indulgences?

Antoine sorted through all of the baggage associated with
Cora and found himself deep in thought as to why someone
would go through so much trouble in the first place. Had it been
love that compelled the senator to brush Cora's wigs and touch
up her nipple paint with a soft sponge? Or had tinkering with her
appearance been a distraction from his own fading image? Had
brushing her hair been a way to ignore the fact that he was losing
his own? And had her silent compliance released him from feeling
responsible for anyone else's pleasure? Cora would never judge,
and could never be dissatisfied. But had the senator truly been
satisfied? No matter how infatuated he may have been with this
creation, there had to be a part of his mind that acknowledged
the harsh reality of the situation: he was a human being having
sex with a silicone replica of one. It was difficult for the antique
dealer to fully understand that compulsion, or to truly empathize
with the senator's values.

Then again, Antoine had been celibate ever since Giuseppe
died, before that even. He could have gone hunting for a casual
hookup at a number of bars in the Quarter, but Antoine didn't really want sex. He could go weeks, even months, without so much
as masturbating. What he really yearned for was connection. He
wanted the intimacy of sharing ideas with someone he loved, the
warmth of human touch, the sound of a laugh or the sight of a
genuine smile that sparkled in the eyes. He wanted to feel safe
with someone again; safe enough to shed his armor and allow
his vulnerable self to fall asleep in the arms of another person.
The senator could never have experienced that with Cora. Instead
of helping him become a better version of himself, this doll had

likely prevented him from ever scrutinizing himself enough to grow in the first place. And by only serving his base animal instincts, this indulgence had likely led to others, eventually leading him to the one that stopped his heart. But that certainly wasn't the doll's fault.

A friend of a friend would be picking her up soon. "By the end of the week," he said. Antoine was putting the finishing touches on his painting, feeling a bit melancholy that Cora would soon be leaving.

"Isn't it strange to want a used sex doll?" Antoine asked.

"Most of us have sex with used people," the friend replied. "At least you can put her parts through the dishwasher."

It all seemed so horribly crude. That's why Antoine was painting Cora's portrait. He didn't want to think of her as a Pandora, just existing for a mindless fuck, void of spirituality by a man who couldn't face his own crippled soul. He sought to elevate the doll, if only through art. And so he painted her as if she were Pygmalion's Galatea, the sculpture that Aphrodite had granted life by virtue of the carved marble's unparalleled beauty and the profound love the artist felt for his creation. Cora was so beautiful, so well-made, Antoine figured she was worthy of such a gift from the gods. And so he painted her in that image, as a material thing granted human consciousness to serve as a giver of love.

Sadly, his friends were likely to make jokes if they saw the work and heard the story. For years they had been begging Antoine to date. Even his best friend, a lively widow named Estelle, had recently gotten remarried, and her first husband had died long after Giuseppe had. The difference was that Estelle was eager to find union with a new mate. In fact, she damn near badgered her sole prospect until he conceded. Antoine begged her to leave that poor priest alone, but she couldn't help herself. Once she discovered that he was deeply concerned for her soul, and gave her more and more attention with every outrageous confession she made, Estelle was sure to return to the confessional every time that man was scheduled. She would dream up more and more outrageous stories, all completely false, just to tempt the man to leave the priesthood altogether, if only to save her from eternal damnation. When he finally did, she laughed to Antoine, "It took me three years, but I finally convinced that man that the only way I'd treat my body like a temple was to put a priest in it!" They were now happily married.

Antoine looked down from his canvas to see Lorelei frantically humping her plush olive toy on the ground, only to grip it between her teeth, growl and jerk it about. *Was* it time he moved on and found someone else to share his life with? The handsome writer who had stopped by earlier in the day had surely caused something in Antoine to awaken. That man's silver eyes and cold restraint had caused him to feel the rumblings of urges he hadn't experienced in decades. If he hadn't known better, he might have suspected that he was in danger of an internal bleed; but he hadn't had one of those in fifteen years.

Harper's liver had not only saved him from hepatitis C, but had cured his blood disorder as well. For years Antoine had been expecting to die, to join Giuseppe once and for all. He thought that he'd never find a liver transplant, that hepatitis would eat away his body and soul until life seemed positively pointless. Then, once he had been given half of Harper's organ, he expected it to be rejected by his body entirely. Instead, within twenty-four hours he'd been miraculously healed from his hemophilia altogether. For someone who had been told all of his life that he could die "any day," the sixty-six-year-old man had outlived them all. The problem was, deciding to live was much harder than accepting the fact that he'd eventually die.

He told Theodore Walsh the whole story, as best he could anyway. The middle-aged playwright had asked such probing questions that Antoine found himself sharing memories and thoughts he hadn't voiced even within himself for decades. Over a glass of pomegranate juice, he seemed to pour out his soul to the stranger, as if that past had been trying to find release for years. Theo just sat there, sipping his water, soaking it all up with his silver eyes and tape recorder. Antoine didn't often confide in people he knew. He preferred to speak with strangers. But there was something so hauntingly familiar about Theo that he felt himself both compelled to speak while afraid that he was sharing too much. He hadn't realized that he too had stories to tell, even if he had sealed those stories behind a hard, crystallized exterior. But somehow, this strange man from Chicago had tuned to the proper frequency so that everything could flow out of Antoine and finally be broadcast into the ether. It was as if Theo had grabbed hold of Antoine's shadow and pulled it towards the light.

First he remembered the pain of hemophilia. Internal bleeds seemed to follow the flood cycles of the moon, with his knees, ankles, elbows and other joints filling up with blood more often than they did not. As an infant he was often covered in bruises, and something as simple as a loose baby tooth could send his frantic parents rushing him to the emergency room. Even the simple act of growing caused internal bleeds, as blood vessels broke in the process. Antoine was helpless against these floods, and all his parents could do was bring him to the hospital and pray that the bleeding stop. As a result, Antoine knew that he had no control over his physical structure before he could even talk.

The pain he endured could transition from dull to acute to excruciating in a matter of hours. And while blood gave life, it could also prove corrosive, destroying his bones and crippling him over time. Each hour that passed was an hour closer to leg braces, an hour closer to a cane, an hour closer to amputation. His knee could expand to the size of a personal watermelon, allowing him to mentally trace the lines of every blue-green vein beneath stretched and tortured skin. Before he had even turned two, he'd been in the hospital over two hundred times. And each time, he'd been tied down and attached to a bag of whole blood, forced to endure the agony of overflowing rivers threatening his very life.

Even as a boy, he understood the history of his blood, how hemophilia had existed on his mother's side of the family, and how he had been the unlucky one to be given "the curse." His ancestors seemed to belong outside of time, yet they existed within that dark, congealed sap causing devastation within his root system. He believed that he would never escape the history of this condition, which had been encrypted into his genes, the very code of his making. The past found a mirror in this blood and, through never-ending pain, forced Antoine to make peace with it. At first he would cry, until he reached an age where tears no longer mattered. Those drops of bitterness and betrayal evaporated over time, leaving behind nothing but the residue of wisdom in the form of salt.

It was through this crippling pain that he was able to search his own chthonic depths, independent of society and even the freedom of movement. He began to see the world differently from his parents, and even the children of the neighboring oncology ward. Slowly, Antoine came to understand that he was neither his body nor his mind. He was not the pain nor the blood. He was the one observing it all. "I am the observer of the observed," became his mantra. "A stone that is no stone." In silence and stillness, observing each drop of whole blood slowly drip into his body in the vain attempt to stop a bleed, Antoine found something else, something almost no one else understood.

There, during the darkest nights of his soul, he discovered the fabric of creation, woven in black, red and white threads. White, he imagined, was the thread of science: the lab coats, the walls, the sheets, the ceilings, the floors. Red was the thread of blood: the constant drip, the internal floods, the past holding him to its chest. And black was the thread of magic: the internal world only he could visit, deep within himself. It was blacker than black, darker than the darkest night. Through his condition, that black thread required that he dismember, dissolve, and disintegrate all that he thought he knew. In that white world with those red drops, he descended into a new reality, deep within the sediment of matter.

In this darkness, all that had once existed—the world of his parents, the world of school, the world of stores where other women gave his mother ugly looks, thinking that she abused him—all of that faded into the background. Everything, every object, every thought, every emotion, dissolved into the darkness of that night. The pain he experienced was so intense, it allowed him to break the tethers of the material world and pursue the path towards his inner star. And in this utterly deep and seemingly endless black of night, Antoine discovered a tiny vein of gold, a humble spark within his nature. In the presence of that spark, Antoine was forced to face his own shadow: every dark desire, every secret ambition, every wish for death. And by bringing his ego into this light, he felt born again, finally free from the tomb of his broken body. That spark burned away all impurities, allowing his soul to climb an emerging column of smoke towards an eternal Truth. It was through this process that Antoine found himself. More than that, he found himself free of pain.

The only person capable of understanding this was his blood brother, Giuseppe. Both of them had severe hemophilia A, and no one else in the hospital or even in their homes knew exactly what they experienced. So they formed their own language to communicate this shared knowledge, which seemed to whisper its secrets in the movement of their blood. Even after all this time, Antoine still couldn't properly explain his love for Giuseppe, even to Theodore Walsh. It was like explaining that one was really two. They were different people, with different passions and different ways of thinking; yet they complemented each other so easily that their union seemed to override all opposites. There was never friction or tension within their bond; each was whole, independent of the other. Yet when Antoine looked into Giuseppe's eyes, he felt love for his partner as if he were experiencing love for himself. Even in their physical union, they each seemed to dissolve into the other, only to fall into themselves. While they looked so different in the realm of matter, within another dimension they were reflections of the same. And when they kissed, their souls awakened, only to entwine their auric energies and bring them closer to Source.

Together they endured the crude treatments of whole blood during the 1950s. They discovered the bliss of cryoprecipitate, a new medical advancement that enabled a bleed to stop within a matter of days rather than weeks or months. Then within a few years, each jumped at the opportunity to use a new clotting factor that hit the market in the 1960s. At the time, Antoine was twelve and Giuseppe was fifteen. And thanks to this "miracle drug" known as Factor VIII, they were both able to spend the next fifteen years living as normal people: going to school, playing outside, traveling away from hospitals and doctors. If they felt a bleed coming on, all they had to do was mix the Factor VIII powder with the included saline and infuse themselves—at home, at school, on an airplane. Antoine was even able to travel with Giuseppe to Sicily and across all of Europe to meet with contacts for his uncle's antique store. Life became so easy that both the red and black threads of creation seemed to fade from their consciousness entirely. Both he and Giuseppe put their total faith in the blinding white light of science as true believers of progress and innovation. But it didn't last.

The day they moved into the shop, Giuseppe got a fever. They had always been warned of a risk of hepatitis with Factor VIII, so the family physician suggested the fever may be related to that infection. After a simple test, both Giuseppe and Antoine realized they were positive for hepatitis B. Safe sex was recommended, as had always been recommended by their unusual if not cooky local doctor, being that both men now had relatively fragile immune systems. The warning was heeded, as it had always been, and life continued as usual. However, Giuseppe continued to decline. The fevers came back, time and time again. His lymph nodes became swollen and hard. He couldn't eat, and lost an unnatural amount of weight in a short period of time. There were rumors circulating

throughout the French Quarter that gay men were getting sick
with similar symptoms. Neither Antoine nor Giuseppe had ever
actively partaken in the gay community of New Orleans. Instead,
they had always surrounded themselves with women. Neither
was interested in such sexual adventures; they were completely
devoted to each other. Why would they fall prey to the same disease? Then lesions began to appear on Giuseppe's skin, and they
couldn't ignore it anymore.

Giuseppe was diagnosed with AIDS in 1983. Doctors believed that he had contracted HIV through Factor VIII around
1982. Miraculously, Antoine had not been infected. Both men
were instructed to stop using Factor VIII and switch back to cryoprecipitate; but cryo was nowhere near as easy to use as Factor
VIII. It was a frozen product and a single internal bleed might
require up to fifteen bags of the protein mixture. Regardless, the
doctor argued that while Factor VIII was far easier to integrate
into their lifestyle, it was made from pools of plasma collected
from over 60,000 donors. Even if only one donor had HIV, it
would contaminate the entire pool. And even if that pool were
diluted ten million times, it would still be infectious. Cryo, on the
other hand, was made from a single donation, greatly minimizing
the risk of contamination. Giuseppe figured that he already had
AIDS, so why switch? He insisted that Antoine return to cryo.

Together the men confined themselves within the protective
walls of their fourth floor living quarters. Estelle ran the daily
operations with the help of Harper on weekends, and Antoine
nursed Giuseppe in private. No one was to speak of the diag-
nosis, as just the mention of AIDS, and eventually hemophilia,
would run their business into the ground. Most of the customers
during that period had no idea that there were gay men hiding
in the attic. Yet day after day, both Giuseppe and Antoine read
the news and talked with activists to learn what was being done.
Scientists at the CDC had been warning industry leaders and the
FDA since before Giuseppe's infection that a new bloodborne ill-

ness was threatening the blood supply and the U.S. population. Leaders of the National Hemophilia Foundation were skeptical and failed to pressure the FDA to change national blood policy. Meanwhile, industry leaders decided to wait, assuming they could take proper action once more data had been collected. Even then, it was too late. AIDS was already in the blood supply and thousands of innocent people were going to die.

As Antoine explained to Theo, when Factor VIII was put on the market, it was such a revolutionary medicine that no one bothered to ask how it was made. They just assumed it was safe. Unfortunately, as Giuseppe slowly died of AIDS, they both learned exactly what had been the true cost of their freedom. The plasma used to create the product had not only been collected from at-risk communities in skid-row neighborhoods but also from prison populations across the country, both of which were breeding grounds for hepatitis and other infectious diseases. These donors were all paid for donating their plasma, mere pennies compared to the profits to be made by the drug companies; however, this payment also gave donors the incentive to lie about their health. And all of this affected the quality and safety of Factor VIII.

Furthermore, American manufacturers knew that heat could purify the plasma used to make this product; but they somehow managed to convince regulators that heat would damage the fragile proteins needed to produce an effective clotting factor. This was only partially true. While heat could damage a percentage of clotting proteins, a heat-treated Factor VIII had already been created in Germany. Still, American companies waited three years to adopt this viral inactivation technique, relying on market pressures to convince the marketing department that an AIDS-free version of Factor VIII was needed to stay competitive. But it was too little, too late.

Contaminated Factor VIII was never officially recalled. Instead it remained in homes and on pharmacy shelves, enabling parents to unknowingly inject their small children with AIDS, all while believing they were helping their young sons and daughters in their battle against hemophilia. And when relatively silent recalls did occur years later, the pharmaceutical companies shipped surplus tainted product overseas, knowing it contained a lethal virus, all because they were unwilling to suffer a financial blow for their own negligence. As a result, those drugs killed thousands more. This had been a completely preventable plague; yet at the height of the epidemic, one hemophiliac died from AIDS every single day.

Meanwhile, Antoine watched as the love of his life withered away. Their few friends tried to help, but Giuseppe hated how they all listened sympathetically and sent him music that only depressed him more. Then he felt guilty for being so selfish. "How are you?" they'd ask, but no one really wanted to hear the truth of what happens when your body is starved of oxygen, begins to drown in its own mucus, and becomes too weak to ward off infections that storm the gates of your dismantled immune system like an invading army from hell. He lost his sight, suffered oral thrush, then slowly lost his mind. People brought flowers to the apartment, but those only served as a constant reminder of mortality. "If anyone can beat AIDS, it's this guy," one friend said. It took everything Antoine had not to kick him out of the apartment. Still, a world filled with fake laughter, harmless jokes, dull banter, and legalese was better than the outside world, where people might pull away in disgust at the very sight of a lesion. In a way, it might have been easier just to die from hemophilia, from slipping on a rug and letting a brain bleed take life away.

Those final moments together were far darker than the moments experienced in childhood. They were more painful as well, especially since only one of them was dying while the other was independent of that experience. Before, they had been in matching beds, side by side, watching those drips and drops of reddest blood, talking each other through the pain. Now Antoine was forced to watch as his partner dissolved into nothing, as if he were a fluff of cotton candy carelessly thrown into water. But even while Giuseppe faded in and out of consciousness during his final days, he still remembered their shared language, of the forever twirling threads of red, white, and black, as well as that hidden vein of precious gold glistening from the light of an internal spark.

Both found themselves plunged back into the darkness of that black thread, but only Giuseppe's light was going out. And when he took his last breath, it was as if all of his pain relocated to the buried chambers of Antoine's heart. Within the four rooms of that vessel, their shared history found a home, in all its glory and all its suffering. Their words carved themselves into the flesh of that beating organ, as an entire world and language collapsed, leaving Antoine alone amongst the wreckage. They had become whole on their own; but the world had glowed with such brightness when they were together. Now that light had dimmed to a fading ember.

Across the years that followed, Antoine wanted to die. Everything was a memory, a shadow, a wound. He spent day and night in their shared closet, holding Giuseppe's clothing, locked within that forever fading garden of textiles, metals and gems. He didn't want to think of the hospital bed that had once existed in the other room, or the painful emptiness left behind from the beeps which had once echoed signs of life down the halls. His nose searched for Giuseppe's cologne, his eyes for stray dark hairs upon the carpet, his hands for deviations in the fabrics. He sought all ethereal symbols of past purpose and momentum, while pocket squares were transformed into delicate flowers, luggage into prized pottery, and Giuseppe's vast collection of suits into burnished gemstones of fading colors. In Sicily, and then New Orleans, they both had suits made: light, beautiful suits designed with soft construction for smooth if not excessive movement. Those suits had been made for the vibrancy of life and all its many pleasures. Now they collected dust in this space, in gentle shades of white, seersucker, navy, tan, cream, pale pink, and softest blue.

Antoine held those fabrics, from cotton and linen to wool and silk blends, praying that his profound longing for his lover's return might somehow take root. He burrowed himself into this world, surrounded by insects represented by gleaming cufflinks, buckles, clasps and more. The plush carpet which lined the floor became the soil, watered daily with his tears. He knew that Giuseppe could never return in the same form, in the same way. No matter the outfit combination, a soul required flesh and blood to be reborn into this world. A hat of woven straw could never host the living. No walking stick could recreate its owner's weight. And while Antoine could hold those ashes of a past life in his hands, nothing could regenerate the fire that had slowly been snuffed out. It was as if Giuseppe's ghost had flown in and out of this tomb of matter as a weightless bubble, and once it had burst, all of him had dissolved into the invisible mist.

The only surviving remnants of their life together remained in the colors of their world. Those vibrations seemed to keep Antoine alive through his profound sadness. He found himself surrounded by the happy hue of pink sapphire, the juicy red of cherry opal, the brazen orange of carnelian, and the nurturing purple tones of jasper. From the possessions in their closet to the paints he applied to canvas, Antoine healed himself with shades of garnet and ruby, orange calcite and tangerine quartz, yellow citrine and rich amber, bubbling malachite and pure Tibetan turquoise. Each raised his vibrations, as if holding up his spine until he could manage to straighten it on his own. He wrapped himself in jade and celestine, lapis and sapphire, amethyst and moonstone, until the past dissolved into the night, reduced to a mere whisper.

In time, Antoine returned to Factor VIII, once a heat-treated option was put on the market. Eventually, life returned to a sort of stable constant. Slowly he gave Giuseppe's clothes away, piece by piece, as if each represented a week of mourning. He spent more time with friends and tried to be merry, but there remained the nagging urge to die. And when he awoke one day to discover the strange sensation of acid rushing through his veins, he thought his time had finally come. Estelle forced him to see a doctor. He was diagnosed with hepatitis C. Apparently, even heat-processed Factor VIII still carried some strains of hepatitis, despite being AIDS-free. The patent for a detergent method to remove this virus entirely from clotting factor had existed since 1980. Of course, American pharmaceutical companies had waited twelve years to adopt it.

Cirrhosis slowly shut down all of Antoine's bodily systems. He became overwhelmingly tired and could no longer think with anything resembling clarity. It was as if an eagle had been sent down from heaven, or up from hell, to inflict even more pain on his already wounded emotional self. He begged his friends to just let him die. "It's time," he pleaded; but his friends were mostly women, and wouldn't take no for an answer. Within the year, Harper donated half of her liver. Despite her gracious donation, Antoine still went into surgery praying that he wouldn't wake up, if only because he couldn't handle any more disappointment in this lifetime. But he did wake up, not just with a new liver, but with his hemophilia completely cured. He cried when the doctor told him the news because, for the first time in his life, that red thread finally represented life.

Antoine shared all of this with Theo in their interview. Just thinking about it had stirred up so many emotions, ones he hadn't realized he still needed to make peace with. Over 10,000 American hemophiliacs were infected with HIV, and over 15,000 with hepatitis C, due to contaminated Factor VIII. Most had died; yet Antoine, for whatever reason, had lived. "This isn't ancient history," Antoine explained. "I'm evidence that it just happened, almost yesterday."

"So how does this story about Blue Lotus and contaminated plasma sit with you, then?"

"I think that all material things are the shadows of our true values," he said. "Factor VIII could have truly been a miracle treatment, had it not been for the greed of others and the ignorance of those protecting the sick. In the case of Blue Lotus, what has her 'golden elixir' revealed? Does it not show us her true values? Society's true values? Are they not the same as those of the companies that killed Giuseppe and nearly me?"

"Those who cannot remember the past are doomed to repeat it," Theo offered.

"More than that," Antoine said. "I think those fancy people over in Silicon Valley opted to eat the lotus, all to forget that they'd forgotten the past, and induce some new dream for the future. But it was never going to work. They're too isolated in a bubble of ignorant thought, never thinking of the people they'd inevitably hurt along the way. It's the same story. The same twisted values propped up by a search for meaning."

"And what is it that you value, Mr. Bergeron?"

Antoine paused. "Life, I suppose. I guess that's turned out to be my greatest art, hasn't it? Staying alive."

When the interview was over, Theo shook his hand and thanked him for the story. Antoine watched the writer leave the shop, then turn onto Royal Street before disappearing into the crowds. What a difference a day can make, Antoine thought to himself as the sun descended into its dark house beneath the horizon. Such talk of the past made him curious about the future, which was why he couldn't sleep. If life was his true value, then why wasn't he living it? All night he wondered what to do next, and now that night was ending, he still wasn't sure.

Lorelei was curled up in a fluffy white ball, sound asleep on the fainting couch beside Cora. Antoine walked past them towards the window in the apartment overlooking Royal Street. The sun was now breaking through the darkness, bathing the entire Quarter in red. For Antoine, that light represented new embers throbbing with a warm hue. By telling his story to Theo, he had cast his own history into a lake of fire. And by speaking those words, breathing life into those painful memories of the past which had weighed him down for so long, Antoine burned that emotional baggage until all that remained were the ashes. He could almost see their essence rising above the rooftops like a column of smoke and fog.

He listened to the city as he leaned against the window. Those whispers were fading, finding peace within the building rays of the morning sun. The gray of the Quarter dissolved into the subtle mist of the day as the light reached his tired eyes. Antoine realized that he would never know why Giuseppe had to die while he was allowed to live. He would never understand why Estelle had to seduce that priest, or why Cora was purchased by the senator. He still didn't understand why Harper had volunteered to give him half her liver. And he'd never understand why some businesses did such awful things to people, despite having good, caring individuals working within the gates. But Antoine didn't have to know the answers. The world was absurd, he thought. And one day, he *would* die; but not today. Today, he would live. He would live as if it were the beginning of an eternal Spring.

*Editor's Note: Ms. Vivienne Shaw was in a romantic rela-
tionship with Mr. Charles Price from 1983 to 1987. They haven't spoken in nineteen years. Mr. Price declined to comment.*

THAT WAS THE ADDENDUM to the article; but of course,
the truth was complex. Vivienne could write an entire
memoir on her relationship with Charles Price and
the way that his family had impacted her life. Had it not been
for her stellar reputation as a tireless investigative journalist, her
editor might very well have taken her off this story. That would
have been fair. Only, no man in the newsroom wanted to go after
Delilah Russell for fear of being labeled sexist or accused of mans-
plaining, while the young women in the ranks were hesitant to go
after such an iconic female entrepreneur, worried they might be
accused of betraying their own kind. And the whistleblower *had*
reached out to Vivienne directly.

However, while an editor's note might serve to disarm Delilah
in some fashion, there was no denying that the roots of Vivienne's
connection to the Price family went very deep. In fact, the fif-
ty-four-year-old journalist had been running from that past for
decades. Now she was not only forced to face it, but to defend her
own personal choices, which had always been in direct conflict
with what Charles had to offer. Naturally, he wasn't the target of
the story. He had been lied to by Delilah, same as everyone else;

but Vivienne feared wounding the man she had once loved. It was something she never wanted to do, not ever again.

Editor's Note: *Ms. Vivienne Shaw had been highly suspicious of Ms. Delilah Russell since first meeting the Blue Lotus founder at a charity gala, months prior to learning that Ms. Russell was in any way affiliated with Mr. Charles Price.*

Vivienne thought that note should be added to the mix, even if it never would be. Then again, she was always suspicious of people who loved fancy parties like that. She hated attending them herself, but she'd been doing it since she was a child at the behest of Charlie Price. Back then, parties only served to put her directly in the crosshairs of her Mama, and that was something Vivienne never appreciated. Her mother, Cecile Brown Dupuis—former Yambilee Queen of the Louisiana Sweet Potato Festival—believed that appearances were everything, and held young Vivi to a very high standard when it came to attending parties at the Price mansion, just across the pond from their Acadian shack along the bayou.

"How you gonna get any man to listen if he can't stand the sight of you?" she'd say, running a metal comb through Vivienne's knotted curls. "People listen with their eyes. Don't you forget it."

"Charlie says I'm pretty just the way I am," the girl would reply.

"Rule number one: don't you be taking nobody's word for nothing. I'm your Mama. I'll tell you the truth, even when it hurts. Ain't nobody else got an interest in telling you like it is, ya hear me? Don't trust nobody but your Mama."

"Yes ma'am," she mumbled.

"What's that?"

"*Yes ma'am!*"

"Good. That skull of yours is awfully thick. Don't make me beat them words into you."

Cecile was awfully fond of beatings, "to make you tough." She toughened up Vivi's hide alright, with leather straps, fly swatters, and rubbery China ball or fig tree switches slapped across her bare ass or the open palms of her hands. That woman was also fond of putting hearty drops of Tabasco on the girl's tongue if she spoke back, then making her count to one hundred with her tongue sticking out and tears streaming down her dirty face. If she made bad grades, she'd have to kneel on hard rice in the corner of their shack until her little knees were embossed by the grains. But even with switch marks on her thighs or acid burns on her tongue, Vivienne had to remain as poised and perfect as a Southern Belle on a nasty swamper's pay.

By the time she was old enough to work a needle and thread, Cecile had Vivienne sewing, stitching, and mending clothes. Together they made all the shirts, dresses, pants and socks their family would ever need, and all without a pattern. Her Mama would sit at her sewing machine with a cigarette in one hand and fabric racing past the other. They'd sit and knit, crochet and quilt, while Cecile would lecture Vivi on the virtues of a good reputation. "That's all you got, girl, is how people perceive you, which is why I ain't none too happy about you running 'round town with Charlie Price. You're gonna scare all them other boys off, and you know Walter ain't never gonna let you be with his boy. You ain't got the right blood, and that ain't nothing you can change. Get that through your head right now. Still, I'll be damned if my baby ain't gonna dress to impress, ya hear? Charlie's been inviting you to all them fancy parties—make use of it. Listen, don't talk. Figure out what you need to know to get on out of here, you understand?"

"Yes ma'am."

"You're lucky you got my looks. Don't waste 'em like I did. To be beautiful is to be virtuous in the eyes of a man. Take care of your looks and you'll do just fine. Only ugly women can't hide their minds."

Those lessons from Mama sure did come in handy once Vivienne moved on to Washington, D.C., where everything is all about appearances. Right out the gate, Vivienne was determined to impress those fancy people of the capital, if not become dazzling enough to blind her competition. Like a strike of lightning, she emerged as a flashing star on the scene, sure to put on a magnificent show with words pouring out of her mouth like pure sugar, if only to disguise the fact that she was overflowing with raw ambition. But in order to elevate her appearance to a personal brand of advertising, Vivienne was forced to use every trick she'd learned from her beautiful Mama to make the best sort of first impression she could. "You're built like a little boy," Cecile would complain. "Make sure you always look like a woman." That was the true reason why Vivienne draped her athletic frame in soft fabrics dyed to a dark blue or regal purple, and kept her long blonde locks inching towards her small yet perky breasts. A strategic slit in a long Grecian gown allowed her tan, sculpted legs to peek out for a seductive advantage at political parties, while her mother's gift for painting faces came to good use as Vivienne highlighted her dramatic cheekbones and softened her forever tight jaw. Blunt bangs disguised her large forehead while delicate shades of pink made her thin lips look about as innocent as that little-girl giggle she used to disarm the men. As a result, Vivienne looked like a starlet on screen and in person, burning with virtue from the inside out.

But relying on beauty and the tricks of Mama's trade was about as bad as relying on Fortuna to rescue her from insignificance. No, Vivienne had lofty goals and absolute confidence in her ability to meet them. She wasn't going to rely on anyone, let alone chance, to make those dreams come true. After all, Vivienne Dupuis wasn't just the daughter of a down-on-her-luck beauty queen, bitter from disappointment; she was also the child of a third-generation swamper, and knew all too well what it took to survive. She recognized that same hunger for success in the eyes of Delilah Russell, who also seemed to shine from the inside out. That's why Vivienne, knowing full well that it hurts to be beautiful, was highly suspicious of the founder's attempts at playing coy.

At the charity gala in question, Vivienne had been laughing with colleagues about her recent Botox injections before going on television to discuss her new book, when Delilah, a dermatologist, interrupted: "Oh my, did it hurt?"

"I'm sorry?" Vivienne asked.

"Did it hurt to get Botox? I've never done it."

Vivienne looked at the glamazon standing before her, with a face as frozen as ice, void of all facial movement apart from a general look of surprise, and smirked. "I don't know. You tell me."

"Oh," Delilah giggled. "I honestly wouldn't know."

In Vivienne's mind, if a woman would lie about something so stupid, so trivial, and so blatantly obvious, what else was she lying about? That's when the wheels began to turn.

Editor's Note: *Ms. Vivienne Shaw was a successful hunter of game long before she became an accomplished journalist renowned for hunting down compelling stories; but it was Ms. Whitney Dugas who provided the arrows Ms. Shaw needed to finally pierce the balloon of fraud that was Blue Lotus.*

Vivienne thought that was worth saying as well, even if she couldn't. She'd promised to protect Whitney's identity, after all. However, it was important that people knew where she came from, and what exactly she was capable of doing. Her father, Alcide Dupuis, had been a swamper, as had been her grandfather and great-grandfather before him. Unlike Cecile, who was all about money, refinement and beauty (or a lack thereof), Alcide loved to be outside. He never made much money as a swamper, but he loved hunting and fishing as much as Mama loved to complain. Year-round he was hunting, either on the Price land or in the Atchafalaya Basin where he grew up. Vivi would join him in his old beat-up truck with a floor that was mostly rust, along with their red leopard Catahoula dog named Roux, who had a rare set of marble eyes and a liver brown nose. They'd travel to the family's camp in the swamps, which was just a bunch of plywood held together by scrap pieces of tin. And while her Daddy would spit dip and mend nets, Vivi would sweep out the leaves and dirt with an old broom that was little more than frayed whiskers at the end of a stick. They'd sleep on the floor in handmade sleeping bags, listening to the wilderness sing as Vivi held onto her beloved Roux while he snored. Good Lord that dog stank! Still, being at the camp was glorious when she was a child, mostly because Mama wasn't there to wash or brush her hair, and because Daddy let her be as wild as any child of the swamps.

It was Alcide who taught Vivi how to hunt with a bow and arrow. He made the bow himself out of cypress harvested from the Basin, then taught her to make her own cypress arrows using feathers plucked from the wild turkeys and geese they killed. Together in their matching white rubber boots, father and daughter would journey through the maze of the Basin on foot and by boat with Roux often by their side. As her Daddy set his lines and traps, Vivi would keep a watchful eye on their surroundings with her bow and arrows, looking out for wild hogs, bobcats, black bears and gators. She'd be as still as a stone in that calico mud, focused on the wilderness, listening for Roux to whimper or bay.

Unlike the family shack, which was often dark and filled with the smell of cigarettes, the Basin was colorful and alive with all sorts of smells. The sunsets would submerge behind the painted surface of the still water, looking like fire rising up in the fog on a canvas broken only by the cypress knees and scattered clouds surrounded by peach and blood orange hues. There were banana spiders as big as her hand, weaving webs with golden spit, and beetles as small as a grain of milo wheat, dancing along the water's surface in groups of a hundred or more, looking like wild bubbles playing near the shore. There were bullfrogs as round as her head, eating anything and everything in sight, and Nutria almost as long as the dog, having thirty babies a year. At night she'd listen to the male alligators croaking for their harem of females, only to hear the babies chirping during the day. There were hundreds of frogs, even more types of birds, young cypress trees wrapped in robes of moss, and lush carpets of green sucking the oxygen up.

As the months passed, those waters would rise and fall, with each season dictating a different kind of life. Vivi would help her Daddy catch and clean alligator gars for their white meat hidden beneath a heavy armor. Then she'd hunt with him for deer, turkey, geese, ducks, squirrels and rabbits, always using her bow and arrow to kill quickly and without fuss. She'd wade into the waters with her Daddy to noodle for catfish, or stay up late into the night to gig for frogs. They'd catch crawfish and river shrimp, eel and perch, even the odd gou fish on occasion. No matter the catch, Vivi would help her Daddy clean the meat then cook a mess in a big ole black pot over an open fire, where he'd tell her stories about magic oak trees and swamp queens, rougarous and ghosts. Alcide's world was nothing like Cecile's and that suited Vivi just fine.

While Mama was obsessed with the blinding radiance of a beautiful appearance, Daddy loved the art of disguise. He could talk for hours about fishing bait, camouflage, duck calls, and secret smells. "You've always got to be ready for anything to happen," he said. So he prepared her for every sort of situation in the Basin, from snake bites to feral pigs. "You can't be letting nothing get the upper hand. Stay calm, but have a plan. Them animals out there tryin' to deceive you, but you gotta deceive 'em first." He told her that relying on chance to get out of danger was foolish. "That's a sure way to get killed, my baby. Always stay one or two steps ahead. Be strong like a bear, sly like a fox."

These were skills that served her well in Washington, where the same poise and accuracy required to kill a wild boar with a bow and arrow were needed to write stories sure to strike at the hearts of her opponents. In time, she replaced her faithful dog Roux with interns and underlings, young men and women she taught to hunt by giving them positions within her circle.

Those baying hounds would find and hold the stories she most wanted until she could raise her bow and shoot, clean and free. Disguise became her own art form, hidden behind the beautiful appearances her mother had inspired. She made relationships with more established players in the Beltway, all strictly political in nature. None were based on trust or loyalty, but the desire for information. She determined the proper bait, then went hunting for her prey, believing that all was fair in love and war, especially when hunting for stories. And just as her Daddy always caught more fish or game than they could load up in that piece-of-shit truck, Vivienne always had more information than she knew what to do with. Then again, information in that world was its own kind of wealth, and it almost always had to be won through some sort of game.

Of course, to play the game properly you always had to be prepared for a surprise, and getting a phone call from Helen Dugas' daughter, after not speaking with Helen or anyone related to the Price family for nineteen years, was certainly a surprise for the books. It was even more surprising to discover that Whitney was contacting her about Delilah Russell.

"Delilah claims she's changing the world," Whitney said. "But for all her talk of transparency, Blue Lotus is not the organization everyone thinks it is. I've got the documents to prove it. You interested?"

At the time, Whitney didn't disclose that those documents included information related to Price Plasma; but after thirty-three years working to expose fraudulent companies and dirty political players, Vivienne didn't see how anyone else could write this story. She knew all too well that secrecy was the best friend of corruption and incompetence, so she decided to drag Blue Lotus into the light, if only to capture the most destructive boar she'd ever hunted. The problem, though, was that by dragging Delilah's fraud out into the open, Vivienne had to face her own reflection, as well as the past she didn't wish to recall.

Editor's Note: Mr. Charles Price had wanted to marry Ms. Vivienne Shaw. They'd been talking about it since they were kids. All that was left was for him to buy a ring and set a date, then Ms. Shaw left him for an entry-level position at a newspaper in Washington, D.C.

Walter Price had called Vivienne into his office the day after she and Charlie had graduated from college to ask her a simple question: "Do you love my son?" Her impulse was to say, "Yes, of course I do!" Those were the words she had been waiting to say for years. In private, she had rehearsed that moment dozens of times, waiting for Walter to corner her and tell her that she wasn't worthy of joining his family. She was prepared to fight for Charlie, to scream from the rooftops that she loved him more than she loved herself. Then the moment arrived and Vivienne felt frozen in time, like a bug trapped in a web, just waiting for a spider to fill her with venom so she wouldn't have to lie; or worse, tell the truth.

She did love Charlie. He was the first boy she'd ever loved. Everything her Daddy had taught her in the Basin she had in turn taught Charlie in the woods surrounding his house. At their respective ages of ten and eleven, he declared her the Queen of the Swamps and crowned her with an abandoned bird's nest they'd found in a live oak. She held in one hand a cow's dirty femur for a scepter, and in the other a living bullfrog for an orb. When Charlie crowned himself King of the Woodlands, they sealed their childish union with a kiss. "We'll always be together," he said, "because we were made for each other." Vivienne wanted to believe that fairytale more than any other, that they could rule over this land in their glittering mansion between the old shack and the road.

She'd never felt safe in anyone's arms before, or comfortable enough to share every little thing on her mind. Part of her wanted to prove her mother wrong: that she could be with Charlie Price, that little Vivienne Dupuis was good enough to move into that big house filled with all them fancy antiques, and that Walter would be proud to have her as his daughter-in-law because she'd been valedictorian at school. But as the years fluttered by, Vivienne found herself suffocating in union with Charlie. For some reason, the more they talked about their love for each other, the smaller the world seemed to get. Like those aquatic plants in the swamp, their promises to each other seemed to grow over her like a weighted blanket, sucking up all the oxygen in the room.

At first, she had wanted everything Charlie could offer; then suddenly, she felt trapped by what that offer might mean. She didn't want to be Mrs. Charles Price any more than she wanted to be Vivienne Dupuis. She didn't want to be stuck in Louisiana. She wanted to be free to play, to live a life as messy, difficult, crazy, beautiful and challenging as she possibly could. She didn't want to be constant, or constantly proving herself to her mother. Vivienne wanted the freedom to change, to grow, to fail, to *experience* everything. She wanted to take her bow and arrows then run into the sun, forced to rely only on her own virtues to win or lose the biggest game of all, which was life itself.

"Do you love my son?" Walter asked.

Vivienne's heart raced faster than ever. "No sir. I don't. Not the way I should."

She and Charlie parted ways that evening. She didn't think either of them had ever cried so hard in their lives. The entire process felt like tearing two trees apart after they had woven their root systems together for centuries. It was brutal, *exhausting*, but necessary. Vivienne believed that they'd both known for some time, subconsciously, that they couldn't stay together forever, that the myth they had created long ago was finite and had to end at some point, and that they had been silently growing apart as their paths diverged over time. She took the job in D.C. She didn't see him again before she left, finding a sort of comfort in the idea that she had been brave enough to blink first, to sever their connection with the coup de grâce neither of them wanted, but both of them needed. It wasn't easy to do, but she felt a deep sense of relief after that painful cut had been made, destroying their bond forever.

Of course, Vivienne didn't know that she was pregnant when she left Louisiana. Charlie's baby was probably only the size of a poppy seed; but by the time she figured it out, it was too late to turn back. She'd already broken Charlie's heart, and she was six weeks in on a job that about a dozen other people would kill to have. She couldn't reverse the wheel of Fortuna; she just had to keep moving forward, and so she did. She buried the profound pain of that decision beneath the weight of work, and tried to rise above the nagging emptiness that her loneliness stirred. The game became all that she had, so she played harder than ever, climbing her way to even greater professional success.

Then Walter Price died. Vivienne hadn't seen Charles in fourteen years. During that time, she'd gotten married then divorced; but he'd opted to remain a playboy, as if he'd been holding space for her all that time. When they first locked eyes at the funeral home, Vivienne knew that he still loved her as much as he had the day she left for Washington; but she also knew that she didn't miss him at all. She realized that she could only love Charlie like a brother, and never anything more. Still, the night before they put Walter in the ground, Charlie came to her hotel, stinking drunk and desperate to know why she didn't want him. What had he done? What could he have done differently? Now that she'd had her little adventure, could she please just come home? He wouldn't take no for an answer. He refused to believe that she didn't love him. So she told him the truth, the awful secret of what she'd done, so that he'd finally leave her alone.

His face hardened and his eyes glazed over. He was breathing, but barely. With a few words, Vivienne had managed to drive her sharpest arrow directly into the center of his heart, and there it stayed as he stumbled out of the room. As the hotel room door closed and locked behind him, Vivienne collapsed onto the bed and let out a gut-wrenching howl, followed by the tears, anger and sorrow she had held onto for so long. She let that fire of regret and resentment consume her until her entire body was twitching with overwhelming pain.

She didn't attend the funeral. Instead she caught a flight back to Washington, all the while remembering something Walter had once said. "You can't outsource the struggle to truth," he told her. "It's too risky. You can be tricked, cheated, or led astray if you trust the wrong source. Form your own opinions, then make choices based on that. At least then, right or wrong, it's your decision. And even if it's a bad one, you'll gain wisdom from it, eventually." Vivienne felt that she had made so many difficult decisions in her quest for personal truth, but the most painful one of all had been choosing the path she most wanted to take, instead of the one that stayed with Charlie. She knew she'd made the right decision for her, even if it was the wrong one for him; but she swore, then and there, that she would never hurt Charlie again. Then, almost two decades later, Whitney Dugas sent over two hundred pages of original source material outlining the fraud committed by Blue Lotus. Nearly half of those pages mentioned Price Plasma.

Editor's Note: Mr. Charles Price is the son of Mr. Walter Price. It was Walter who had taught Ms. Vivienne Shaw the ways of the world. While Ms. Shaw hated to hurt Charles again, she was willing to play by the rules as Walter had defined them. If Charles couldn't play that game, he was worse off than she thought.

It would almost be *too* cruel for Vivienne to drag Charlie's father into this mess, but it was Walter who had first gotten her dreaming about a life in D.C., where he spent plenty of time lobbying for his blood business. "Politicians are cheaper than horses," the Price patriarch once laughed. "That's why I've got a whole stable of them. I've got horses from each political party, every moral soapbox, and on both sides of the aisle. I've got horses on committees, in coalitions, and on TV. I've got Ivy League horses and state college horses, do-gooders, optimistic runners, and cut-throat motherfuckers. The beauty of it all is that I don't really care which of them wins, as long as one of them does. That's how I get my returns." Of course, the only horse Vivienne had was the stick-thin nag as black as night her Daddy had bought from the slaughterhouse, and he wasn't gonna be winning much. Instead, she'd have to be her own horse and place all bets squarely on herself.

By the time she was a senior in high school, Vivienne had learned that everything was a game to Walter Price, but he couldn't play those games alone. That's why he roped everyone else into them, including Charlie and herself. For Walter, games had a clear beginning and an agreed upon ending, mostly with him winning. "No one is forced to play," he'd say in his defense. "Everyone plays freely and the rules are always crystal clear from the start. That's why no one gets to cry when they lose. They knew the risks when they entered the ring. Just because they chose to forget that they knew doesn't mean that I did."

Power, as defined by Walter, was something you gained by winning. You certainly didn't win *because* you were powerful; but by winning, you could *become* powerful. It was all theatre in his mind, with certain players taking on certain roles and agreeing to constraints as obvious as the edge of a stage. And to increase the fun, there was always conflict between two equal yet opposing forces, *like in all theatre*, with each side seeking to outwit or out-play the other. In that world, to win the audience was to win the game, with power bestowed by applause. And because no one was ever applauded quite to their satisfaction, those games continued in gross repetition, with the same scripts being played out again and again with different players. Change was just a concept, and never fully embraced. Just like in politics, there was nowhere to go but round and round, the only difference being the horses and the weather, never the game itself.

"Who are we to change things?" Walter once hollered at Charles, with Vivienne listening by his side. "And why would those in power want to, if the current order serves their interests? Yeah, the 'people' could rise up and demand real change; but have you ever seen sheep rebel against the dog working the herd? Or the farmer who controls the dog? No! The herd simply splits into smaller and smaller groups until they're absolutely ineffective at whatever it is the herd thought they might accomplish in the first place. Those sheep love to forget that all systems of oppression require voluntary compliance. They agreed to be oppressed, son! And just as they were completely free to sign up for the game of victimhood, they're free to stop it too. Hell, all it takes is thirty percent non-compliance to kill a game. But that thought scares the shit out the sheep, which is why they'll never, ever rise up. They'd rather complain about the *type* of dog nipping at their heels than figure out the goddamn gate. It's *more comfortable* for them that way. Trust me son, you're better off behind the curtain with me, rather than veiling yourself with that beautiful lie. If you limit yourself like that, well, you'll never win a game."

According to Walter, we were all competing for life, to win another day if not the immortality of our name. He wasn't concerned with the soul, but with the glory of continued triumph only possible through the winning of titles and the avoidance of death in the ring. He wanted his name to live on in the theatre of his games, to become immortal within the scripts of his victories. Death to him was defeat, something deserved for losing a match. It represented a sort of obedient silence within that theatre of power in which we limit and oppress ourselves in order to forget our freedom. That's why it was so shocking when Walter died— Vivienne didn't think he was capable of such a loss. He'd never lost anything before. "You do what you did," he once said. "You get what you got." Those words hardly made sense in the face of his absurd death: killed by a drunk driver at seven in the morning on the way to the office.

Vivienne couldn't deny the influence Walter had had over her upbringing, and even the way she saw the world up to this very day. She assumed that's why she had been able to climb the ranks so quickly. Walter had helped her see that by understanding the rules of the game and playing them well she could speed her ascent that much faster. And as a woman who wanted to play with the boys, she needed to make damn sure that she not only played fair but accepted the consequences of her decisions as they made themselves apparent. "Respect is earned," Walter once said. "Never given." That meant something to Vivienne, and she welcomed accountability because of it. There would be no double standards for her.

That's probably why Delilah Russell disgusted her. Not only did that failed entrepreneur play dirty, she refused to accept the consequences of her own decisions, instead choosing to hide behind that paper screen of modern feminism, which enables the very worst of women to scream "oppression" instead of accepting accountability. When the story first broke that Delilah had been selling contaminated blood plasma, and had likely infected thousands of early adopters with a fatal disease that was spreading through blood, spit, and sputum, the startup founder blamed everyone else: the research lab, the well-respected biochemist Eliot Lawrence, the men in competition against her, and even Vivienne Shaw herself, whom she declared "a handmaiden to the patriarchy, actively holding women back." The beautiful dermatologist hoped to get lucky, that the press would stay on her side and fight her battles for her; but as Walter Price once said, "Fortuna doesn't favor the bold. She only smiles on the prepared." And Delilah Russell was comically unprepared to face the truth.

Editor's Note: *Ms. Vivienne Shaw had no knowledge about the source of photographs recently purchased by her employer. She had no part in the decision to publish photographs of paid donors at Price Plasma, or in the decision to attach them to*

her article regarding Blue Lotus. She also did not know that
the photographer in question, known simply as Ms. Natalie
Rose, is the only child of Mr. Charles Price.

Even if that could actually be an editor's note, it wouldn't make much difference to Charlie. He'd see it as a betrayal either way; yet another betrayal at the hands of Vivienne Dupuis. He wouldn't care one iota that Vivienne had never wanted to hurt him. The fact of the matter was that she had, repeatedly. She had hurt him so many times, there was nothing she could do to make it any better. To make matters worse, those photographs were an enormously helpful weapon against Delilah, providing a much needed visual aid for an audience grappling with the science and numbers behind the shimmering Blue Lotus façade. Maybe Charlie could appreciate that. Probably not. Vivienne could always fly down to Louisiana to talk with him, but there was no reason to do that. She had no reason to be in Louisiana at all.

Both of her parents were dead. Daddy died on an oil rig in the Gulf. "Freak accident" was how the situation had been explained to her. His death certificate said he drowned. A few years later Mama died in Rayne, Louisiana, after falling asleep with a cigarette in her hand, causing her brand new house—and all of the past memories stored within—to go up in a cloud of smoke. In fact, all of Vivienne's past seemed to be charred earth; but she never seemed to notice that destruction until a lull between stories would force her to be still.

Time and time again, once a game had been won, and her victory had been turned into an immortal title, that empty space would again announce its presence. She would suddenly feel that dark weight deep within her bones, forcing her to remember that her mother's greatest regret was marrying a man just because she got pregnant with him. Vivienne could remember countless occasions where her mother would sob on the porch or in the kitchen. She'd scream at Vivi, "Don't you make the same mistakes I did!

You get a good education and you get the hell out of here. Don't let any man hold you back, you understand? I should have never had children," she'd cry. "I should have never had you." Vivienne knew she could never guarantee that she wouldn't have become that same resentful woman, crying on the shoulder of Charlie's child, wishing they'd never been born. Saving a baby from that kind of life seemed to justify her actions, but only about half the time. The other half she couldn't remember: had she really wanted to be with Charlie? Had she made the biggest mistake of her life? Should she have taken the other path?

A part of her wished that the glittering Price mansion would have been enough to make her happy. Isn't that what all poor Cajun trash was supposed to want? The life of a wealthy Anglo, or a Creole with elite European blood? Why didn't she want it? There were so many beautiful moments shared with Charlie, from running barefoot in the rain to their first kiss while swimming half-naked in the pond. During college, they often slept completely intertwined with one another, the nook of his arm serving as her home. She had told him everything there was to tell about herself back then. There were no secrets between them, apart from the biggest secret of all.

For years, she had felt that schism growing as they slowly pulled apart. She didn't want to believe that she would never be fulfilled by a life with Charlie, that she was meant to go her own way, independent of him; but deep down, she knew that the life he offered her wasn't the one she was meant to live. Even now, Vivienne still loved the loud, frantic newsroom in comparison to the polite decay of life at the Price mansion. She loved the smell of ink on paper more than the scent of luxurious perfumes, the company of books and files to the collections of decorative antiques, and the hunt for stories far more than the search for meaning in a world that seemed to have everything figured out.

She'd never found success in love, but she'd found it in a career that she loved instead, in the world she was meant to be a part of all along. She didn't want to hurt Charles any more than she had wanted to hurt her Daddy by moving so far away; but she had found something within herself, something that offered the promise of the future rather than those familiar shackles of the past. She had no choice but to chase it. And maybe one day, when there were no more stories for her to hunt, or her mind became too weak, she would sit alone in her empty house and regret rejecting those other roads. Maybe she would regret not having children, not marrying Charles, not becoming a Price; but she didn't think so.

Her work was all the meaning she needed. The games she felt called to play were enough. Helping people expand their vision, while holding the powerful to account, was enough. And exposing a fraud like Delilah Russell, *whose face was full of Botox*, and who had spread a fatal disease out of pure ignorance, pride and greed, was a goddamn honor. Vivienne would be merciless when it came to taking her down, because she was the daughter of a beautiful woman and a sly Cajun swamper, and she'd learned the art of power from one of the most successful men in the State of Louisiana. Moreover, she had sacrificed so very much to be on this path, at this moment, with this acquired knowledge. That's why Vivienne would win this battle against Delilah. She would win no matter the cost. It was what she had been born to do.

CHARLES PRICE COULD STILL RECALL the last plague that had affected the family business. He was finishing up high school when that strange new disease had first captured his imagination. Originally known as GRID, or Gay-Related Immunodeficiency Disease, that mysterious virus had found its way into his father's phone calls, their lunch dates, and even gossip in the kitchen with Ms. Helen. Initially, there were only a few isolated incidents, seemingly random cases which many tried to explain away as Lady Justice balancing her scales. At dinner parties and political functions, rumors swirled about the room that only those who deserved to be punished for their sins would be affected, while the moral and virtuous would remain immune. It was far more comforting, even then, to believe that those in pursuit of socially appropriate behavior, language and lifestyles would be fitted with armor against the cruel indifference of disease, while those who failed to abide by such strict moral codes would be purged from society by AIDS. The idea that anyone could be affected—gay or straight, loyal or promiscuous, moral or immoral—was avoided, if not banned from discussion altogether. The message was clear: if you believed in certain things, spoke a certain way, and behaved appropriately, you would be spared. If you dared to color outside of those lines, you deserved to die.

Plague, or really any unexpected event, had a way of dialing up the intensity of such divisive thought. Charles believed it was because the weak were afraid, that they feared not being able to control their future, and so they fought to control everyone else. His father had voiced similar frustrations back in the 1980s. "People would rather be in than out," he said. "That's the problem." He argued it was precisely this human impulse that resulted in the scourge of groupthink, in which certain people are all too willing to follow whatever egocentric fool screams the loudest, confidently pushes their way to the front of the conversation, and hides behind an immaculate résumé that means nothing in terms of true experience. If presented with enough bravado behind the slick sheen of notoriety, such "experts" would seldom be questioned, even as they led their followers right on off a cliff.

"Some people are so desperate for acceptance," his father argued, "and so terrified to be rejected or kicked out of their social club, that they'll gladly abandon critical thinking, anchor to someone else's ideas, and bow their heads to a ridiculous fool, assuming they won't have to face the consequences if that fool is wrong. Then they'll go on whining about how the chains are so tight, how they couldn't possibly budge, how they have no choice but to comply. Secretly they know those chains are so loose, they could easily sneak out of the devil's lair, if only they had the courage to reject blind conformity. But no, they *choose* to be obedient to save themselves the social cost of a disagreement, and in the process, commit the greatest sin of all: inaction in the face of what they know to be wrong. They commit evil in the name of popularity, while crying that they're only human."

Charles was scrolling through Natalie's photography as published online by the *Journal*. The title of the collection was "Going Back to Source." Based on the articles and commentary he had read over the course of the day, Charles knew that he was being lined up perfectly to be Delilah's scapegoat. The media, and Delilah's followers, were already constructing their narrative, independent of the objective truth. Unsurprisingly, they were extremely monolithic in their coverage, using the same phrases, arguments, and talking points. Delilah Russell was their goddess, the figurehead of a secular religion based on a specific idea of progress, with worship requiring the bloodthirsty desire to tear down all that had come before. There could be no compromise, discussion, or debate. This religion required absolute servitude to the cause of dismantling the so-called "patriarchy," while lifting up those who identified as women, no matter how deeply flawed. Anyone who stood in the way of this goal was not only a problem, they were an evil that must be snuffed out without mercy or reprieve.

This celluloid façade, supported by an intolerant public's opinion, reminded Charles of the Nazi regime, through which the leading scientists of Germany, most of them Jews, had been silenced, sterilized, or murdered in the name of progress and purity. That same desperation for power had devolved into distorted language, reworking and manipulating scientific research to support a narrow-minded agenda. At one point the regime even decided that the B blood type should be used as a marker for undesirables, initially associating it with the Jews and Eastern Europeans, then those with less than ideal temperaments or intelligence. That was *their* narrative: to achieve utopia, science says purge this blood. It didn't matter that blood types have no correlation to habits or mental acuity, or that Aryans living in Berlin at the time exhibited B type more than Jews; but because of this racially motivated purge, German medicine slid back into the darkness of antiquated thought. It wasn't progress, but a violent ignorance that took decades to correct. Unfortunately, Charles knew that the quacks of today would never heed this message, and especially not from him. He was now the devil, the enemy, the treacherous villain of their beloved story. Even his own daughter had turned against him, or so the public howled, as if Natalie's photographs had presented his Achilles' heel for the mob to pull 'n' peel like a Twizzler. As with the Nazis, it didn't matter if their beliefs made sense, or if they were even true. All that mattered was whether or not such actions could be made to fit within their all-important narrative, that golden calf they worshipped at Delilah's pristine feet.

Charles had known that Natalie was not his child since the day she was born. Both he and Matilda had Rh negative blood while the infant was Rh positive. He'd chosen to raise her as his own anyway. He'd never told Natalie the truth and neither had Matilda; but that was changing. When he put the eighteen year old onto the company's Cessna Citation for a flight to Chicago earlier in the day, he had been assured by his soon-to-be ex-wife that she would be telling Natalie the truth, and nothing but the truth, once she arrived. He wanted to believe her, but Charles knew that Matilda often stalled when it came to revealing anything about herself. They had been married for three years before she told him that she had been raped. Natalie's sudden spurt of red hair had been the tipping point. Five years after that, Matilda revealed that she considered herself bisexual, with strong leanings towards being a lesbian. Ultimately, they decided to stay together for Natalie's sake, while Charles did everything in his power to help Matilda heal and recover from what had been done to her, even if trust remained an issue. Over the course of nineteen years, they had tried everything from therapy and retreats to romantic holidays—anything to salvage the marriage; but they never could stop fighting with each other, if not purposely hurting one another. Sexually, they never did mesh. As a result, they'd grown absolutely intolerant of each other over the past few years, sleeping in separate rooms and spitting words at each other like a couple of quarreling cobras. Still, their divorce was as amicable as it could be under those circumstances, and Charles was going to make sure both Matilda and Natalie had sufficient funds for the next stage of their lives, at least until they could take care of themselves. He wasn't a monster.

Then again, Charles honestly didn't know what was worse: that the girl he'd raised as his own daughter had been foolish enough to fall in love with an older man suspected of being a closeted homosexual, or that she genuinely thought she could live off of $800, the measly amount she had accepted for her now infamous photographs. Actually, the true tragedy of it all was that the public seemed to believe that Natalie's actions had been the work of a bold revolutionary, when in reality they had been done by a silly, lovestruck teenager whose grasp of power extended no further than a powder puff. Of course, the truth behind Natalie's actions meant nothing, as the narrative required a hero, and so a hero she would be. Natalie's true identity and motivations didn't matter outside of the story actively being written about her. Her participation was neither wanted nor needed. The spin masters of the world would take it from here, ignoring the ugly truth as best they could.

Charles had yet to find any coverage detailing the full scope of Delilah's deception, apart from Vivienne's initial article. He could say a great many things about Vivienne Dupuis, but he knew that she wouldn't spin a thing. She might withhold information, for years even, but when it came time to tell the truth, she'd hit you square between the eyes. As for Delilah Russell, and the extremely elaborate lie she had constructed, only Vivi could have gotten to the heart of it, and Charles was relieved that she did. He didn't have a written record of Delilah's exact pitch to him, but thanks to the source documents acquired by an anonymous whistleblower and published by Vivi's paper, he had documentation of the exact same lie she had told to him, this time to her board and investors. None of those suits had any real knowledge of medical, pharmaceutical, or laboratory sciences, and if Charles was honest, neither did he. That's probably why no one had questioned Delilah's claim that plasma could be used to identify toxins in her precious elixir.

Over a business lunch, the mysterious founder with jet black hair and bright green eyes had compared her discovery to LAL Testing. She told Charles that, while the blood of horseshoe crabs had been approved by the FDA in the late 1970s to create an effective test for bacterial contamination with certain pharmaceuticals and medical devices, plasma's clotting proteins could do the job just as well, at least in terms of her anti-aging treatment. "I think we're at the tip of the iceberg when it comes to studying plasma," Delilah said, and Charles believed her. In truth, he was only vaguely familiar with the Limulus Amebocyte Lysate Test, which requires fishermen to catch those ancient crabs during their breeding season to collect a portion of their copper-rich blood worth well over fifteen thousand dollars a quart. During the test, the cells of that blue blood quickly coagulate should a product have any trace of endotoxin. It was a safety measure widely used within certain industries, but Charles had never heard of using plasma's clotting proteins to replace it.

The only knowledge Charles had was the history of plasma, and based on that knowledge, Delilah's claims seemed *plausible*. In the beginning, the biggest problem with plasma had been bacterial contamination, earning that amber-colored gold the nickname "liquid dynamite." Years of intensive research, as well as the invention of plastic, were needed to solve this specific problem, which incidentally produced the innovation known as plasmapheresis, a technology Price Plasma relied on even today. At all fifteen Price collection centers along the Gulf Coast, donors reclined back while that ingenious machine removed a certain amount of a donor's blood, centrifuged it to collect the plasma, then re-infused the donor with their own oxygen-carrying red cells. The plastic tubes prevented contamination while the automated machine prevented human error, ensuring a bacteria-free supply to be fresh frozen, packaged, and shipped around the world to research labs and pharmaceutical companies desperate for that vital resource. Since the material was quick to grow bacteria, it made sense to Charles that a tainted pharmaceutical or medical device would ignite further contamination. Then again, he wasn't a scientist, just a second generation supplier.

Of course, plenty of people could shout that the plasma industry was "immoral and distasteful profiteering," or accuse Price

Plasma of exploiting the poor through a form of modern cannibalism. Charles had even been equated to a vampire on more than one occasion. None of that was new. Those arguments had been made time and time again since the 1950s. The truth was that the entire world depended on plasma, specifically the plasma sourced from the paid systems of the United States. That's why the U.S. was known as the "OPEC of Blood Plasma." Its citizens bled for all the world to live, even those who seemed to believe that their nation's socialized healthcare systems and voluntary blood donor programs equated to self-sufficiency on all fronts. As Charles knew all too well, the plasma industry itself was a giant international web of often American plasma pools shipped around the world, fractionated for components, then made into lifesaving drugs bought and sold across borders as part of life-long therapies for the rarest diseases and disorders known to mankind. It was real easy to look at a couple of photographs and judge an entire industry. It was much more difficult to stomach how the sausage is made, and why. Yet headline after headline practically screamed, HOW PRICE PLASMA STARTED A MODERN PLAGUE.

The U.S. blood supply had been clean since 1985; but Delilah Russell argued that it was a repeat of the negligence witnessed during the AIDS epidemic that had cost her business its flawless reputation. She claimed that voluntary standards had made the plasma industry as a whole complacent, resulting in her product becoming infectious. She never responded to claims that her product didn't really exist—that it was just source plasma repackaged with a shiny blue label. She never discussed where *all* of her plasma had been sourced from either. Delilah simply claimed that she was under attack, while pointing her perfectly manicured finger directly at Charles Price. Now, Charles could admit that when it came to blood and its components, the idea of "zero risk" was not attainable, as there would always be viruses, each able to mutate into an infinite number of evolving threats over time, and the human race would always be blind to the next unpredictable event, the next infectious disease, the next epidemic. No matter how advanced, humanity would never be able to protect itself completely. New pathogens would always be discovered and new treatments would always be necessary to conquer them, each requiring an enormous amount of time, money, and willpower to create. But Charles firmly believed, as did his parents, that scientists should do everything in their power to prevent its spread, starting with source plasma. Sure, the novel virus connected with the Blue Lotus elixir could have been delivered by a Price Plasma donor. As with AIDS in the early days, there was no way to test for this new pathogen, so of course *it was possible*; however, plasma sourced from Price was never supposed to be infused into patients by that company in the first place.

According to their contract, the relationship between Price Plasma and Blue Lotus was meant to focus strictly on research and development. Price would provide an extremely specific amount of fresh frozen plasma to the startup, on the condition that it be used as an experimental testing protocol for bacterial contamination. The contract also outlined every preventative safety measure Price Plasma had in place, from monitoring their plasma collections for more than eighty pathogens that could be transmitted by transfusion, to the use of robust donor screening questionnaires that had been put in place in the 1990s. However, once he sold that plasma to Blue Lotus, the "means and methods of production" using that raw material became Delilah's responsibility, according to the precedent set in 1968. As an addendum to the contract, three detailed methods for inactivating viruses and purifying the plasma to ensure minimal risk were recommended for consideration, such as old-school heat-treatment, a solvent-detergent method, and ultraviolet irradiation often used by pharmaceutical companies. Charles even made it a point to warn her about hepatitis E and Creutzfeldt-Jacob disease, which were both immune to these efforts. In response, Delilah repeatedly reassured him that she was buying the raw material purely for testing bacterial growth, not for use in patients. He still encouraged her to be vigilant, as unknown threats were always a risk with biological products; but she reminded him that she was a doctor and didn't need to be badgered. Reluctantly, Charles acknowledged that Delilah might know more than he did, then ultimately decided to trust her judgment over his own. After all, she was the physician supposedly trying to treat disease; he was just a suit. As for the overarching narrative claiming that Delilah was a genius, that Blue Lotus would revolutionize medicine, that her elixir *was real*—all of that had also influenced his decision, since he could not know what he did not know. All he could do was trust what he'd been told.

Charles assumed that's why narratives existed in the first place, to soothe our nerves in the face of deep uncertainty. We would all have to make choices, and those choices would have consequences along a spectrum of positive and negative results. In terms of the AIDS epidemic, yes, that dark period in the history of the blood industry had taught them all extremely painful lessons at an immensely high cost; but that same tainted blood era had also resulted in pasteurized blood products and extensive testing that should have prevented the Blue Lotus situation from ever taking place. In fact, Charles had spent his entire career learning from his father's fight to build and maintain Price Plasma in the face of those very struggles. He even bought into the narrative that smaller pool sizes, stricter screening methods, and robust disinfection procedures were enough to keep us all safe from another pandemic. That's why Charles had waited to change things, to implement what he believed was the next step for the family business. In the back of his mind, he figured something would happen eventually—a catastrophic event that would force the hand of the blood industry, pushing them all to change the status quo. He just didn't think he'd be at the center of it, or that he'd have to lead the charge. Then again, leading was exactly what he'd been raised to do.

Throughout his childhood, his father had reminded him that their bloodline was like a ship. All of his ancestors and potential descendants were aboard, and one by one, they had been or would be offered the opportunity to steer the collective. "When it's your turn," Walter warned, "know that we will all pay a price for your decisions. You can either steer us into the rocks and destroy everything we've worked for, or bring us safely into the next harbor. The choice is yours. Choose wisely." Charles knew that he could never escape his blood, or the history enclosed within his veins. For centuries, his family had been involved in medicine, specifically the study of blood itself. And for years, Charles had been strategically formulating ways to make their business model an example for other plasma collectors to follow. Day after day he had meticulously studied and documented historical examples of paid systems that had produced unrivaled quality of product. He sought to design a new kind of plasma center based not on academic speculation or philosophical theories, but systems that had actually worked.

Charles knew that those suffering through unemployment, or employed but living paycheck to paycheck, would almost always exist within the United States. He'd personally benefited significantly from recessions and economic downturns, even a weakened social safety net; but he also believed strongly that the pursuit of profit should not come at the expense of safety. Most of the nonprofits and academics screamed against the idea of paid systems for this very reason. Charles, however, was a realist who understood that the American middle class had collectively rejected the idea of volunteering for plasmapheresis. He also knew that once a donor had been paid for donating, it was almost impossible to switch them back to voluntary systems. Furthermore, the demand for source plasma was so great, American donors weren't even capable of providing all of the necessary supply, paid or unpaid. But those weren't the problems he deemed most important. Instead, Charles wondered what could be done to ensure the highest quality plasma in the marketplace. How could Price Plasma become known for providing the safest raw material to their customers?

He envisioned a plasma center that took talk of morality and benevolence and put them into action by cultivating a community of professional donors treated with the respect, dignity, and care they deserved, by focusing first on their health and then on the plasma they provided, with a small stipend offered to encourage continued participation. Charles envisioned himself becoming an advocate for paid donors, who rarely received credit for their part in a global network of scientists, doctors, and patients. He wanted to educate them on their role, explain why their donations mattered, and share stories with them from real patients whose lives had been changed forever because that one person had taken the time to donate their plasma, which then went on to become a life-saving drug for a previously untreatable condition. He even wanted each donor to receive a text message in real-time when their plasma was used to help someone else, ultimately connecting the Price Plasma donors in Louisiana, Texas, Alabama, and Mississippi with patients across the United States, Canada, Britain, and Europe who all relied on their showing up to serve.

The new Price Plasma would include a medical clinic offering free preventative healthcare to professional donors who volunteered to donate at least four times a month. As soon as a donor became ill with any condition, Price Plasma would know immediately and be able to quarantine their plasma until further tests in the company's fully equipped lab could be completed. An in-house cafeteria serving iron-rich, plant-based foods would also be available to donors on donation days, or when they came into the clinic for routine check-ups and bloodwork. An app on their smartphone would serve as the donor's registration book, containing a completely encrypted record of every donation, payment, health examination, and lab test. Scanning the app would be required for entry to any Price Plasma location, similar to a passport for entering foreign countries. Charles also wanted to offer continuing education programs focused on health, nutrition, and exercise. He believed that if he informed donors on how their plasma was used to make specific products by pharmaceutical companies, and connected them with the recipients of their plasma, the donors would become more disciplined about maintaining optimal health for the patients who relied on them as well as for themselves.

Ultimately he wanted to inspire individual responsibility by giving purpose to those consistently looked down upon as the scum at the very bottom of society's barrel, so that those donors could become as proud of donating as their volunteer counterparts, inspired by being able to help their fellow men and women while simultaneously helping themselves. Their payment would then represent a sign of professionalism for those already known as professionals, albeit tongue-in-cheek. More than anything, he wanted to nurture personal relationships with these donors through the help of highly trained medical personnel in the clinic and collection center. Price Plasma could then become a sort of family united by the common purpose of providing the highest quality blood plasma to the patients who desperately needed that resource to fight against debilitating health conditions. His contract with Blue Lotus had been meant to fund these efforts, and he was weeks away from an initial launch; then the horrible reality of Delilah's deception was dropped into his lap.

Yes, Price Plasma was the name on everyone's lips; but Delilah had sourced even larger quantities of plasma on the cheap from India and China, two darlings of the Valley for affordable manufacturing costs and dirt cheap raw materials. Then she mixed all three sources together to form her precious elixir. Only, plasma wasn't the same as cheap imitation leather or bits of plastic. As a physician, Delilah should have known better. It frightened Charles even more to consider that she didn't. In his opinion, both countries were extremely problematic sources for blood products. India, for instance, had been struggling for decades to establish a voluntary blood system, and while there had been improvements in recent years, the country was known for facing the largest blood supply shortage in the world. Paid systems were illegal and voluntary donations were often in direct opposition to the nation's cultural beliefs, with husbands and wives fearing an adverse affect on fertility and their immune systems. As for the blood being used out of desperation by physicians across that country, in 2008, the international community learned exactly how the supply gaps were being filled.

Throughout the agricultural regions of India, desperate farmers faced with horrible poverty and failed crops appeared to have two options: commit suicide, as thousands of farmers had already done, or get into the blood farming business. Doctors were willing to purchase blood from these dealers, illegally, for the equivalent of $20 or less per pint; but where exactly was this supply coming from? Blood slaves, imprisoned in barns like cattle, "milked" twice weekly until they died, as disease spread round and round. The situation in China was worse. Poor farmers in the Henan province did the exact same thing, only they would pool all whole blood of the same type together, centrifuge the plasma to be sold, then re-infuse the leftover mixture of red cells back into their blood slaves. It was the equivalent of Two Girls, One Cup, HIV-style, and more than 50,000 "donors" contracted the virus. Still, it wasn't until the early 2000s that the Chinese Communist Party even admitted that AIDS had reached their borders during the global epidemic. Who could say that such blood slaves weren't the norm in these countries, even today? Could anyone prove that Delilah's foreign plasma hadn't been harvested by similar farms? The companies mentioned in the source documents had no website, documentation, or credibility. Charles had been trying to lift up the plasma donor to a more respected position in society; but it was highly likely that, in the process, he'd unknowingly gotten into bed with a business that was secretly trying to turn a profit off of modern slavery. The thought alone disgusted him.

After everything his family had been through, Charles did not want to be the one to fail. His grandfather, Edward Price, had served as a surgeon on the battlefields of France during World War One. He had planted the acacia tree outside of their kitchen window to remind himself of the lives he'd saved with Bayliss' gummy solution, a primitive treatment for traumatic shock made from the amber sap of that ancient tree before the miracle of plasma had been discovered. Walter often said that Charles should view that tree as a symbol of their family and the great fortitude of the many physicians and scientists of his bloodline who had sacrificed everything in the name of medical progress one century after the next. He claimed that their struggles would never be for nothing as long as each descendent remembered their dark battles against their own ignorance. "All they ask," Walter told his son, "is that we take what they've learned to create something new." It was a request that Charles had never taken lightly.

Their family tree seemed to have sprung up during the earliest days of Western medicine, in which folk cures and superstitions aligned with the stars and were pulled from the earth by way of herbs, roots, and powders ground from precious stones. For thousands of years, Charles' ancestors had viewed blood as a magical substance to be removed from the body, as dictated by the ever shifting scales of bodily humors, in combination with all other forms of purging. The cut of the lancet, lengthwise into a vein, allowed that dark, spiritual substance to drain out into measuring bowls, so to balance those mysterious energies once more. Then there were cups used to form blisters meant to be pierced by that sharpened blade, and shimmering leeches fished out of ponds with bare feet so to drain pooled blood from odd and complex places. In this way, rivers of blood were spilt, for within a world of ignorance and illness, removing that life-force was the only element doctors could control. And so they bled, and they bled, until their patients bled to death.

Then physicians began to ponder the virtues of *adding* blood to a patient by sharing it between husband and wife, or changing

their personalities with the injection of that vital essence collected
from dog, lamb, or calf. Through this infancy of thought, transfusions were first attempted with hollow reeds and quills attached
to salvaged bladders now filled with animal blood, all injected
into the poor and sick who lived in wretched filth. Soon reeds and
quills became silver tubes and cylinders joined by newly manufac-
tured sacks; still patients reacted to this pioneering medicine with
furious fevers and urine turned rancid and black. Doctors hoped
to cure the pox and leprosy, even madness and tumultuous mar-
riages; but so many patients died from these transfusions that the
governments of Europe, in combination with the then all-pow-
erful Catholic Church, chose to forbid the procedure for more
than one hundred and fifty years. It wasn't until the start of World
War One that blood transfusions once more gained traction, with
Edward Price himself serving as a pioneer in the field.

At the time, transfusions were coarse and crude. In order
to transfer any amount of blood from one patient to another,
Edward had been forced to cut down into the arms of both, dis-
sect the necessary veins, then connect the two patients together
with rubber tubing, while each individual remained close enough
to feel the other breathe. The procedure could last for well over
two hours with blood constantly clotting in the tube. There was
no way to measure amounts or maintain the flow from one patient to another, while many died and others lost use of their
arms. Yet wounded soldiers were carried into the medical tents
day in and day out. There was never enough time, there was never
enough morphine, and there was never enough blood to replenish
all that had been lost, while a great number of Edward's patients
succumbed to the haunting pallor of their traumatic shock.

Day after day, Edward would walk the length of their make-
shift hospital to find patients in recovery, young doctors, and even
strangers who might be willing to part with some of their blood,
often in exchange for money. At the time, no one in those tents
knew of blood types, even though the reality of distinct groups to

be named A, B, AB, and O had recently been discovered by a man named Landsteiner who worked in Vienna. No one in the tent had heard of his research, as news traveled so very slowly, causing fatal mismatches of blood types to continue, despite the knowledge being available to prevent it. Then glass bottles of freshly acquired blood quickly cultivated bacteria through contact with air, dwindling supplies of acacia gum hardly worked at all to prevent traumatic shock, and the wounds were unlike anything Edward had ever seen before. His humble civilian knowledge of medicine was completely inadequate in the face of mustard gas, barbed wire, and the violent carnage of horrific wounds filled with shrapnel and mud. Young boys would be brought to the overcrowded medical tents from those gray battlefields screaming in pain as their life-force fled the scene. There was rot between their toes, panic in their eyes, and metal thrust into their flesh. They begged anyone and everyone to help them, save them, fix them. Edward would frantically try to sew their mangled tissues back together; but like a twisted game of Russian roulette, each soldier's survival depended purely on fate, whether they made it to the medical tent or not. For within a world reduced to violence and death, deep within those trenches painted with the rotten stench of wasted blood and charred by the heat of lead, ignorance was the greatest killer of all.

According to the stories Charles had heard all of his life, his grandfather had remained haunted by those memories of the medical tent, and feared those same screaming boys he had failed to save would eventually be replaced by his sons during the next World War, and they were. His eldest, Michael, was very badly wounded on the battlefields of France and received a transfusion with blood of the wrong type, causing a reaction that, in combination with his injuries, led to his untimely death. Edward's second son, Nathanial, then received a yellow fever vaccine tainted with hepatitis while stationed at Camp Polk. The injection would affect over thirty thousand soldiers in all; Nathanial was one of sixty-two who died, long before he could ever step foot on European soil. Then Edward's third son, Ethan, often described as the most gentle and friendly of his brothers, was captured by the Japanese. He disappeared among rumors of medical experiments and freeze-dried plague bombs, never to be seen again, a mere one of thousands thought to have been killed in the name of such "research." But Edward's youngest son Walter never left the United States. Instead, through various strings that Edward madly pulled in his capacity as a recently elected Louisiana senator, his most temperamental son was sent to New York City to work with government teams shipping blood plasma to the troops overseas. As a result, Walter was the family's sole survivor of that conflict, hardened by the wisdom won through the great sacrifice and tragedy of his family's history—something he never let Charles forget.

His father often shared stories from the birth of the plasma industry, which emerged through necessity during World War Two. At the time, each nation sought a competitive advantage not just with their weapons but through medical innovation. The crude techniques of Edward's day quickly evolved from dissections of veins to the use of slender needles, while clots in bottles were prevented with a few measly drops of sodium citrate, as early voluntary blood donor networks were organized by British allies and financed with tin foil collections redeemed for cash. Across the world, entire governments were collapsing, yet the women of each nation fought to supply their struggling medical establishments with fresh blood in the hopes of saving the lives of their husbands, brothers, lovers, and sons. In London alone, the women not only donated blood but drove that chilled substance from collection depots to hospitals in need during the nightly bombings of the Blitz, dodging explosions, crumbling buildings, and gas lines ablaze, all while wearing their pearls. As for Walter, he knew that American women could not send whole blood to support these efforts. Red cells could only survive for roughly forty days outside of the body, while platelets would begin to self-destruct within a week. The only way Americans could send much needed biological assistance to their troops and Allies overseas was through plasma, which could be freeze-dried, frozen, or delivered as heat-treated albumin to help medics and surgeons alike treat burns, crush injuries, fractures, and shock across the war theaters of Europe and the Pacific.

Working with government teams, Walter ensured that whole blood donations were quickly transported to industrial laboratories across the United States where that dark substance could be cracked into three separate parts: the heavy red cells which sunk to the bottom, the thick buffy coat of white cells in the middle, and the precious amber-colored plasma that hovered near the top. It was like magic to Walter, unlocking hidden secrets that his ancestors had struggled for centuries to comprehend. He watched in awe as the future began to unfold before his very eyes, starting with those three components of human blood. That's how Price Plasma was born, as an idea in the mind of a young man riding the train to a laboratory, clutching an ice chest filled with blood. Every choice made by their ancestors had brought him to that very moment, that very decision, just as Charles was being brought to the precipice of a new struggle, which would determine everything moving forward.

For fifty-five years, up until the day he died, Charles' father had collected plasma. He'd made many mistakes over the course of that period, such as collecting from prisoners at the Louisiana State Penitentiary known as Angola, where hepatitis B was practically guaranteed due to dirty needles, homemade tattoos, intravenous drugs, and unprotected sex. Thankfully, he'd ended his contract with Angola right at the beginning of the AIDS epidemic; but even then, it was too late. The silver lining, Charles supposed, was that Walter had married Eleanor, an expert on hepatitis who'd often shared her scientific knowledge with her husband so that he might recognize red flags when they arose. She died from a postpartum hemorrhage about a decade before the first few cases of HIV in hemophiliacs; but during their brief marriage Charles' mother had always warned Walter that if hepatitis B was in the blood supply, there would always be the risk of something else. When they'd first met, she'd been working at Stanford University alongside Dr. Judith Pool, who would go on to discover cryoprecipitate. That discovery would then lead to the creation of Factor VIII, a miracle drug that would end up killing half of the American hemophilia population through tainted plasma. But even in the face of his own unbearable grief at the loss of his wife and daughter, as well as the chaos of a global epidemic, Walter continued to do everything in his power to right the wrongs of the past by supplying the highest quality plasma available for the patients who relied upon it, to continue moving forward in the face of cutthroat competition, and to carry the guilt of never being able to do enough. And now it was Charles' turn, and he felt horribly unprepared to take it.

Charles looked around the empty house as he stood in the foyer near his home office, smoking the remnants of his cigar. The presence of the dead always seemed to demand acknowledgment within their old Antebellum home. Hallways were decorated with their browning portraits, their notes were scribbled in pencil and ink on the yellowing pages of aging books, and Charles had once found his father's name carved into the baseboard of the narrow closet beneath the stairs, along with the names of his uncles. These ghosts seemed to haunt the place, dancing in the dust hovering above the crystal chandeliers in luminescent particles, and hiding behind the heavy folds of the custom curtains, running their invisible fingers along the faded burgundy tassels affixed to the walls. Their collective sorrow softly sighed in faint repose within the ornate swirls of gilded frames, painfully creaked between the boards of the oak and pine floors, and remained forever trapped by the copper screens on the sleeping porches. Charles had felt their presence all his life, and he feared, more than anything, that he had failed them. At the same time, he felt compelled to move forward in spite of these fears. He may not have been able to save his marriage, or to win the love and respect of Natalie; but he could damn well fix this problem and save his business. He had to do it; there was no other choice.

Now that Vivienne's article had been published and read by millions, hundreds of early adopters, who had fought to be the first to use the Blue Lotus elixir, had come forward to announce their illness, previously unaware of the true connection between that golden medicine and their current state. Family members spoke on behalf of those attached to ventilators, or still fighting for their lives in an intensive care unit. Charles wondered how many of those early users had traveled to other nations before the appearance of symptoms? How many people had made contact with them, had sex with them, shook hands with them? How many innocent bystanders had been infected? How long was the true lag time between initial infection and the appearance of symptoms? How many would die? What was this strange new virus being mixed in those vats and then injected into the veins of Delilah's eager customers? Was it a mutated form of HIV come to finish what it had started all those years ago? Charles didn't know the answer.

He retrieved his violin from the cabinet beside his desk, opened the case, then removed the instrument from its silk bag. As he tightened his bow then applied rosin to the hair, a memory caught his attention. Roughly a month ago, he'd been in Katy, Texas at the Pin Oak Charity Horse Show with Natalie and Pine Grove Farms. Renée Benoît had found a new prospect horse for Natalie to consider, if she wanted to move up from the Children's Jumper division to the Junior/Amateur Owner. The gelding was white with red freckles, although grey was the appropriate description, and he was well over 17 hands high, or six feet tall at the withers. Renée had volunteered to ride him in a fun Friday night class called a Gambler's Choice as a way to test him out, and see if he was safe for a rider of Natalie's caliber. Of course, Natalie had run off with David, leaving Renée and Charles alone before the course walk. He'd seen plenty of riders over the years walk the course before a class, but he'd never done it himself. He was surprised when Renée invited him to join her in the arena.

She quickly taught him how to walk the distance between jumps to measure the number of strides, then how to check the footing, the cups holding the rails, and the timers measuring each round. Charles felt that Renée was the only person who thought the way he did. She could tell him everything about the history of show jumping, often arguing that the way she sat in the saddle had been informed by everything and everyone that had come before, from Genghis Khan to the Italian cavalry officers of the late 1800s. "Nothing is by accident," she said. "And every time I sit in the saddle, I'm continuing that history of war, struggles for power, the techniques for speed and agility in combat. I'm paying homage to the decisions made centuries ago, constantly seeking the balance needed to move forward, while somehow remaining perfectly in the moment." She explained that every show jumping class was a test of skill, but the Gambler's Choice was the greatest test of communication between horse and rider. She compared it to life. "It's unpredictable. You know there are certain obstacles you'll have to overcome, but you have no idea in what order they'll pop up, or how many times you'll have to face them. Anything can happen in a Gambler's, just as anything can happen in life. The clock is always ticking down and you never realize you're out of time until the buzzer sounds."

She laughed at all the young riders glued to the piece of paper outlining the obstacles on course and how many points each was worth. Usually riders would be studying a course designed by someone else; but in this class, and only this class, they got to decide where to go, with the goal being to collect as many points as possible within the time allowed. "I bet they're all scheming fancy plans," she said. "They're wondering how they can hit the big numbers as many times as possible. Fifty points, one hundred, one-twenty. Watch. They're gonna knock those jumps down first, freak the fuck out, have no clue what to do, then run their horse off their feet trying to do *something*. That's why they're gonna lose." Renée then pulled Charles aside and whispered to him, real close. He could smell her winter fresh breath. "Here's the secret," she said, each word making the hairs on his neck stand up. "This isn't a test of best course designer. It's a test of how well you face the unexpected. And you can't face the unexpected if there's friction or confusion, which is exactly what happens when you get attached to your fancy plans. You need to flow, in perfect sync with the rhythm of the horse—with the momentum you build on course. You need to flow straight, forward, and calm, because ignorance is actually a form of freedom."

"Ignorance?" he asked.

"Look, I have no idea what's gonna happen once I enter that arena. I'm ignorant of the future. But if I get attached to a certain plan in my head—you know, my big idea of how things are *supposed* to go—when they *don't* go that way, I'll lose because I'll be too busy fighting to keep my plan alive. I won't see what's right in front of me. On the other hand, if I know I don't know anything, I'll flow with the opportunities as they present themselves, and maintaining that flow is the only way to win."

Charles watched from the stands as she entered the arena on that massive white horse, which was pawing at the sand before the buzzer sounded. Once she picked up the canter, it was as if she had tapped into something ancient and true. He felt his heart match the rhythm of that big white horse, same as Renée was in sync with it. He felt a longing for something long forgotten, a connection he had once had. As he watched Renée flow with that animal, he wondered why he couldn't flow with himself. What was stopping him? The answer was his mind, and all of its elaborate plans. That's why he seemed to be pulled in two directions, as if two voices were fighting within him, above him, around him. He felt pulled apart by his heart and mind, which were not in sync. They were hardly even talking. Standing in the middle of his home office, which had once been his mother's music room, Charles took a moment to ground himself with that realization, to find his center; then he began to tune his instrument, flipping through a mental catalogue of possible compositions, starting with A, then D, G, and E. When he tuned to that highest pitch, he recognized what he most wanted to play in this moment.

The public now saw him as a devil, and so a devil he would be. He would face his shadow by playing the Devil's Trill. Supposedly given to Giuseppe Tartini in a dream, this sonata had been offered to the composer in exchange for his soul. Tartini claimed that he had given the devil his instrument, then listened as that supernatural being played a beautiful piece the artist admitted that he could "never have conceived in his boldest flights of fancy." Alas, once he awoke, the musician never could play the piece exactly as the devil had done, probably because he had lost his soul. Now Charles wondered if such a piece could be used to win one's soul back. He hoped that, maybe, if he could play this composition with brutal honesty, not once shying away from what might arise in him, he could finally balance his mind and heart to dance with his fears, the same way Renée had merged with that white horse. He yearned to merge with his own soul, hoping that the rhythm of his heart might guide him forward through this mess. Everyone was betting on something; but Charles would bet on that. And so he picked up the instrument, raised his bow, then began to play with such passion, even the devil would blush.

THEODORE WALSH WAS CONTEMPLATING the nature of truth as the airplane began its descent towards O'Hare International Airport. He'd been considering the subject ever since he'd met with Antoine Bergeron at his antique shop in the French Quarter. For most of his life, Theo had been in pursuit of pure objective truth, believing that there was an absolute that could be dug up, uncovered, and known. Every play he'd ever written had served this quest for such elusive knowledge, yet every play he'd ever written had fallen short of that goal, with feedback from audience members, fellow playwrights, and even critics only serving to make him feel even more alone, if not horribly misunderstood. In time, he realized that no one saw the world exactly the way that he did; but he refused to give up trying to find that common ground where communication might actually occur.

That's what had led him to study Ludwig Wittgenstein and his writings on the failures of language. The philosopher had argued that miscommunications happen because the words we use to communicate form "pictures of facts" within our minds, and the same words might form two completely different pictures within the minds of two different people. In fact, such mismatches were almost guaranteed to happen. That's why Theo wondered if words could ever express truth, or even represent it. Words seemed to focus more on trading pictures as an exchange, not the exploration of a shared reality. Perhaps that's why Theo had never been able to fully communicate what was on his mind. It was almost impossible to articulate the exact picture he wished to share, or for another person to piece it back together themselves. He wondered if humans had ever really communicated *anything* at all, limited as they were within those harsh constraints of language.

As he approached Chicago, Theo began to wonder if that's why he had stayed with Sarah for so long. It didn't make much sense to anyone else. His parents never thought they'd last more than a few months, his siblings questioned his choices, his friends were even confused. Time and time again he'd been reassured that their relationship would never work and that it would never last. Maybe that's why they had stayed together for nearly twenty years—to prove everyone else wrong. No, that wasn't the truth, although it may very well have been a part of it. For the longest time, he felt that Sarah was the only person who "got him." She seemed to understand his motives and struggles, his obsessions with work, his desire to be accepted and loved unconditionally. There were good memories shared between them, sure. There were romantic kisses in the rain, countless nights tangled together, inside jokes and funny stories created during late night Chicago adventures. They'd shared their dreams over cocktails, big ideas in a haze of marijuana smoke, and passionate love backstage, in bed and in the shower. His vocal cords retained the muscle memory of every long conversation, every quirky debate, every heated discussion. Hours upon hours of his life had been spent communicating with Sarah, over every little thing; but had any *real* communication taken place at all? How many times had he told her that things needed to change? How many times had he encouraged her to pursue her purpose, her own goals, her hidden dreams? How many times had he begged her to stand on her own two feet instead of leaning so heavily on him?

Loving Sarah felt like karma. He felt bound to her, in some spiritual sense, as if he had to pay an extremely heavy karmic debt from the past in order to gain his freedom. He never felt that he could just *leave*. There were too many strings holding him to her, even if they were always superficial. That was another truth he'd had to face: that he'd never seen his relationship clearly. Had he fallen in love with Sarah, *the actual human being*, or had he created a version of her in his mind that met his standards of perfection? If Theo were being truly honest with himself, he'd admit that he had fallen in love with Sarah's potential, an imaginary version of her that she could one day become, with his help. As a result, he'd ignored every deviation from that perfect image, only to reaffirm his fantasy and secretly pray that any glitch would eventually dissolve. Whoever Sarah really was, he was more than happy to ignore, if not judge. That's why every time his fantasy version of her would fade, chip, or peel away, revealing the ugly truth underneath, he'd comfort himself with thinking, "if she only changed this or that, or stopped doing *that one thing*, then I could love her, then she would be *perfect*."

That was a dangerous word: *perfect*. Even his pursuit of a "perfect" truth was flawed. He had naively believed that if he could capture that absolute truth, if he could express it, if he could make an audience *feel* it, then he might be able to change the world in his own little way. That had been his intention with every play he'd ever written, including *Blood and Sand*. However, trying to change the world, to make it "perfect," seemed to be the most dangerous dream of all. Sarah and Greyson's sabotaging his work had made him see that more clearly. They'd helped him see his own fictional identity, forged through suffering and sacrifice to represent his model of perfection, as a writer, playwright, and partner. He'd turned writing into a form of activism, telling himself that "people like us do things like this," while morphing his own Self to fit that identity, no matter what pieces had to be cut along the way. He had lost himself in that perfect image of himself, the one handcrafted by his ego, and really, that's all he'd ever wanted to do—to lose himself in his relationship, in his work, in his message to the world. He'd gone chasing after utopia, only to have it crash down in his face with a Sally Rand-style feather fan dance to Lesley Gore's *You Don't Own Me*, with Sarah wearing a barely-there pink negligée a few shades lighter than cotton candy pink. Had *he* driven her to this?

Theo had often criticized people in search of utopia. He'd listen to their conversations as they outlined their own visions for a perfect world, then he'd mock them: "*Our* utopia must be this way, not that. *Our* utopia is only for those who believe this, not that. *Our* utopia is nonviolent, except when violence serves our needs. *Our* utopia is for freedom and diversity of thought, until you disagree." He accused them of expecting everyone to shape-shift to meet their own ever evolving criteria while ignoring the countless subcultures that exist in this world and online, as well as the infinite possibilities for self-expression. He'd waxed poetic about the true path of creative expression, through which any culture could be kept alive by living it, embracing it, *feeling it* to create something mutated, adapted, and infused by a different perspective. He'd consistently preached tolerance in the name of exploration, curiosity, and expansion; but the second someone mutated his work or deviated from *his* ideal, he lashed out with brutal intensity. It wasn't that Sarah had cheated on him. No, Theo was angry at her for expressing her own creativity, for changing his work to fit a different ideal, for threatening *his* vision of utopia. That's why he was a hypocrite.

In his mind, society was painting its own picture, envisioning itself as its own ideal, all while closing the gates on creativity and self-expression. At first the gatekeepers would whisper, "If you only changed a little, if you just believed this instead of that, if you would simply apologize for x, y, or z...*then* society could be peaceful, *then* nature could be protected, *then* everyone could live in utopia." But society can't control culture, or its many mutations, deviations, and changes—mostly because not everyone has the same vision of utopia, not even the people trying to build it! That disconnect, that uncertainty, that was why those whispers quickly turned into the screams of violent mobs trying to force their own "pictures of facts" down your throat. *That's why the best day for utopia is the day the idea is formed,* Theo had thought in perfect smugness. *It's all downhill from there.* He didn't realize that he was guilty of that exact same behavior in his own relationship, with his own idea of perfection, with his own dreams of a better world for himself and others. No, for the past week he'd been stewing in his anger, contemplating every possible retort, devising every possible insult for Sarah and Greyson, planning his next selfish move to prove everyone wrong. His wounded ego was more than eager to point the finger of blame at every other person, anyone but himself.

It was so easy to get wrapped up in those energies. For almost his entire life, Theo had been trained *not* to trust his own instincts, but to submit to the beautiful vision of utopia created by society, starting with the promise of a stable future sold to him by school. Theo was older now, and wiser, especially since he now knew that the theory behind public school was only about a hundred years old, originally designed to get kids out of the workforce so that adults could claim their low-wage jobs. The entire purpose of school was to take those same kids and transform them into even more compliant workers for the future. That was their goal: make kids like Theo obedient, compliant, and productive workers for the larger industrial system. It wasn't designed to *educate*; school was designed to *train*, right on down to the multiple-choice test—a test for "lower order thinking for the lower orders," as said by the guy who'd invented them. Meant to be a temporary solution to a supposedly temporary problem, those tests caught on because employers didn't need their future workers to *think*, they just needed them to know enough to maintain a certain level of productivity over the course of their lifecycle. That's why multiple-choice became *the* test for the masses, those sheep in search of a cage. Theo didn't like cages. He wanted to be free to roam.

That's why he'd run off to join the world of theatre in the first place. Theo told himself that he didn't need safety or stability; he wanted connection. Let the others fight for the dwindling spots available for careers that come with instructions. He didn't need a babysitter to learn or pursue the things he was passionate about. After finishing school, he decided that he was done with being stuck in that mold, depending on someone else to tell him what to do, how to do it, and when it was due. He thought those cages offered nothing more than a beautiful lie: if you do what you're told, raise your hand, and play by the rules, you'll be rewarded with security, stability, and success. That's why everyone was fighting to stay within those stone walls of mediocrity; they thought it was *safe* there. And when they got pushed out, or when they weren't picked, after doing everything they'd ever been told to do, they were the first ones to scream foul—that it was sexism, racism, or some other kind of -ism that hadn't been invented yet.

All Theo saw was a crumbling industrial world in which society pressured the young to spend more and more time *in school*, while school only became more expensive, without ever instructing them on how to think critically, communicate, or hold two conflicting ideas within their increasingly narrow worldview. That's why they were all screaming at each other, without anyone ever communicating a goddamn thing. All they'd ever been trained to do was choose between A, B, or C. They didn't know how to think for themselves, construct an argument, or even look beyond what was being offered. School was nothing more than rote memorization and playing games with chance. And if someone lost that gamble, betting that they were good enough to become an assistant, administrator, adjunct professor or part-time critic safely stowed within a bureaucratic institution, they'd succumb to the most debilitating form of dread, all because they had let their creativity and passion atrophy in the name of obedience to school. That's why they screamed so loudly—they couldn't handle the fact that everything they'd been told was a lie. They'd rather watch the world burn than find their true purpose in life, knowing it's so much easier to destroy with a match than to create something new. And even if they pulled the world to its knees, at least they were still being productive with some sort of busy work—the only thing they'd ever been trained to do.

But, according to Theo, that same industrial model wasn't limited to public school or university. It had taken over the theatre world too. He couldn't remember how many times Sarah had pushed for him to go to graduate school, to get an MFA in Playwriting, if only to seem more "legitimate." He'd considered it, over and over again, against his better judgment. Then one by one he saw his friends go off to get a higher degree in the arts only to lose their gifts entirely, if not give up on their passions in the name of *maybe* getting a teaching job a little further down the road. Most of them weren't even writing anymore, almost all of them were hundreds of thousands of dollars in debt, and when they did produce a play, it was academic drivel. He'd even stopped seeing plays at the major theatres because the only playwrights they seemed to take a chance on these days had résumés that boasted names like Harvard, Oxford, and Yale. Half the time he'd bail by intermission, frustrated if not bored. Becoming an artist wasn't something you could do in a classroom, where it was "safe." True art could only be discovered on the tight wire between life and death. And in his mind, theatre is not and never should be a *safe* space. Still, that's what people sought and the world provided: machines, cages, and comfort.

Yes, he thought, *school trains you for cages, so the world makes cages, luring you in with the idea of fame, notoriety, and engagement.* Theo assumed that's why the actresses he knew dreamed of becoming Hollywood stars, or even the *assistants* to stars. They seemed to think that Hollywood was freedom from the machine, when really Hollywood is just a more grotesque form of that exact same system. That's why Rita Hayworth was known as the "most obedient girl in Hollywood," he thought. She may have played a femme fatale on screen, but behind the scenes, she did exactly what she was told, even when it came to sleeping with certain men in positions of power. That poor woman hated everything about Hollywood, but never could escape it. She didn't know how to be disobedient, or creative for her own sake. Theo could see those same traits in so many actresses throughout Chicago, and they weren't even being controlled by promises of fame and fortune. No, they were being controlled by the promise of a *possibility* at an *opportunity* to *maybe* grasp fame and fortune, using Chicago's reputation as a process city to launch their ascent to New York or L.A.

As a result, so many of those theatres were fueled by people desperate to participate for free, with artistic directors knowing that those poor actors and actresses, determined to escape the industrial machines school had prepared them for, were more than happy to hand over their remaining morsels of dignity for a chance at anything else. Of course, that eagerness also attracted people who wanted to take advantage of their desperation, to prey on those weakened emotional states. That's why so many theatres depended on abuse. If you spoke up against it, you were pushed back into line by being told that you were bitter for not "making it" because you weren't "good enough." In essence, they said the same thing as the industrial world: you're just jealous because you weren't *obedient* enough to get picked. That's why men and women alike were selling themselves part and parcel, all for the opportunity to shine for fifteen minutes. Theo had no doubt it was even worse in Hollywood, especially today, where the desperate are glad to sell someone their body and soul for a mere glimmer of fame, if not a hint of validation.

And what was fame anyway? *Celebrity?* The first celebrity had been a woman named Florence Lawrence, who hardly anyone remembers. In 1910, she starred in a film called *The Broken Oath*, which nobody talks about anymore. To stir interest, the producer of that film, Carl Laemmle, told the press that his leading lady had suddenly been killed in a tragic trolley car accident. The next day, Americans were devastated by the news, whether they knew who Florence Lawrence was or not. After letting the public stew in that emotional syrup, Laemmle then ran a series of advertisements proclaiming that Florence wasn't dead after all. That she'd survived, and could soon be seen in a new moving picture coming to a cinema near you! Like clockwork, everyone started talking about *The Broken Oath*, while Florence began a tour of public appearances complete with in-depth interviews. The film did extraordinarily well at the box office, giving Carl a high return on his investment and ultimately creating the idea of the celebrity—a new marketing tool that could be used to connect audiences to the people behind the characters. Even if the film was terrible, the audience wouldn't care—they'd already be emotionally invested in the people behind the mask, feeling "in the know" for being able to repeat the narratives as offered.

It was the same for Rita Hayworth, who became famous because of another lie, this time on the cover of *Look* magazine. The article broadcast her to the American public as the "best dressed off-screen actress in Hollywood," mentioning that she'd been recognized by the Fashion Couturiers' Association of America—a fake organization that Rita's husband at the time had made up. In fact, Eddie Judson, that scoundrel she'd married at the age of eighteen, had created the entire wardrobe lie, then ran around Los Angeles to borrow all of the necessary pieces for the photoshoot—anything to fill the aspiring actress' empty closet and impress potential fans. Rita didn't become a celebrity because she was a brilliant performer, but because of a completely fabricated story. No wonder she suffered from imposter syndrome!

In Theo's mind, people wanted to believe these stories because they wanted to be celebrities themselves, anything to justify the sacrifices they had made while chasing their "perfect" dreams, those supposedly hidden truths just waiting to be uncovered for all the world to see. He knew firsthand how people roll into their dreamworlds with empty pockets and a hunger to belong, not knowing anything about themselves, only to get paid peanuts, sleep in shitty apartments with shitty furniture, work crazy hours, survive on Red Bull or weed, and never really live. Eventually, the struggle wears them down until they're no longer pursuing deeply meaningful work but anything that might get them out of the rat race and into the comfort of stable success. They tell themselves that then, and only then, will they *truly* get to live—once they've validated their sacrifices. That's why those kinds of people tend to be overly emotional onstage and off, Theo thought. They repress their feelings completely, thinking they can deal with them some other day, once they've achieved something, once they've reached some sort of benchmark; but the more they suppress what they feel, the more toxic they become. Then they get all wrapped up in various addictions or sexual misadventures while trying to climb their way out of the hole they've been digging from the beginning. They refuse to be truly intimate with others, even the audience, because they know exactly how much shit is bubbling just under the surface. That's why they become violent, angry, cruel and intolerant, he thought, why they explode on people or tell them who they need to be or what they should be doing. It's because of decades of built-up tension resting on a hairline trigger. Theo could see now that he was guilty of this too.

All along, he'd been trying to escape the machine he'd been trained for by school; but he got sucked into the apparatus anyway, like Charlie Chaplin, gobbled up by the mechanism only to tighten the goddamn bolts. That's why he refused to feel, why he had remained so painfully detached from Sarah and the rest of the world. It wasn't because he didn't want to; it was because he thought he couldn't afford to. He'd gotten himself stuck in a machine, as a machine, and machines can't feel. Those sacrifices made at the altar of impossible goals had simply formed another cage, designed specifically to separate human beings from their own intuition, making them the most dangerous animals of all, because once they lost the ability to follow their own instincts, they became much more likely to take direction from someone else, someone eager to take advantage of all those sacrifices and goals. And more often than not, that someone else only has *their* best interests in mind.

Theo believed that's why society itself had become a house of cards, with each desperate individual leaning on another, instead of standing up straight, beaming with their own inner light. Theo thought we'd all become sad little embers of human beings, thrown in a pile of trash, praying for society's approval. "Am I small enough yet? Am I victim enough yet? Have I sacrificed enough yet to be considered worthy of society's love and acceptance?" When it came to his relationship with Sarah, and the work he'd produced over the past twenty years, he knew he'd fallen into that exact same trap. The realization made him remember some strange story about zebras, how researchers were having a hard time telling one zebra apart from another. They started putting a pink mark on their haunches or a tag on their ears, anything to make a certain zebra distinctive from the herd. The problem was, the lions killed that distinct zebra every single time. Turns out, the zebra's stripes weren't meant to help them blend into their environment. All along that pattern was camouflage designed to help the weak hide among the strong. School had taken an entire ark of animals and morphed them all into zebras. That's why criticism was now considered violence. If you criticized a member of the herd, you might as well have marked them with a bright pink line across their ass, telling the lions where to hit, as more and more extremely niche subject matters were given power in academia, as more pigeon-holes were created, as more super narrow lenses were affixed, as more smoke and mirrors were applied through language. If you were to criticize one, you were considered to have criticized all, putting the entire herd at risk. That's why lions had to be destroyed by society—that culture of strength, critical thinking, and fortitude threatened the delicate zebras hiding behind their mismatched stripes, even the zebras guilty of fraud.

All along Theo had considered himself a lion, when really he was just another zebra, desperately trying to blend into a certain herd. That's why he didn't trust himself. That's why his ego was so badly bruised by Sarah's edits to his play. Her chiffon negligée might as well have been a can of spray paint, marking him so that he'd soon be devoured by fear.

That was partly why he was so fascinated with the woman sitting beside him on the plane. She reminded him of Tinker Bell in her short skirt and tank top, her light brown hair pulled back into a bun with a few loose pieces playfully flirting with her lashes. He found himself staring into her almond eyes as they chatted over the course of the past hour and a half. They had both been reading the same article in the *Journal*, the second story written by Vivienne Shaw on Delilah Russell, this time outlining the virtues of Price Plasma and pushing for greater transparency regarding the source of additional plasma purchased by the startup. If Theo had learned anything from this Blue Lotus debacle, it was that the public doesn't care about the source of things, as long as there's pretty packaging and mention of the final product in fancy magazines. Actually, he'd already learned that lesson by exploring the dark underbelly of the chocolate industry, where children between the ages of six and ten are often forced into slavery all to harvest cacao on the Ivory Coast. It was the same problem with plasma. Consumers simply don't care about the raw material, any more than they care about the sweatshops manufacturing their sneakers. He didn't really know whose fault it was; maybe it was a world at fault. And maybe it stemmed from the fact that we don't really want to know who it is that we are, underneath all the bullshit. We don't want to get to the root of things, but that's exactly where we need to go.

It was the mischievous pixie sitting beside him who suggested that every human being was actually an equation unto themselves, and that, if x equated to their true purpose, most of them had no idea how to go about solving for it. "That's why most people balance themselves against the expectations of others," she said. "They desire the *appearance* of equality, of likeness, of similarity, because that's way easier to justify than true individual expression, especially if their true identity conflicts with society's vision of what's right or wrong." She argued that people confused their identities with their résumés for that very reason, believing that they're nothing more than whatever's written on that piece of paper. "A résumé just marks all the ways you've bought into a larger system," she claimed. "And the more invested you are, the easier you can be controlled by fear, specifically the fear of being reduced to a blank page."

"That's also the fear of change," Theo offered.

"When change is the only way to discover who you really are," she said.

Countless people on the flight were wearing an assortment of paper and fabric masks. There were lots of suspicious glances and muffled coughs throughout the cabin. Everyone onboard seemed wary of everyone else, whispering about plague and infection, while he and this strange woman discussed what they imagined was the root cause of the problem. The pixie, with her fingernails bitten down to nubs, insisted that women were partly to blame. "It seems like everyone loves to preach that women should be in positions of power," she said, "that female presidents and CEOs would solve all the world's problems, but then they don't want to hold those women accountable for their actions, past or present. If someone like Delilah does something wrong, then it must be because men made her do it, *right?* Those white, power-hungry men eager to destroy a powerful goddess. It's such a grotesque Victorian mindset," she argued. "That women, due to their outstanding virtue, are incapable of doing horrible, selfish things. As if only men could be guilty of fraud or violence, murder or plague. Really, if women are *that* weak, if they can't face the consequences of their actions, then they should never be put in charge of anything."

Of course neither of them knew of any truly weak women. The pixie argued that such weakness was simply a smokescreen, precisely to hide the nefarious actions most women didn't want the world to see. "No puppet master wants you to see the strings," she laughed. "That would ruin the whole thing!" As for all the women furious with Vivienne Shaw and screaming to defend Delilah, the pixie—revealing that she was *itching* for a cigarette—started to rant out of frustration. "Look, there are thousands of cases of this pneumonia, this *AIDS-like pathogen* if you will, with more than half in California. It was already burning its way through China and India; but no one was paying attention. The source documents published online detail Delilah's deception from start to finish, but no one is reading those. Instead, they're screaming that those documents were stolen and should not be read, or that they're fake and should not be trusted, or, my personal favorite, altered by men who were intimidated by Delilah's success. HA!

"I'll tell you exactly what it is. Think of it this way: you're a woman and you look up to Delilah. You think she's the *perfect* woman, someone you can *really* admire. If it turns out she's a fraud, that perfect image is shattered. Or maybe you see yourself as a Delilah. That if she could do it, so could you! All of a sudden, if someone dares criticize Delilah, you think they're criticizing *you!* You think people are telling *you* that you can't do it either. That *you're a failure.* Those people telling you that Delilah is a fraud, what they're really doing is telling you that you were *stupid.* They're saying you were wrong. And those kinds of egos can't handle being wrong. The very idea of being seen as stupid— *publicly*—ensnares them in a blind rage. That's why those women are screaming like some hellhounds in defense of Delilah, and why the men who hope to sleep with those women are screaming too. They're not defending Delilah, *the human being*, a person they've never actually met. No, those screams you hear are the death throes of their own wounded egos—because they never really wanted the truth, or for true female leaders willing to take a chance and face the consequences if they failed. No! They just want celebrities, all because they'd rather be a celebrity themselves than dare to do something significant."

"Follow the stars," Theo said. "And hope to become a star yourself."

"That's the problem with stolen documents, I guess. I thought they'd make people face the truth—acknowledge some sort of truth—but they don't want that. If they have to face the truth about the people they admire, then they have to face the truth about themselves. They could make the time to dig, to read, to investigate; but they don't even take the time to explore themselves, let alone the truth about other people. Instead they give that power over to the pundits, politicians, and celebrities of the world who tell them what to think, how to feel, and why they'll *never be safe*, unless they get in line."

She was right, Theo thought. The public were absorbed by machines as machines. If they didn't have the time to *feel*, they certainly didn't have the time to do the groundwork and research required to fully grasp the scale of any situation. That's why they depended on the media. Yes, they were giving away their power; but in order to question authority, you have to be willing to first question your own. That was another problem. How many people are truly brave enough to ask themselves provocative questions like, is what I believe actually true? Am I seeing the full reality of a situation? Or is it all an illusion? The public had been trained since kindergarten to accept things as they are, to be lectured at and patronized by a professional class. Theo couldn't villainize them; but maybe he could show them a better way.

Of course, he didn't believe the journalists could get us there, not even Vivienne Shaw. In his mind, that was the job of the artists, the poets, and the true storytellers—not the masters of spin. True artists couldn't be trained to be obedient because they only answer to their hearts and souls, viewing culture through their higher selves and forever gathering the skills needed to nurture their own innate gifts. Unfortunately, those people had been driven underground over the years. They'd been punched in the gut by harsh judgments, slapped in the face by the critical and proud, and pushed aside for the world of empty entertainment; but Theo believed that those were the people who would inevitably rise up from the ashes of this chaos. Those were the people we needed—not the trained, maybe not even the educated. He felt we need the *inspired:* the creatives, the people who do not destroy, do not tear down, do not burn the cities, but plant gardens, write songs, and lift up society through a mosaic of cultures. They were the outsiders, but also the linchpins. The pundits and broadcasters couldn't see because nowadays they were practically paid to be blind; but a poet doesn't work for money, they work only in the service of their higher calling. And because they follow that calling, it's their vision that forms the horizon. Theo wanted to follow that too. He wanted to write something worthy of that. And so he decided to surrender, with newfound clarity and ease. He would surrender to the Universe and let everything unfold in its own timing.

Perhaps that's why he was so drawn to the woman who'd been sitting beside him for this flight. They'd covered everything from the difference between art and entertainment, the genocide of the Acadians, the hypocrisy of Silicon Valley, the abuse of Cajun children who spoke French in school, resulting in their being labeled as "stupid" by their Anglo peers, to the current problems facing biotechnology—all within the first thirty minutes of knowing each other. He liked her vision for utopia, using her own bloodline as an example. She said that the Acadians had been brutally removed from their beloved home known fondly as Acadie, only for it to be renamed as Nova Scotia after they'd been expelled. The British wanted their abundant farmlands for themselves, so they separated Acadian men and women onto separate ships and scattered them across the world. Only a small number made it to New Orleans. From there, they reestablished themselves in Acadiana, mutating, adapting, and deviating to survive. They weren't French, they were no longer Acadian, but they had become something else entirely, separated from the land they loved, the land that had made them a people.

"I believe that Acadie lives on in our hearts," she said. "That we always have the freedom to embody that culture, to live that way, to work our asses off then sing and dance and play. We're always free to be who we are, no matter what anyone says. And really, the Cajuns will always be a bunch of scrappy motherfuckers, because we know how to survive no matter what, precisely because we've struggled and suffered so much. We'll eat frickin' swamp rats if we have to. It's *that* history—*that* fight to endure— *that's* what's in our blood, no matter where we go or who we become. We live on in Acadie, which will never, ever die because we'll just keep on living, completely wild and free."

Theo couldn't help but agree with her vision for a future enriched by the past. And through their winding conversation, he came to the sudden realization that utopia must exist within each individual, for each individual, based on their own personal stories, if not history. He finally understood that we can no more demand another person fit that vision than we can carve it into the material world with our words, those imperfectly shared "pictures of facts." He now believed that all of us must find our own vision for tomorrow, based on our own dreams and passions, our own personal paths. We must shape it with our hopes, desires, and love; but we can't push it on someone else, or force them into a cage, for there are an infinite number of possibilities and none are right or wrong. And for every Delilah Russell, capable of such disastrous fraud, there is always her equal counterpart—the other side of the energy field, that opposite polarity. If Delilah didn't exist, then neither would he or she. For every darkness, there is light. For every fear, there is hope. And for every individual, there is a true counterpart. As Theo looked at the woman beside him, gazing out of the window with childlike wonder as they flew past the Chicago skyline, his heart beat frantically with a strange rec-ognition. He felt that he finally understood the love that Antoine Bergeron had described, the connection experienced with a shared language and a physical attraction that only brings you closer to understanding yourself. Theo felt closer to an ancient truth, if not a familiar yearning and desire to remember to know and be known. He couldn't let the moment pass, but he felt that he had nothing to offer her. Still, he was moved to move.

"Have dinner with me," he said.

"*Tonight?* I have a job interview in the morning, remember?"

"I won't keep you out late."

"You say that now," she laughed.

"Well, would you prefer I share the end of the story before it's written?"

"Never," she said with a mischievous smirk. "I'm having far too much fun."

"So am I," he replied, locking his gaze with hers.

"I'm Whitney, by the way. Whitney Dugas."

"Theodore," he said, extending his hand to meet hers. "But you can call me Theo."

He was in love with this woman, exactly as she was, and while he didn't understand it, he somehow knew *that* was the goddamn truth.

MADELEINE LEBLANC WAS LISTENING to Jonathan and Margot Karl as they shared their ideas, confident that the pair of copywriters were the right fit for her project. Producing an effective gene therapy treatment for Hemophilia Type A had been a lifelong dream of hers, ever since the idea of healing genetic disorders had first captured her attention at the age of eleven. She had spent almost her entire life studying molecular genetics, marveling at the beauty of the double helix known as DNA, and deciphering the code to what she believed was the Book of Life. She was forty years old, her company was on the verge of gaining FDA approval for the experimental treatment she had spent the past five years perfecting, and life as she knew it was about to change.

She now understood how every event in her life had brought her to this very moment, sitting with these writers, discussing the future of not only medicine but the blood disorder that had come to define her existence. Yet she found herself unable to truly focus within that white room with dry erase boards for walls. She could smell hints of the chemical stench from Expo markers, see the black grunge left over from their smudges, and sense shadows of past messages hidden within the surface of each board; but her mind was somewhere else. Jonathan and Margot were taking turns speaking, sharing their strategy for the materials requested. She knew their words and ideas were important. Still her mind's eye remained forever fixed on an image, an image she had known from the age of ten. It was the image of an egg suspended in the air, with a silver serpent wrapped around its girth four times. Her aunt had informed her that it was called the "cosmic egg."

"What does it mean?" she had asked as a child, still clutching her mermaid doll in one hand, the only toy she'd brought with her from home.

"Oh, I can't tell you what it means," her aunt said. "Words couldn't possibly describe it. But if you look at a symbol long enough, it begins to speak to you. If your heart and mind are open, that symbol will share its secrets in a language all its own."

Why now was that image burning into her brain? Why today, of all days? Madeleine didn't know. Thirty years had come and gone without that symbol ever once demanding her full attention. And now, in this very important meeting, it seemed to be all she could think about.

"Just to be clear," Jonathan interrupted, "these materials will be sent to decision makers at insurance companies and government programs?"

"That's correct," she replied.

"And what do you hope to achieve? What's the goal?" Margot asked.

"We need their support to cover patient costs. My solution is designed to be a one-time treatment for hemophilia A; however, that single infusion of gene therapy could cost several million dollars. It's not a question of profit, but expense. Granted, prices are already inflated for clotting factor, and your average patient requires hundreds of thousands of dollars worth of factor each year; but our product is an experimental treatment and this is new technology. Compare it to the early computer. Those models were extremely expensive. Hardly anyone could own one. Today, almost everyone has one in their pocket. Our hope is that, with time, our costs will decrease and these treatments will become more affordable. And personally, I want to ensure that anyone interested in this gene therapy will be able to afford it; but until that time comes, our patients need financial support, whether through government assistance or their health insurance policies. And those decision makers have a huge knowledge gap. They're not familiar with the science, the technology, or the need. Your job is to educate them so that they can make an informed decision and see a clear ROI."

There was that snake again, as if separate from the egg, slithering through her mind. Its undulating energy seemed to navigate the folds of her brain, its forked tongue tickling certain regions until they glowed with an understanding she could not describe. It almost danced on the very spirals of her DNA, as if it had been coiled in each and every cell, waiting for this moment to rise. Its shining skin seemed to glide against her own with a familiar chill. It was smooth, never blinking, always knowing; but what did it mean?

"And you've included everything in this file drop?" Margot asked.

"Yes. We've included more than eight hundred pages of source material. Everything from the results of our phase I/II trials to our current phase III study, as well as background material on hemophilia, the tainted blood era, data on Factor VIII, and other areas of opportunity, such problems with recombinant Factor VIII. You can consider that to be a sort of GMO product. It's still clotting factor, but it's not sourced from humans, or blood plasma to be more specific. Part of the struggle with recombinant factor are inhibitors, meaning patients need a great deal more factor to stop a bleed because their body is actively working against the medicine. It's viewed as a foreign body, an attack to their immune system; and our therapy could, theoretically, make that an experience of the past. I think that's a major selling point to be honest, especially for patients."

"Should we lean on these documents then," Jonathan asked, "to create educational material for patients?"

"*Absolutely.* We're offering to infuse trillions of genetically engineered viruses into their bloodstream so that healthy genes can be carried into their livers. This is scary stuff, which is why I want complete transparency with patients. For as long as I can remember, hemophiliacs have been regarded as the 'shut up and die' community, and a lack of transparency has always been part of the problem. That's exactly why there's so much distrust in the community, even though these patients and pharmaceutical firms ultimately rely on one another. I want to regain that trust, step by step. Don't hide, sugarcoat, or over exaggerate *anything*. Give it to them square between the eyes. Be honest, but write to them as you would to one another. Share this information as you would with someone you love."

"We can do that," Margot reassured her.

"And we just hired a new member of our team this morning," Jonathan added. "Her name is Whitney Dugas. She's a biochemist. She'll be helping us with this project, making sure that we fully understand the science and communicate it accurately."

"*Dugas?* Where's she from?"

"Louisiana, I believe; but she's been working in Silicon Valley for years," Margot offered.

"Fantastic!" Madeleine looked at her watch. "It seems like we're in agreement here. Take the next thirty days to go through the material and flesh out some rough copy. Just play with it! We're not in a rush. I'd rather take things slowly and do them correctly than speed up and make a mistake. But I'm afraid, if I'm going to make it to the Monadnock before a certain store closes, I need to be heading out."

Jonathan looked at his watch. "Oh dear, yes. I need to be heading that way as well. I can walk with you if you'd like."

"Great! I love to walk and talk."

She was listening, she was present, but Madeleine felt entranced by that ancient symbol on prominent display in her aunt's cluttered shotgun house just outside the French Quarter. Now her focus was on the egg—a golden egg—as delicate as a womb, full of shimmering energy. She was pregnant. She knew that might be the connection. If

she hadn't dreamt of the image the night before, well before going
to the doctor this morning, she might very well have believed that
symbol represented just that: birth, renewal, fertility. But something
told her that the meaning extended even further than that. That egg
was not her womb, that yolk was not her embryo, that energy was
not another's. It was something inside of her, something deeper than
the news, which she planned to share with Gabriel tonight, once he
joined her in Chicago for the weekend. She was excited, but she was
also afraid to be excited. It was early, she was older, so much could
happen, and she was a carrier of hemophilia.

She said her farewells to Margot and shook her hand, then
joined Jonathan in the elevator. "I think this is going to be a fun
project," he said.

"I hope so," Madeleine smiled. "This treatment could change
the lives of so many hemophiliacs, even those with extremely rare
variations of the disorder, those missing factors I, II, and IV. I'm
not exaggerating when I say that it's been a *very* long road to get
us here, to this exact point in time with science, so I hope you and
Margot can both appreciate the gravity of the situation."

"Oh, of course. We completely understand. You don't mind
my walking with you, do you?"

"No, not at all. I'm glad to have the company."

The elevator doors opened. The pair walked through Merchandise Mart, past the food court, and out onto the street. The weather
was cold but not frigid, the streets wet but not icy. The river was
slowly rippling with the passing of boats and water taxis as the pair
crossed over the trembling bridge, which was jolting with the traffic.

"Tell me," Jonathan started. "What drew you to genetics? To
working in a lab? Margot and I read an article about you, about how
you lost your parents, and we were very sorry to hear about that; but
aren't there other ways to help hemophiliacs? Why gene therapy?"

As they walked down Wells Street, then turned onto Lake Street,
Madeleine tried to express herself. "When you're working on a bit
of copy, like a tagline or a slogan, what's that experience like?"

"Oh, well, Margot and I go over every phrase we can think of. We fill entire notebooks with ideas, phrases, idioms, words. We gather crumbs until we can piece them together into bread. It's all about the turn of phrase, the memory that certain words elicit in the brain. We're playing with pictures, ethereal snapshots, all formed in the customer's mind. What best paints that picture? How can we speak the right words to conjure a certain response? It's an arduous task; but that's our craft. We study everything that has been to create something that could be. That's how we make art."

"I look at my work in the lab the same way," Madeleine said. "Everything is white, almost like a canvas. And my paint is the code. Every time I hold my brush, so to speak, I think, what is it that makes us who we are? What are we? What is 'I?' That concept of I? If i is an imaginary number in math, then couldn't 'I the person' also be imaginary? Who are we? And why? Every time I enter the lab, I get to dig deeper into those questions, and that's really what drew me there to begin with."

"Because of your father?"

"Yes, but also because of myself. I may have started out trying to determine why my father died the way he did; but eventually, that desire turned into a need to understand why I am the way that I am. Am I the code as it's written, with my fate predetermined by my genes? Or am I more than the code itself?"

"Code being your genome?"

"Yes, but are you a compilation of your traits, of the genetic material passed on through your bloodlines, of the beads strung along a chromosome's string? Or is there something larger than that to consider?"

Madeleine could almost feel the serpent tightening its grip around the girth of that egg; however, the egg's shell seemed to be cracking from the inside out—as if the snake had merely been holding that shell together, incubating it until this very moment. And as she walked beside Jonathan, she could almost feel the release of tension as the exterior gave way to the pressure, revealing the slightest hint of warmth from an interior light.

"Are we more than just a map of code, you mean?"

"Yes," Madeleine answered. "Are we more than just hemophiliacs, or someone with Huntington's disease, diabetes or cancer? Are we defined by our mutations, our malfunctions, our disorders, or are those merely obstacles we must overcome to discover our true natures? Are they the wounds that open doors to self-discovery? Or do they define our true Self?"

"What could be more true than the code of our making?" Jonathan asked. "And if we *can* change it, or improve it, why shouldn't we?"

"Honestly, I can't answer that, and I know I should be able to; but we are only at the very beginning of this research, and we're blind to where we're going, or what the consequences might be as we edit the human genome. If you study the history of hemophilia treatments, or even the blood industry as a whole, you'll see that it took a very long time to get us from cutting veins for bloodletting to the highly sophisticated blood and plasma systems we have today—and we still don't even know what blood types are for! In comparison to the study of blood, the study of genetics is still in its infancy. We're practically fishing for leeches in ponds at this point. We're still at the dawn of genetic discovery, even with gene therapy; but our capabilities are evolving so much faster than any other evolution in science. And I think the study of technology helps us better understand how we can approach this rapid progression of innovation, to see how we can move at that speed but more carefully. If we've learned anything over the past hundred years, it's that there can be very serious consequences to acting out of ignorance and pride."

"Like Waterfall versus Agile methodologies? I think I read that somewhere in your notes today."

"Exactly. Look at those methods," she said. "Before, with Waterfall, it was a slow, arduous process to create a product, get it to mar-

ket, and see how well it did with consumers. You had one shot to
get it right or wrong. Today, we have Agile methods, in which you
create a minimal viable product, test it, learn from it, then start
the process all over again. I see Agile more and more within the
world of genetics, specifically in how scientists demand a 'pause'
when a new technology is discovered, like CRISPR. During the
early days of the blood industry, the only pause was demanded
by the Church, and governments followed suit. There were never
considerations for the true consequences of science or innovation;
today we feel that dark shadow, constantly. For every positive,
there is a negative. For every glimmer of light, there is a shadow.
The same is true for gene therapy. Really, for anything within the
field of genetics."

"Such as eugenics," Jonathan offered.

"For every transformative development, I think there are stages.
At first, your curiosity is piqued. You pursue a new science, no
matter the cost. You merely want to solve a problem; but in trying to solve a problem, you may cause even more. We're human.
We're imperfect. We see the world imperfectly. And even though
we create amazing technologies, we don't know what the true consequences of those technologies will be, even when it comes to
me and my product. We are all wandering in the dark, unsure of
what's to come; but it's the only way forward, so we go. We wade
through the muck, we fight with dragons, and hopefully we come
out stronger in the end. But you don't know the ending when you
begin. You don't know how your best intentions can be morphed
into evils you never imagined. So yes, I'm an artist when it comes
to genetic code. I see the beauty in it. But beauty can be distorted,
good intentions can be twisted, and miracles can carry the kiss
of death. We're all playing with fire, whether we realize it or not."

They turned the corner onto Dearborn Street, right along
the edges of the Goodman Theatre. Jonathan stopped dead in
his tracks. There was a man with reddish hair, sprinkled with
shades of grey, holding a woman in a white dress as a photog-

rapher snapped a photograph. When the strange couple noticed Jonathan standing on the corner, they froze in time, then smiled.

"J.J.," squealed the blonde woman with large breasts pouring out of her white dress. "My God, I can't remember the last time I saw you!"

"Hello Sarah," Jonathan offered. "Greyson," he acknowledged through his teeth. "What are you two doing? Creating promos for a new play?"

"No, silly," Sarah said, playfully slapping Jonathan's arm. "We just got married!"

"Married?"

"Not even an hour ago," Greyson boasted.

Madeleine held back and watched, studying the groom's blue eyes and the bride's eager hands.

"J.J., aren't you happy for me?" Sarah pouted, holding onto Greyson like a stranded sailor hangs from a buoy. "You look like you've seen a ghost!"

"Yes, yes! I'm sorry," he recovered. "Of course I'm very happy for you both. Congratulations!"

"I don't think he means it," Greyson suggested, practically elbowing his new bride in the ribs before taking a swig from a leather-bound flask.

"No," Sarah whined, stomping her foot playfully, causing her cleavage to jiggle. "I don't think he does. I don't think he means it at all."

"Oh, of course I do! I'm just *surprised*."

"Everyone will be surprised," Sarah shrieked with delight. "I can't wait to see the looks on their faces, although I hope it's a better look than the one you're giving me now."

"I'm sorry," Jonathan laughed. "I'm actually heading to see my sister. This is all just…unexpected. Last I heard you were with Theo."

"Oh, she's here? Tell Tilly I said hello," Sarah laughed, throwing her left hand out in front of him. "And be sure to tell her all about my ring!"

"Will do," Jonathan said, holding Sarah's dainty hand in his own, studying the two-carat diamond. "I'll be sure to tell her."

"We best be going," Greyson nudged, after downing the last of his flask. "The party awaits!"

"Greyson's entire theatre company is throwing us a party. You're more than welcome to come, and bring along your...I'm sorry, who are you?"

"A client," Jonathan offered before Madeleine could speak. "We're on our way to another meeting, and I'm afraid we're running late. Thank you for the invitation, but of course we must decline. Congratulations though! You both look very happy." His words seemed forced, if not fake. Sarah kissed him on the cheek regardless, leaving behind a bright red smudge, then Greyson shook his hand before they both scurried down the street, like two rats hurrying to a feast.

All the while, Madeline envisioned more cracks in the image of her mind, of the egg and the serpent intertwined. For the first time, she began to see the world through a strange filter, as if everything were being bathed in the warm hues of red as the sun began to descend towards its home in the West. It was as if her eyes were closed and all she could see were the sun's rays highlighting the blood vessels within her eyelids. The shell was cracking, the serpent tightening, her eyes covered by the sensation of red, as those two fools danced down the street, barely giving her a second glance as they passed her by, cackling together, arm in arm. "Friends of yours?" she asked.

"I hardly even know anymore. Acquaintances from a past life, perhaps. I don't know how I'll tell my sister about this."

They continued down the road, making small talk about genetics and human pride. "I've got a great example for you," Madeleine offered. "About twenty years ago, there was this famous bet in the field of genetics. At this point, scientists had cracked the code of the human genome, at least in terms of identifying certain sequences, but we still didn't know how to really read the thing. It was like being handed the Rosetta Stone after it had been translated, but still being unable to decipher the true meaning of hieroglyphics. We knew what certain things meant, but we didn't understand why they meant that, or if a deeper meaning or purpose existed. And at the root of all this, we had no idea how many genes human beings actually have within that code. Now, we knew that a fly has around thirteen thousand and a poplar tree, like a cottonwood, can have around forty-five thousand. So how many does a human have? We seem far more complex than flies and poplar trees, right? We build cities and create symphonies and write novels. Shouldn't we have more genes? So this bet takes place. Scientists pretty much created a range between thirty thousand and one hundred and fifty thousand genes. Guess who won the bet?"

"The person who bet on the cottonwood number? Forty-five thousand?"

"Nope. No one won."

"What? Why? Is it more than one hundred and fifty thousand?"

"Nope. We have around twenty to twenty-five thousand genes. An onion has more than we do!"

"And nobody bet that low?"

"Human pride. We always think we're far more complex and sophisticated than we actually are, that we're superior to a fruit fly, when really we're all connected. We're all written with the same code, and the complexity or simplicity of that code doesn't make you superior to any other life-form, whether we like it or not."

Madeleine could see the Monadnock building in all of its red glory along the horizon. "You know," Jonathan started. "My brother-in-law was involved with this Blue Lotus mess."

"I knew you'd worked with Delilah in the past…"

"Yes, but my brother-in-law, Charles, his company was involved with it too. I think that's why my sister's here."

"Your brother-in-law is Charles Price?"

"Yeah, he's been married to my sister for the past twenty years."

"I get the feeling you don't like Charles very much."

"It's not that," Jonathan said. "It's just, he's a very difficult man to know."

"I've only met him twice," Madeleine began. "And yes, he's very quiet. A very solemn man, honestly. Although I've known him to be very funny too, once he gets a few drinks in him anyway."

"Now funny is not a word I would use to describe Charles."

"No, no. With the right people, he can be very funny. In a boyish way. But I do admire him. Price Plasma is the most well-respected company of that size. He has a stellar reputation. I don't think what's happening to him right now is very fair, but Charles is great at solving problems for other people. Maybe this time he'll be pushed to solve his own."

"I heard he's cooperating with the CDC."

"I'm sure he is," Madeleine stated. "If he's not in the wrong, what does he have to lose?"

"We didn't know what Delilah was up to," he offered. "I had my suspicions, but we had no idea. That's why we hired a scientist, so we won't make the same mistakes again."

Madeleine laughed. "Military generals and former Secretaries of State had no idea what she was up to! Of course you didn't! But don't worry, my treatment is legit. I've worked far too hard for far too long for it to be a fake. Let's just finish strong, okay?"

"Agreed," Jonathan said as they reached the Monadnock. "I promise, you won't be disappointed with the work."

"I have no doubt," she said, extending her hand. "Looking forward to what you create."

They shook on it, then he went into Intelligentsia to meet his sister and niece for coffee, while Madeleine walked into Optimo to collect her husband's hat. As she entered the crisp, clean and modern environment, surrounded by glass yet nestled in seductive light, where John Lee Hooker's rich, buttery voice reached her ears in soothing tones, Madeleine felt calm for the first time all day. Through the large windows shared between the hat shop and Intelligentsia, she could see Jonathan hugging a woman who looked very similar to him—short brown hair, large golden eyes, the same mouth. Her daughter, on the other hand, stood out with strawberry blonde hair and china-blue eyes, with an appearance very much like the man they'd encountered at the Goodman. On the table rested a large Nikon camera. Mother and daughter had been fighting when Jonathan arrived, and didn't show any signs of stopping.

"Hi Madeleine," Alexander said from behind the counter. "You're here for Gabriel's hat?"

"Yes sir," she replied, studying the Panama hat display on the table, trying not to get caught as she carefully observed the copywriter with his extended family.

"One minute," Alexander offered, before heading into the back room to locate the proper hat box and tag.

Madeleine's fingers explored the loose bits of toquilla palm protruding from the rough hat bodies that had been carefully arranged along the back table. Under the light, the yellow straw seemed to glisten with a golden hue. It could take months, if not years, for a weaver in Ecuador to form the tight patterns of a Montecristi Superfino, the finest straw hat in the world. Madeleine's fingertips lightly grazed the rough textures of those unfinished hat bodies while her eyes remained fixed on the café. She watched as Jonathan's niece rose from the table, tossed her empty paper cup into the trash bin, then crossed the hallway between the café and hat shop. She hardly noticed Madeleine at first. Instead, the girl's eyes were transfixed on the elaborate display of beaver fur felt and straw hats lined up along metal wires or resting their brims along wooden spokes. They resembled jewels in a jewelry box, calling their future owners forth through the vibrations of their colors and felts. As the girl reached the counter, so did Alexander, carrying the black oval hatbox that belonged to Gabriel. "Here we go," he said. "As good as new."

Gabriel had his hats re-blocked and cleaned at least once a year. Madeleine was collecting his own Superfino, which had been shipped to Chicago in advance of their trip. As Alexander handed it to her from across the counter, she admired the hat's faint patina which had been acquired over time. The brown leather sweat band on the interior had been replaced with a new one, freshly branded with the golden Optimo logo as well as Gabriel's monogram. Madeleine carefully studied the delicate hat while keeping her focus on the teenager circling her like a shark, as the girl glanced at the various sizes and shapes of hats.

"What's that one?" the girl asked, pointing to a pale pink lightweight fur felt directly across from her.

"That's the Mia," Alexander responded. "Our first hat designed specifically for women." He collected the delicate creation then handed it to her over the counter. Immediately, the girl plopped it onto her head, then turned to greet the standing mirror, adjusting her long strawberry blonde locks as she admired her reflection.

"Are you happy with the work?" Alexander asked Madeleine, as they both kept half their attention on the strange girl in the mirror.

"Yes, very. I'm sure Gabriel will be delighted with it. Thank you."

"I don't like the shape of this one," the girl announced. "Do you have another one? Another one in pink with a different shape?" She carelessly tossed the hat back onto the counter.

"Actually, this one changes shape," Alexander replied, reaching inside the hat to return it to an open crown while smoothing out any dimples in the felt. "It's a lightweight material, so it's very responsive to touch. You can shape it to any style you'd like."

"May I?" Madeleine asked, reaching for the hat.

The girl nodded as Alexander handed the pale pink hat to Madeleine, then watched as she presented the styles. "I have one of these," Madeleine offered. "It's my favorite, probably because it can become any hat, and I can roll it up when I travel." With a slide and a pinch, Madeleine changed the hat's shape from an open crown to a center crease then a front pinch fedora, all by manipulating the material fold by fold. From there, she transformed the hat's crown into a three-knuckle diamond, then a teardrop, before ending with a porkpie shape by wiping the fold into a circle in the crown while applying pressure underneath. The teenager watched with detached curiosity. When Madeleine handed over the pink porkpie she asked, "You're Charles Price's daughter, aren't you?"

"Ha!" the girl jibed. "Depends on who you ask."

"I've only met your father a few times, but I know he'll get through this scandal unscathed."

"If you're going to lecture me about my photographs, trust me," the girl replied. "I've already gotten an earful and then some, so save your breath."

"Photographs?"

"Yeah, in the *Journal*."

"Natalie *Rose?*"

The girl smiled, then feigned a curtsey. "That's me."

Madeleine looked across the glass windows into the café. Natalie's mother was now sobbing on Jonathan's shoulder as he tried in vain to comfort her. He seemed angry. Furious even. "Maybe you should go check on your mother," she suggested.

"There's nothing I can do for her," Natalie replied, still admiring herself with the pink porkpie in the mirror. "I've just gotta bide my time until I can go to college and then I'm done. I'll never have to see that bitch again."

Madeleine was taken aback by that response. The words seemed to bounce off the mirror and hit her in the face. She wanted to pull that hat off of Natalie's head, then drag the girl back to her mother, anything to knock some sense into her; but she knew that would accomplish nothing except make a scene. It wouldn't change that girl's mind about anything. Madeleine looked at her watch instead. "Have it your way," she said, then took a seat at the counter.

Natalie was still admiring herself in the mirror when Madeleine decided to speak again. She hoped the teenager might listen, but she also knew that if she spoke directly to her, she never would. "How's it going with your play, Alexander? Have you finished writing it?"

"The sock comedy?"

"Yes," she laughed. "I'd love to see it."

"Oh no," he said. "I'm taking a break with it. Looking for something else to write about in the meantime, maybe a drama. Heard any good stories lately?"

Madeleine pretended to think it over, drumming her fingertips along the matte black counter. "Did I ever tell you about what happened to my parents?"

"No, I can't say that I've heard that one."

"Well, my dad had a very mild case of hemophilia."

"The blood disorder?"

"Yeah. His blood couldn't clot properly. It's caused by a genetic mutation, which is something my company is working to fix. The funny thing is, hemophilia didn't run in my family at all. His was a random mutation, just a fluke really. It happens, rarely. Of course, most people with hemophilia have more severe issues. They have to inject clotting factor on a regular basis to prevent or stop bleeds, especially as children, because growth causes micro-tears in tissue. But my dad had never used clotting factor in his life. His case was so very mild, he'd never needed it. And even then, he was a nerd, so he pretty much lived in the library. He never played sports or anything. And my grandfather's fishing business had gone under, so he'd never had to do any hard labor either. His dream was to become a lawyer, so all he really did was study, and paper cuts aren't really as big of a threat to hemophiliacs as some might think. He was the first person in his family to go to college, let alone law school, but he did it. Graduated top of his class. That's where he met my mother." Madeleine softly touched the string of pearls around her neck, which was the only possession of her mother's that she had kept. "They were both lawyers, completely dedicated to reason and logic. That's all I really remember about them."

"What happened?" Alexander asked, half-watching Natalie as she continued to experiment with different folds in the crown of the hat. They were the only three people in the store, and

Madeleine could sense that Natalie was listening, even if she pretended otherwise.

"Well, when I was two, my dad got in a car accident. It was nothing, really. A fender bender. He was able to drive away from the scene. Didn't have a scratch on him; but he knew he had this blood disorder, and that an internal bleed could kill him if he wasn't careful, so he went to the emergency room, told them he had a mild case of hemophilia A, and that he needed treatment. He'd never been treated before. He didn't even know what the treatment was! But the nurse came back with a single shot of Factor VIII, a new miracle drug for his condition. He got the shot, they put a Band-aid over the spot, and he went home. No big deal, right?"

Madeleine could feel Natalie slowly inching closer and closer to the seat beside her. She could sense the girl's attention hovering over her, as she slowly reeled her in. "A few weeks later," Madeleine continued, "he started feeling sort of sluggish, like he had the flu. He didn't think it was anything serious, so he went on with his life, built his practice, continued trying to have another child with my mom to give me a brother or sister. Nothing in our life changed, yet everything was changing. Over time, he really started to deteriorate; then my mother started getting sick too. It seemed like the flu, but it wasn't the flu. They knew it wasn't, and that recognition was scary for them, and really, became scary for me because I could sense the shift happening. I could feel the tension between them. They knew something was deeply wrong, but they didn't quite know what. Fast forward four years. I'm six years old. It's about a week after my birthday. My father finally convinced his doctor to test him for a new type of disease, which he shouldn't have even been at risk for. The results came back. My father had AIDS. He'd been infected by that single dose of Factor VIII, which had been made from tainted blood plasma sourced from America's prisons."

"Oh my God," Alexander said. "That's terrible. What about your mother?"

"She tested positive too. So my aunt, who's always been a bit of a whack job, moved in with us. She'd trained to be a nurse, but hated it, so she quit and 'fell off the deep end,' as she likes to say. Two years later, my father died. It was horrible to watch him slowly fade into nothing, along with his struggles against pneumonia, wasting syndrome, candida esophagitis, and all sorts of other words my memory has since blocked out. My mother watched him disintegrate into nothing, then she faded too. About a year later, she died. Same condition, same horrible end. My aunt was the only person I had left, because at nine years old, I'd been made an orphan by a single virus in a single injection given to my father because of a random genetic mutation threatened by a fender bender. Talk about life not being fair, right?"

"Jesus. So you moved in with your aunt?"

"My aunt decided she wanted to move to New Orleans, leave Halifax behind, start over. So we packed my things and off we went. We left the only home I'd ever known, a house built on a bedrock of logic and reason, for a townhouse right outside of the French Quarter, filled to the brim with symbols of myth and magic. Like hats. My aunt loves hats. She says they're reflections of personality, a map of human expression shaped over many cultures in time. Take the Mia, for instance. Every shape, every fold, every crease has a history behind it, a reason for being. One leads to the next, and then the next. It's a shapeshifting form of creativity through which we can explore everything we are, and everyone we'd like to become. It's a sort of mirror, helping us understand that we do the exact same thing with invisible masks, personas, attitudes. We're always changing, shifting, shaping ourselves into the next version of who we'd like to be, with the history of those changes hidden in the folds."

Madeleine turned and looked at Natalie, who was now standing beside her, holding the pale pink hat in her hands, covering her torso, completely enchanted by the siren's call. "My dear, your family is the only constant. You are going to change and shift so many times throughout your life. You will wander through hell in the process, if not absolute darkness where you don't know up from down. You will experience tragedy, heartache, pain, and suffering. We all do, in our own time, in our own way. But how you respond to those events will define you, and ultimately shape you into whoever you're meant to be. And your mother, crying in that café right now, she may never be able to help you through that process; but she's here now, and she probably needs your help to get through this moment in time. I'm not saying she's perfect. She may very well be the villain in your story. I have no idea. But she might also hold the key to the questions you're asking, deep within yourself. And right now, she's alive. You can ask her those questions. You can get answers, and fight to know the truth. Then you can use that information to solve the mystery of yourself. So go, listen to her, find the source of her pain, because it might very well be the source of your own. Then choose to love her, for all her faults, because you will never fully understand yourself until you've made peace with where you've come from, and why. But, then again, that's a choice only you can make."

With that, Madeleine nodded to Alexander, grabbed the cord of her husband's hat box, and exited the store. A rush of chilled air hit her face, and with it, she finally understood that image of the golden egg seemingly threatened by a silver snake. The revelation had come to her in code, as if the answer had been inscribed within the inner spirals of her Self all along. Of course, Madeleine knew herself on many levels, starting with the very genes she had worked so diligently to understand. Her parents might have died long ago, but they were still with her, even today. Their own dominant and recessive traits had been discreetly stored and shared, just as her own genes, seamlessly mixed with Gabriel's, were being given to their own child, now growing in her womb. Through these genetic blueprints, they were all connected, generation after generation, spinning round and round, forever evolving within each revolution.

Yet their family was but a drop in the ocean of genetic material, a mere sequence within a realm of infinite possibilities. For Madeleine knew that all life on Earth was written in the very same script, encoded in amino acids to produce all the proteins in the world. The very same genetic code encrypted within her DNA was the universal code of life itself. Still, having studied that code, she knew that she was no more her script as written than a patient with severe hemophilia A was their blood disorder. She was not a disorder, a mutation, or any trivial spelling mistake. She was not the patterns within her own genome, or the diseases for which she was at risk because of the way certain letters had been written across more than three billion DNA pairs. She was not her genetic inheritance any more than her unborn child should be defined by his or hers. No one should be defined by their chromosomes, she thought. No one should be judged by the supposed flaws within their code.

After all, every life form shares these chemical phrases, yet each and every thing is completely unique at the very same time. If all were uniform, we would not have the diversity of life, or the creativity born of such differences. Yes, she could edit this code. She could cut, copy and paste as one might edit a manuscript; but this particular manuscript was far more complex than any one human being could possibly comprehend entirely. This was the Book of Life and Death itself, written in a living language humanity had only just begun to translate. Such a language could be altered, damaged, even wielded over mankind. It could provide the greatest enlightenment and understanding, or shackle all life to the disgusting pursuits of better and best, often in the name of material gains. That sort of engineering could have the power to destroy all life, if driven by ignorance, ambition, and greed. Such actions could do more than trigger a plague—they might spark a genetic holocaust.

These were dangers Madeleine did not take lightly. She knew all too well the urge for dissolution, to break something into fragments only to sort, separate, and discard. She had faced the genetic mutations responsible for hemophilia A with the same single-minded focus. And she knew how easily good intentions could become obsessions, morphing a desire to prevent evil into evil itself. The history of eugenics in the United States was one such example, in which a desire to improve the human race had evolved into legally required sterilizations of more than sixty thousand "unfit" Americans, mostly women. These actions went on to inspire Adolf Hitler's Nazi regime, first with the sterilization of undesirables with "inferior" genes, followed by mass murder. With the speed and precision of modern data processing, in which anyone's genetic profile can be quickly mapped in the name of hyper-personalized treatments, such as the one advertised by Blue Lotus, Madeleine feared what might happen if such detailed information were to fall into the hands of another ignorant extremist, obsessed with purifying mankind to meet their own specifications. She knew that she was not her code, that those struggling were not their disorders or genetic mutations, yet how easy it would be to group others by their "inferior" code or spelling errors. For every advancement, there is danger. For every miracle drug, there are unknowns. For every vial of hope, there exists an ecosystem dependent on trust, whether that trust is warranted or not. And for every gene, there is a window into suffering, with as many opportunities and possibilities as the diversity of life itself.

The history of life could easily be viewed through the lens of this suffering; however, through the lens of transformation, life could be seen as all the more beautiful because of the darkness once imposed upon it. Such trials and tribulations had not destroyed life itself. Instead, periods of pain and struggle had served to make life forms more unique, colorful, and well-defined. Like the many potential folds created within the crown of a lightweight fur felt hat, so too did we all evolve into a plethora of sizes, shapes, colors, smells, and perspectives. We didn't become this way in a flash. Humans, if not all life, had evolved fold by fold, all while remaining linked together by almost identical genetic material. We all changed to suit our environments and needs while remaining forever connected by our code.

Madeleine understood that the entire history of life had been written within her molecular structure; and more importantly, that the embryo growing with her now was actively living that evolution, which spanned a timeline of more than 300 million years. What had started as a single cell had divided again and again, forming fold after fold until its early physical form had taken shape. In these early stages of growth, remnants of past aquatic ancestors had made themselves known through the appearance of gill arches and a tail. Even the head and body of this young fetus resembled those of an embryonic fish. Of course, those same gill arches would eventually shape her baby's lower jaw and middle ear, just as what would become a fin in a fish would actually become her child's hand, as dictated by the signals within the code.

Even the yolk sac in Madeleine's uterus gave a gentle nod to the evolutionary process of life. While empty of nutrients, this sac mirrored those found in eggs—the very eggs laid by our genetic relatives. Even the fluid sac in which her baby was growing shared similarities with the eggs of amphibians, reptiles, and birds. The baby's skin, teeth, and hair also found connections with such creatures, with the differences between them dictated by the many folds in the child's making, each predetermined by certain genes. Her child's ears would be formed by the movement of three tiny bones, differentiating those ears from those of reptiles, which only required one, finding more use for the other two within their powerful jaws. And like the child's fellow mammals, he or she would have hands agile enough to climb and forage. According to certain scripts, the child's eyes might even be able to see a world of color, starting with red, so to pick ripe fruits and feel subliminal messages shared through those rich emotional tones. And even though highly sophisticated, her child's brain would still share a similar architecture with the fish brains that came before. Such was the marvel of genetics.

However, for all this complexity masked by simplicity, that double helix of DNA, coiled within the hearts of every cell, was neither egg nor snake in her vision. It was but a spiral of smoke deep within that egg upon which all physical structures were built. There, encircled by her own animal nature, Madeleine's awareness grew, just as her child's physical form developed within her own. No, she was not that code, even though the code was a part of her. She was something larger than that, larger than the Book of Life. As she turned onto State Street from West Jackson Boulevard, heading back towards the river, it was as if her thoughts had blown smoke onto the web of her own existence, so that she might see its shape more clearly. And as she walked down the bustling street, she focused her attention on her body, her living machine in which the code took form, as if crafted on a spinning wheel.

First she considered her head, that revered seat of reason and logic, along with her delicate face, through which she often channeled emotion or hid her true feelings. She thought of her brown eyes and the way she saw the world. Madeleine observed the many people walking up and down the street, as well as the myriad of faces that rushed past her in quick procession. To her, they were no more than their faces, if not their garments and shopping bags, markers that might express who they were and how they thought. Her ears heard their voices and tones, their language and passion. Her nose could smell perfume, cologne, fried foods, and filthy stench. She licked her lips and felt the air upon them, as her teeth opened and closed, her tongue still spiked like a cat's from being burned by tea at the airport. She could see out as well as she could look in, as her brain processed any and all data; yet Madeleine knew that her Self was not her head any more than those fleeting strangers were their faces.

Madeleine cleared her throat to the scorn of a few around her. She knew their fears of the mysterious respiratory pathogen and rumors of pandemic. She could sense the tension in the air, radiating off of those terrified of the unknown. They did not understand the science nor did they possess the proper language to communicate their suspicions, or the knowledge required to comfort each other's fears. And forced to rely on their sources, each with various agendas, those schools of strangers floated en masse— towards what, they did not know. They simply swam with the current believed to match their ideals, until those ideals dissolved into the growing collections of fading foam, leaving them even more confused. She tuned into the frantic energy surrounding her, covered by a surface of calm. Each stranger's information highway from sensory organs to brain seemed overwhelmed by conflicting data, and as she walked she listened. Highly charged conversations about plasma and politics, transfusions and fraud, life and death, all fluctuated in frequency to match their rapid fire fears and doubts. What was the truth? Who could you trust? And more importantly, how might this all affect *them*? Strangers were talking with their hands, texting with their fingers, and clutching their chests out of the panic eagerly fed to their anxiety with every scroll, glance, and click while stress rumbled in their guts with sickly sour waves of acid nurtured by befuddled dread.

Madeleine could hear the tension in the voices around her, layered with melancholia, defeat, and rage. Such emotions seemed to form blockages within each individual, like concrete walls built to halt the fury of a turbulent sea. The energy was building, surging, threatening to break through those fragile dams of civility, obedience, and calm. Madeleine could sense an impending flood with every careful step she took forward. Still her heart went out to each and every stranger who connected with her through their worried eyes. She wanted to comfort them, to explain that she understood their fears and apprehension, and to guide them towards their own heartbeats, which can offer some solace in times of universal expansion and contraction. Madeleine wished to show them compassion, from the homeless man sleeping on the corner to the exhausted mother of three small children chasing their tiny hands with baby wipes and sanitizer as they grabbed and touched every possible surface within reach. Madeleine wanted to hug the elderly gentleman waiting at the bus stop in a blue mask holding nothing but a battered briefcase and a state of vacancy in his eyes. She wanted to kiss the cheek of the puppeteer trying to bring joy and humor to the street with his humble yet colorful puppet bike. Instead, she focused on her gratitude, now flowing through her body in a figure-eight, following the path of her blood. As she opened her awareness to each stranger, she tried to send them love.

But it was in that moment that Madeleine felt forced to acknowledge the limitations of her physical being. She was not her body, nor the organs operating inside. At forty years old, most of the cells of her making had already been replaced six times or more. Her red blood cells alone, able to live for a mere one hundred and fifteen days, had regenerated nearly one hundred and twenty-seven times. Like the Ship of Theseus, could Madeleine even be considered herself, after all these years? How many versions of herself—physically, mentally, and emotionally—had already lived and died? How much waste had her lymphatic system removed? How many wars had been won by her immune system? How many eggs had been shed before this one had formed life? And how many ethereal seeds of good and evil had she inadvertently planted with her thoughts, words, and actions over time? She did not know. But if she removed her physical body and her genetic code from the equation, then shed her fears, doubts, and confusion, what would remain? If she no longer craved fame and fortune, or ceased to acknowledge her fatigue, if she abandoned her frustrations and surrendered to the flow of life, what might she find? What if she ceased wanting to have more, and instead chose to *be* more? And what if she already was?

Just as evolution was a story of folds, her own personal journey within had been one of unfolding. With each act towards improvement and understanding of her true Self, Madeleine had inadvertently lifted multiple veils of ignorance, as if by traversing a system of planets. The lessons she learned in the icy darkness of Pluto had taught her the laws of transformation and that not all darkness is bad, just as all light is not good. The vibrant blue of Neptune, the very color of the sheath dress she was wearing now beneath her cream wool coat, represented the gifts of inspiration and dreams, even the mysterious symbols that can be used for good or evil. The pale blue of Uranus, on the other hand, represented a surrender to the Divine, and respect for the power of the unexpected. Then Saturn revealed the virtues of hard work and sacrifice, while Jupiter taught her the ways of luck. In possession of such understanding, Mars then lifted the veil on her life's purpose and taught her to fight for what she believed in, while Venus had taught her to love— not just Gabriel or herself, but all of life's many forms. Then Mercury helped her speak her truth. Finally, the Moon had taught her how to embrace change, as all creation moves in cycles and phases. But it was the Sun that held her attention now—that brightest yolk within the egg, held upside down within a serpent's grasp.

The shell of that egg existed so that she might learn her own lessons in her own way. Within that shell, she had been tested, again and again, not to learn new knowledge but to shed the veils of untruth blocking her from the Self. And in this world of spirit, this ocean of living code, she had evolved from her lower Self to her higher, same as her future child was growing now. But Madeleine's flesh and blood had reached its peak, and she had been both Maiden and Nymph. Now, she realized, was the time for a second birth from within a second womb so that she might evolve her own consciousness and see the world in the patterns of its true making. The thought suddenly occurred to her, as she crossed that river once more, feeling the metal construction of the bridge sway with the movement of traffic, that man and woman had never left the Garden of

Eden. We were all living in it now. Yet blinded by fear and confusion, we had failed to see the profound elegance of all creation which surrounds us, or the true power of our very Souls. She could feel that spark within her ignite into three plumes of sacred fire emanating from her heart. The warmth of that fire filled her being with Light as she reached the other side of the bridge, allowing her former self and her old ways of understanding to fade.

For the first time, her mental understanding of the world was felt from her head to her toes as experience. She was experiencing oneness with all forms of life as the shell of that egg continued to crack, giving way to a higher awareness that could no longer fit within the confines of her former Self. She could feel the answer to her question surging from within, bathing her in red hues of a more powerful light shining through. Her energies were spinning, spinning, spinning, as she walked into the lobby of the Langham Hotel and stepped into the elevator. As that steel box carried her to the hotel's bar, she exhaled as she never had before, finally encouraging that heavy shell to fall, revealing the snake to be nothing more than the flow of energy fueled by unconditional love.

Madeleine knew that she was everyone and no one all the same. She was Delilah Russell and Charles Price, she was Jonathan and Margot Karl, she was Natalie Rose and all the people in between, just as they were all mirror images of her, in different bodies, on different paths, their natures written in living code. I AM all, her soul seemed to say. I AM the reflection of all that I AM. That was the true ocean from which we have all emerged, each a single drop, as we are also a single flame from a great and eternal fire. And as the elevator doors opened, Madeleine realized that she had accessed the true door to immortality, the true Elixir of Life, to which we all hold a key, buried within the darkness and confusion of our shells, forever guarded by the flowing energies of movement and Light.

She entered the hotel's bar where Gabriel was waiting, sitting in his grey suit near the floor-to-ceiling windows with his back facing the river and his luggage by his feet. A surge of energy flowed from Madeleine's heart into her veins and across the whole of her physical structure as her soul recognized the presence of her counterpart, enabling a balance of polarities forever yearning to merge. Her body fluttered with recognition, as she glowed from the inside out. There were infinite possibilities before her, and she felt open to them all. There was no friction, no doubt, no fear, but faith. And as she walked towards the man she loved, she smiled like an absolute fool, because she was The Fool, stepping out into the unknown, trusting in the power of Source.

"There you are," Gabriel said, standing up to greet her. They kissed, stirring a kaleidoscope of energies between them, which flickered with the glow of a secret ruby diamond, a sphere of energy holding them in its resplendent embrace. Madeleine felt the warmth of his lips, the strength of his hands as he pulled her closer towards him, and she allowed herself to melt into the folds as their hearts beat together. "Let me take that for you," he said, moving the hat box from her hand to the floor before removing his wife's coat. "Now, how was your day?"

"I actually have something to tell you," she said, feeling the blush on her cheeks.

"Oh, yeah? What's that?"

The river was flowing beneath them. The leaves of trees fluttered against the Chicago wind. People were walking up and down State Street, going about their business, which no one knew but them. There were families and lovers, brothers and sisters, friends and co-workers, all walking, talking, thinking, and hoping—hoping for a better tomorrow. The sun descended into the West, and eventually the moon rose. Its full face, a precious pearl, soon found reflection upon the river's surface, as the constellations glittered from above. The lights in the hotel bar eventually dimmed as Madeleine and Gabriel planned for the future. Theirs was a new science, a new business, and a new family to build; but tonight they would celebrate how far they had come, because a new world was brewing, built not on fear but on a foundation of love and understanding. The flame growing within them, nurtured by their love, they would share with all the world. These lovers would carry that flame burning within themselves, and see its potential in everyone they would meet. This way, flame after flame would be ignited to illuminate the path forward and enlighten the world from within every temple of flesh and blood, until all beat in harmony with the pulse of Eternal Life. Here was the shift, here was the moment. Breathe in, and pause. Embrace the fullness of an Eternal Now, then let all fear dissolve, my love, for the end is only the beginning.

CURTAIN

Image by Jay Deaux Photography

Amber Jo Ann is a poet and storyteller born and raised in Opelousas, Louisiana. She's since lived a dozen lives, from the national show jumping circuit to Chicago's improv scene. She's been a writer the entire time, but her story is only getting started. Join the journey at www.lunasophiapublishing.com.

ADDITIONAL READING

Acadie Then and Now: A People's History
by Warren Perrin, Mary Broussard Perrin and Phil Comeau

Bad Blood: Secrets and Lies in a Silicon Valley Startup
by John Carreyrou

Blood: An Epic History of Medicine and Commerce
by Douglas Starr

*Blood on Their Hands: How Greedy Companies, Inept Bureaucracy,
and Bad Science Killed Thousands of Hemophiliacs*
by Eric Weinberg and Donna Shaw

*Broken Blood: A Reflection of Loss & Hope
in the Hemophilia Community* by Sabrina Mann

Five Quarts: A Personal and Natural History of Blood
by Bill Hayes

If This Was Happiness: A Biography of Rita Hayworth
by Barbara Leaming

*Nine Pints: A Journey Through the Money, Medicine,
and Mysteries of Blood* by Rose George

Sextrology: The Astrology of Sex and the Sexes
by Stella Starsky and Quinn Cox

*Stop Stealing Dreams (What is School For?):
A Manifesto on Transforming Education* by Seth Godin

The Lucifer Effect: Understanding How Good People Turn Evil
by Philip Zimbardo

Documentaries

Bad Blood: A Cautionary Tale (2010) by Marilyn Ness

The Chocolate Case (2016) by Benthe Forrer

The Dhamma Brothers: East Meets West in the Deep South (2008) by Andrew Kukura, Jenny Philips, Anne Marie Stein

The Gene: An Intimate History (2020) by Ken Burns

Tintamarre: On the Trail of Acadians in North America (2004) by André Gladu

Your Inner Fish (2014) by Neil Shubin & PBS

**To learn more about Vipassana meditation and 10-day retreats, visit www.dhamma.org.

THE POEM THAT INSPIRED THIS NOVEL:

RED

Takes two to start a fire
Or rage a bloody war,
With kindling for desire
And wavelengths to explore.

There is that threat of danger
In every call to arms,
As passion can breed anger
And red sounds all alarms.

Still, the energy of Nymphs
And Satyrs dressed as gods
Evokes a sacred glimpse
Into why we're all at odds.

For Life and Death flow aroused
As battle trumpets sound
Find the lock where sex is housed
To see how we are bound.

*To read the remaining nine poems of The Color Series
poetry collection, visit www.lunasophiapublishing.com
to download your free copy.*

SPECIAL THANKS

First, to you, dear reader, for making it this far! This novel was written for you, as will be the next nine novels that form *The Color Series*. These books would not exist without your participation, so thank you.

For this particular novel, a great many people helped form this story over the course of the past decade. These include, but are not limited to, Mark Artall, Ryan Benson, Bart Bernard, Nora Best, Michael Blaney, Anja Boltz, Shirley Brown, Debbie Carlson, Jerry Cleaver, Carolyn Constantin, Roy Constantin, Trena Constantin, Jerry Curry, Bill Daniel, Jennifer Darby, Mary Duhé, Shelby & Victoria Emrick, Dean Evans, A.J. Froeber, Karen Glover, Dr. Lisa Graley, Geza Gyuk, Dwayne & Anita Hargroder, Raymond & Margaret Hargroder, Norm Holly, Emil Ivanov, Linda Joubert, David N. Khey, Kirk Kicklighter, Marina Kozak, Robert Kozlowski, Eugene Kwarteng, Patrick James Lynch, Elizabeth Machen, Susan Messing, Suzanne McManus, Catherine Miers, Brooke Miller, Jason Pettus, Edmund Schenecker, Jacqueline Olivia Scott, John "Pudd" Sharp, John Sorensen, Jennifer Spurgeon, Dijana Starcevic, Graham Thompson, Craig Uhlir, Alexander Utz, Velvet, and Meredith Wright. Thank you to the moon and back!